喚醒你的英文語感！

Get a Feel for English !

喚醒你的英文語感！

Get a Feel for English !

BIZ English

Biz.

搞定
進階 商務口說

Advanced Business
Communication

學會基礎口說，你還要搞定進階商務溝通能力！

熟練本書深入談話、接待、銷售、時程安排、物流處理及解決
問題等進階業務交涉用語，練就漂亮口說能力，迅速敲定生意！

588個商務核心字彙
165個深入談話好用句
128個接待客戶加分句
240個業務交涉必通句
130個商務e-mail好用句 *Bonus!*

Best-seller
《搞定商務口說》
再升級！

附1片實戰MP3

總編審 ⊙ 王復國
作　者 ⊙ Dana Forsythe

作者序

本書所涵蓋的內容是台灣貿易公司或跨國企業最常希望員工能熟練與精通的商務核心用語。

各位可能對 80/20 法則，也就是所謂的帕列托法則 (Pareto principle) 都十分熟悉，它的核心概念是，80% 的成果是由 20% 的原因所造成。以本書的寫作目的來說，我對於 80/20 法則有不同的詮釋：生活中 20% 的事非常重要，另外的 80% 則不太重要。以此推論，不管是在商場還是學習英語時，你所學到的字彙、文法和商業片語，其中只有 20% 對你的溝通真的很重要，且確實發揮效用。本書所挑選的所有商務用語，就是這最實用、有效的 20%。

本書僅收錄了十分常用且影響重大的商務溝通用語，它們也是各位確實需要精通才能和客戶進行有效業務交涉的英文。我對台灣的貿易公司或跨國企業非常熟悉，並教過無數位來自中小型或大型知名企業的學生。這些公司的員工和經理人向我反映了哪些商業用語對他們最有用。我利用了這些寶貴的意見，把最基本且關鍵的商用英文編寫成這本書，並呈現在各位眼前。

希望本書有助於各位和所有的顧客順利溝通，並對自己的努力感到滿意！

Dana Forsythe

本書特色

　　本書介紹商務人士在進行商業溝通時必須具備的核心英文用語。在內容呈現上，本書可說是《搞定商務口說》（*Oral Business Communication*）的進階篇，《搞定商務口說》鎖定基礎溝通主題（包括基本對話、打電話、簡報、開會、談判及介紹自己公司等用語），《搞定進階商務口說》則是除了釐清口語常見問題、深入談話、接待賓客等用語外，更深入業務交涉最核心的部分，包括銷售、時程安排、物流處理、討論問題及解決之道等。此外，本書更增加數位工作者必備的 email 溝通技巧及好用句，企圖打造更完整、實用的商務英文溝通全書。

BIZ 必通字彙、句型、片語

　　本書包含進階商業溝通所必須知道的字彙、片語和句型，在大多數的情況下，這些商務核心用語都是出現在名為「BIZ 必通字彙」或「BIZ 必通句型」的單元中。

Show Time 範例

　　在任何一堂語言課上，大家最常問的問題就是：「可以舉個例嗎？」學習新語言的人需要很多例子，才能清楚了解如何使用新的單字、片語及句型。本書提供了豐富的實例，讓讀者能充分了解並熟悉如何運用書中所提到的商業用語。書中的例子不勝枚舉，絕大部分都出現在「Show Time」單元中。

糾正錯誤

　　排除錯誤是精通英語很重要的一部分。本書第一章特別探討中文母語人士經常會犯的發音及口語錯誤，文中羅列許多易混淆的字彙或用語並詳加解析，幫助讀者從釐清錯誤之中，學習清晰、正確的口語。此外，本書各頁會不時出現「小心陷阱」單元，隨時提醒中文母語人士經常會犯的口語或文法錯誤。

······························ ◇◇◇ 小心陷阱 ◇◇◇ ·····························

☹ 錯誤用法

I can't **down** the price.

我沒辦法降價。

☺ 正確用法

I can't **lower** the price.

我沒辦法降價。

實戰演練

　　"Practice makes perfect." 本書各章結尾皆提供了練習題，第一至六章的實戰演練，是設計來讓兩個人一起練習。每道習題都設計了一至二個情境，兩位搭檔需利用該章學會的商業用語來「扮演」角色。每道習題可按照以下方式來進行：

1. 兩人先決定誰是角色 A 、誰是角色 B 。
2. 兩位搭檔各自閱讀習題，以了解整體概念。接著兩人回頭翻閱該章內容，挑選出本身角色所需的用語。
3. 兩人用剛才所挑選的用語將習題演練一次，並盡量將商業用語運用到純熟的程度。
4. 兩人交換角色，再將習題演練一次。

第三部分 E-mail 寫作章節則另有實戰演練設計。

CONTENTS

作者序

本書特色

第一部 Section One
人際溝通 Interpersonal Communication

第二章 發展話題 Developing Topics

第二部 Section Two
常見商務議題 Common Business Issues

第三部 Section Three
商務 Email 寫作 E-Writing

第七章 E-mail 的標點、段落與格式 Making E-mail Clear

第八章 E-mail 寫作技巧與慣用語 Common Business Usage

第九章 語氣 Tone

Section

ONE

人際溝通

Interpersonal Communcation

第 1 章

清晰的口語

Oral Clarity

清晰的重要性至高無上。筆者必須在此提醒各位讀者,說話清楚並從他人那裡得到清楚的訊息十分重要。不過話雖如此,但是要清楚地與人溝通,你並不一定需要是以英文為母語的人士。事實上,英文母語人士在做生意時,並不怎麼在乎別人是否能說一口十分流利的英文。商場人士做生意靠的是清楚的溝通,而不一定是流利的英語。本章所呈現的用語將能為各位的商業口語溝通形成堅實的基礎。只要好好學習,各位就能超越台灣其他的商務人士,包括那些曾在海外留學過的人。

Clarity is king. Speaking clearly and obtaining clear information from others are both so important that I must remind you here. That being said, you need not be a native speaker to communicate clearly. In fact, native English speakers doing business do not really care if others can speak English with complete fluency. Business people rely on clear communication — not necessarily fluent speech — to conduct business. The language presented in this chapter will form the backbone of all your oral business communication. Learn it well, and you will be head and shoulders above other people doing business in Taiwan — and that includes those who have studied overseas!

1 ┊ 常見的發音錯誤 Common Pronunciation Mistakes

各位的目標應該是盡可能清楚地發出每一個英文字音。這是身為英文學習者及使用者應有的態度。事實上，只有少數的英文發音真的對以中文為母語的人士有困難，因此如果要清楚而準確地把字音唸出來，九成是看你的態度和決心，看你願不願意努力習得正確的發音，並在說話時準確唸出來。

有些商場人士告訴我：「我的發音沒有那麼好，可是這樣已經夠好了。我認為我的客戶能了解我的意思。」我告訴各位，這種態度在國際商務溝通時會造成許多麻煩。假如對方並不是真的了解你在說什麼，你們就無法有意義地交換意見。此外，還有三點理由應該要努力把每個字都說對，而不只是抱著「已經夠好了」的態度。

1. 你不知道哪些發音錯誤會使客戶混淆、哪些不會，因此，唯一合理的作法就是，盡力把「每個字」都清楚地唸出來。

2. 在商場上，你的客戶需要專注在句子的意義上，而不是設法猜測你發錯音的單字是什麼意思。雖然別人可以猜出許多你說錯的字，但你還是應該以盡量減少說錯單字（尤其是數字）為目標。為什麼？你需要顧客把注意力集中在句子的層次，而不是在單字的層次，以確保你的想法能清楚地傳達給對方。不要讓聽者太吃力！

3. 清楚正確的發音是品質的表現。假如你清楚正確地把字唸出來，這就會顯示出你是個注重品質的人。相反地（無論這麼說公不公平），隨便發音會讓人覺得此人比較不聰明，或者根本不用心把事情做好。相信你不希望自己被認為是不聰明、做事不認真的人，不是嗎？

雖然我十分鼓勵各位這麼做，但是你並不需要去精通英文發音的所有層面。就目前來說，我知道各位是工作忙碌的專業人士，所以只需專注在英文發音中最常讓中文母語人士感到頭痛的特定部分即可。我從多年教授商業英文的經驗之中，將英文發音最棘手的重點問題都蒐集起來並羅列於下。對各位來說，相較於使用一本冗長的發音書籍，閱讀本章內容可以讓你只花一點時間即可迅速改善許多常見的發音及口說問題。依筆者個人淺見，單單這一點價值就超過這整本書的價格了。

1.1 字尾子音問題 Final Consonant Review

 track 02

　　我有許多學生誤以爲英文母語人士會省略字尾子音，這種誤解主要是因爲沒有專心聆聽。而讓問題雪上加霜的是，在中文環境裡教學的英文老師不見得都有能力教授英文發音的細節。

　　的確，英文母語人士在發字尾子音時，有時會輕一點，但絕非省略。英文的字尾子音，像是「t」和「d」，對中文母語人士來說可能較難，因爲中文雖然也有這些音，但是在中文裡這些音卻只出現在字首。如果要精通這些發音，在以英文爲母語的環境中的確會有幫助，但不要讓它成爲妨礙你把這些音發對的理由！適當唸出這些音是可以而且應該學會的事。真正重要的是，你要能清楚發出字尾子音，至於能不能像英文母語人士一樣，把力道掌握得恰到好處倒是其次。

　　就我看來，省略英文字尾子音是在台灣最常見的發音問題。當有人不了解你所說的某個字時，大約有一半的情況是因爲你沒有清楚發把字尾子音發出來。

　　下列的練習是設計來幫助各位學習發英文某些單字的字尾子音。仔細聽 MP3，並複誦你所聽到的內容。

　　你也可以先錄下自己的聲音，並拿它來和 MP3 中英文母語人士的發音做比較。這要花一點時間，但這種分析有助於微調你的英文發音。

1.1a 字尾的「t」 Final [t]

　　最重要的字：can't。我在台灣的學生絕大部分都沒有「t」唸清楚，如此可能會使客戶搞不清楚你的意思。練習確實把字尾的「t」清楚地唸出來！

台灣商務人士：　I am a little busy. I [kæn] answer your request today.
國外顧客：　　　Huh? You can, or you can't? Which is it?
台灣商務人士：　I'm sorry. I [kænt].

台灣商務人士：　我有點忙，我今天「能」回覆你的要求。
國外顧客：　　　嘎？你能還是不能？是哪一個？
台灣商務人士：　抱歉，我「不能」。

test 試驗	difficult 困難的	not 不	chart 圖表
repeat 重複	that 那個	product 產品	light 光
unit 單位	list 表	heat 熱度	limit 界限
update 更新	defect 缺陷	count 計數	department 部門

1.1b　字尾的「d」Final [d]

　　我發現許多人把字尾的「d」發成「t」。把「d」清楚地唸出來是很重要的。它的音很類似中文的「的」，所以各位應該很容易發出這個音。

could 可以 （can 的過去式）	did 做 （do 的過去式）	guide 指導	should 應該
hundred 一百	thousand 一千	find 發現	standard 標準
record 記錄	upgrade 升級	world 世界	used 用 （use 的過去式）

　　英文裡有許多單字的差別只在字尾的「t」和「d」，所以老是把「t」和「d」都唸成「t」會造成混淆。例如：

sat 坐 （sit 的過去式）	sad 難過
tight 緊的	tide 潮汐
fate 命運	fade 褪去

1.1c　字尾的「m」 Final [m]

　　確定你可以清楚、正確地發出下列單字中的字尾「m」，注意嘴巴必須閉合：

time 時間	from 來自	program 計畫	custom 習俗
problem 問題	volume 量	item 項目	system 體系
bottom 底部	maximum 最大量	same 同樣的	form 形式

　　以「m」結尾最重要的單字大概就是「name」了。我所教過的台灣商務人士大約有八成都會漏掉「name」中的「m」。注意，這是英文中最重要的單字之一，每當你自我介紹的時候就會用到這個字。

My name is Judy.

我的名字是茱蒂。

My name is Sam.

我的名字是山姆。

1.1d 字尾的「n」Final [n]

發「n」時，舌頭必須穩定地抵在上門牙後方並維持得夠久，才能把音發清楚。我們來練習一下。

can 能	opinion 意見	again 再次	mine 我的
design 設計	reason 原因	fine 好的	phone 電話
concern 關心	presentation 呈現	million 百萬	billion 十億

1.1e 字尾的「k」Final [k]

無論拼字的結尾是「k」還是「c」，以下這些單字都是以「k」的音結尾。跟著MP3 練習唸這些字。

think 認為	back 背面	mistake 錯誤	week 一星期
electronic 電子的	take 拿	mechanic 技工	break 破裂

1.1f 字尾的「v」 Final [v]

這是另一個困擾中文母語人士的英文發音。正確唸出這個字母的秘訣是，在發音時須把上門牙抵著下嘴唇。

five 五	positive 正面的	negative 負面的	receive 接收
improve 改善	save 挽救	give 給	survive 生存

1.1g 字尾的「s」Final [s]

由於中文的「s」音（「ㄙ」）是字頭而非字尾子音，所以造成一些學生在說英文時的一些困擾。我們來練習一下。

process 過程	response 反應	enhance 增加	piece 單位
false 偽造的	influence 影響	precise 精確的	base 基地

　　加「s」變複數的單字可能會特別麻煩，但複數的觀念在英文中是既重要又普遍的，所以不要逃避它。跟著 MP3 練習說出下列單字。

facts 事實	lists 列舉	dates 日期	charts 圖表
chips 晶片	mistakes 錯誤	ships 船	bikes 腳踏車

　　注意，當「s」加在「t」後面時，兩個音應該要一起發，唸成「ts」，聽起來就跟中文的「ㄘ」沒兩樣。

1.1h 字尾的「z」Final [z]
　　首先練習一下字尾的「z」：

realize 了解	customize 訂做	internalize 內化	finalize 完成

有些字的複數型雖然拼成「s」，但是念成「z」。我們來看一下。

heads 頭	needs 需要	problems 問題	reasons 理由
tables 桌子	chairs 椅子	computers 電腦	orders 訂購

　　注意，當「z」加在「d」後面時，兩個音應該要一起發，唸成「dz」，聽起來類似中文的「ㄗ」。

1.1i 字尾的「p」Final [p]
　　這是另一個在中文裡只出現在字首，但在英文裡卻常出現在字尾的子音。

stop 停止	gap 缺口	cheap 便宜的	step 步驟

1.2 字中子音問題 Reviewing Internal Consonants track 02

　　這是我的學生經常遇到困難的另一組發音。也就像本節許多的發音重點一樣，問題在於這些音出現在單字中的位置。中文也有下列的音，但它們不像英文一樣時常出現在單字的中間。因此，讀者應花一點時間聽 MP3 練習，以確切掌握這些發音。

1.2a 字中的「n」Internal [n]

前面提到過發「n」時，必須以舌尖確實地頂著上門牙後方才能完成。記得，假如你太快彈動舌頭，就無法發出正確的音。

analysis 分析	contract 契約	finish 完成	opinion 意見
condition 條件	present 禮物	analyze 分析	contain 包含

1.2b 字中的「z」Internal [z]

字中的「z」經常被我的學生誤唸為「r」。字中的「z」音其實並不難發，只要放輕鬆並慢慢唸出單字即可。你可以把單字拆成幾個音節，使「z」變成音節的開頭。當你放慢速度時，唸起來其實並不難。等你熟悉了發音之後，再練習說快一點，直到你能用正常的速度發音為止。

reason 理由	presentation 呈現	design 設計	thousand 一千

1.3 把「i」錯發成「ɪ」Mispronouncing [i] as [ɪ]

我的學生經常把這兩個音搞混。我們先從練習「i」的發音開始。請聽 MP3 並複誦。

piece 一件	sheet（紙等的）一張	complete 完成	these 這些
greet 招呼	feature 特色	meet 會見	beach 海灘

我納入下列的例子當作笑話，請特別小心這些單字，類似的錯誤可能會很要命！

☺ I received your sheet yesterday.
　我昨天收到你的單子。

☹ I received your shit yesterday.
　我昨天收到你的屎。

☺ I saw a nice beach in Thailand.

我在泰國看到一個漂亮的海灘。

☹ I saw a nice bitch in Thailand.

我在泰國看到一個漂亮的賤人。

1.4 「e」的發音 Pronunciation of [e]

 track 02

對我教過的許多商務人士來說，「e」是個難以掌握的音。它的發音其實與中文的「ㄟ」相同。請聽 MP3，並練習下列單字的發音。

same 同樣的	estimate 估計	state 說明	name 名字
game 遊戲	shape 形狀	create 創造	phase 階段
facilitate 促進	paper 紙	eliminate 消除	shake 搖動

1.5 把「ļ」錯發成「o」Mispronouncing final [ļ] as [o]

 track 02

這種錯誤通常不會造成聽者的混淆，但兩者發音方式相當不同。前者是音節化的「子」音，而後者則是原本就構成音節的「母」音。記得發 [ļ] 時，舌頭一定要確實抵在上門牙後方。

people 人	sample 樣品	stable 穩定的	model 型號
impossible 不可能的	acceptable 可以接受的	visible 可看見的	multiple 多樣的
cable 電纜	vegetable 蔬菜	regrettable 令人遺憾的	incredible 難以置信的

2 聽與唸常見的問題 Common Problems with Listening and Pronunciation

聽與說息息相關。想要清楚地把字唸出來需要先經歷仔細聽別人說並模仿他們的過程。要是聽得不仔細，就會導致不正確的發音。此外，學到錯誤發音的人常常也無法了解許多發音正確的字。因此，盡量藉由多聽母語人士說話來吸取經驗非常重要。廣播、電影、CNN 電視頻道、網路、語言錄音帶，以及這本書所附的 MP3 等等都是很好的學習模仿對象。記得，不要光看，還要多聽！

2.1 區分子音 Differentiating Consonants

 track 03

請聽以下各組單字。試著聽出每對單字在子音發音上的不同，並在必要時回頭多聽幾次，以訓練耳朵能輕易聽出其中的差異，然後自己唸出單字。唸出單字可以強化清楚聽出這些單字的能力。注意：能夠聽出差別並不代表能夠唸得出來，所以務必一面聽、一面練習！

allow 准許	aloud 大聲地
and 和	ant 螞蟻
browse 瀏覽	blouse 女襯衫
car 汽車	card 卡片
fire 火	file 檔案
flight 飛行	fright 驚嚇
made 製造（make 的過去式）	mate 夥伴
pass 經過	past 過去的
suit 套	shoot 發射
year 年	ear 耳朵

2.2　區分母音 Differentiating Vowels

 track 03

請利用 MP3 聽以下各組單字。注意母音的變化如何改變單字的發音。在必要時回頭多聽幾次，以強迫耳朵能輕易聽出其中的差異。然後自己唸出單字。記得，唸出單字可以強化清楚聽出這些單字的能力。

bill 帳單	bell 鐘	ball 球
cheap 便宜的	chip 晶片	chap 龜裂
claim 聲稱	clam 蛤蜊	
firm 穩固的	form 形式	farm 農場
heat 熱度	hit 打擊	hat 帽子
left 離開	laughed 笑（laugh 的過去式）	
leg 腿	lag 落後	lug 拉
paper 紙	pepper 胡椒粉	pauper 窮人
real 真的	rail 鐵路	royal 王室的
snack 點心	snake 蛇	sneak 偷偷摸摸
want 想要	won't 將不（will not 的縮寫）	
wedding 婚禮	wading 涉水	wording 措辭

2.3　區分子音及母音的組合
Differentiating Combinations of Consonants and Vowels

 track 03

請聽以下各組單字。試著聽出不同的母音及子音是如何改變各組單字的發音。在必要時回頭多聽幾次，以訓練耳朵能聽出其中的差異，然後自己唸出單字，以強化清楚聽出這些單字的能力。

agent 代理商	Asian 亞洲人	
checking 檢查	check in 登記	
clerk 辦事員	clock 時鐘	
days 每天	dates 日期	
exit 出口	access 進入	asset 資產

food 食物	foot 腳	
late 遲的	laid 放（lay 的過去式）	let 讓
next 下一個	nest 巢	
percent 百分比	person 人	
pieces 單位	pizzas 比薩	
seat 座位	sheet 床單	
say 說	said 說（say 的過去式）	
thin 薄的	think 認為	thing 事物
waiter 侍者	weather 天氣	
walk 走	work 工作	
yield 生產	ill 病的	
debt 債	debit 借方	

Memo

13

3 聲清對話中的問題 Clarification During Conversation

3.1 聽話者作的釐清 Clarification for the Listener

 track 04

當你在聽別人說話時，你必須確定自己能聽得懂。跟你說話的人不可能看出你的心思，所以當某些地方不清楚時，你就要讓對方知道。此外，你必須清楚告訴說話的人，你到底是哪裡不懂。

大部分的商務人士都知道，當他們不了解某人的意思時，說「Huh?」（嗄？）並不專業。不過，說「Pardon?」（抱歉？）通常也不是好的辦法。為什麼呢？因為這通常無法清楚表達你的問題出在哪裡：是你不懂單字？不懂句子？不懂整個論述？還是說話的人說得太快？

記住，商業溝通的首要原則就是：清楚！你應該用下列的精準用語來增進談話雙方的了解。

3.1a 表示理解 Expressing Comprehension

BIZ 必通句型

I GOT YOU.
我懂你的意思。

I FOLLOW YOU.
我知道你在說什麼。

I SEE Sb.'s POINT.
我明白某人的意思。
例 I see your point.
　　我明白你的意思。

I SEE/UNDERSTAND WHAT YOU MEAN.
我明白／了解你是什麼意思。

I UNDERSTAND YOUR MEANING.
我了解你的意思。

I CATCH YOUR MEANING.
我聽懂你的意思。

I AM CLEAR ON THAT.
那點我清楚。

EVERYTHING IS CLEAR.
一切都很清楚。

3.1b 表示不理解 Expressing Lack of Comprehension

BIZ 必通字彙

- 完全不理解 Complete Lack of Comprehension

I DON'T GET YOU.
我不懂你的意思。

I DON'T FOLLOW YOU.
我不知道你在說什麼。

I DON'T SEE/UNDERSTAND WHAT YOU MEAN.
我不明白／了解你在說什麼。

I DON'T UNDERSTAND YOUR MEANING.
我不了解你的意思。

I DON'T GET WHAT YOU ARE SAYING.
我不懂你在說什麼。

● 部分不理解 Partial Lack of Comprehension

I DON'T QUITE FOLLOW YOU.
我不太知道你在說什麼。

I CAN'T QUITE CATCH YOUR MEANING.
我不太能聽懂你的意思。

I'M NOT COMPLETELY SURE WHAT YOU MEAN.
我不是完全確定你是什麼意思。

● 可能不理解 Possible Lack of Comprehension

I'M NOT SURE I UNDERSTAND.
我不確定我了解。

MAYBE I AM MISSING YOUR POINT.
也許我沒搞懂你的意思。

 ◇◇ 小心陷阱 ◇◇

☹ 錯誤用法
I don't see **you mean**.
我不明白你的意思。
☺ 正確用法
I don't see **your meaning**.
我不明白你的意思。
I don't see **what you mean**.
我不明白你是什麼意思。

3.1c 詢問清楚 Checking for Clarity

BIZ 必通句型

DO YOU MEAN ...?

你的意思是……嗎？

例 Do you mean the containers are the wrong size?

你的意思是容器的尺寸錯了嗎？

YOU MEAN ..., RIGHT?

你的意思是……，對嗎？

例 You mean you would like to open another <u>branch</u> in Taipei, right?

你的意思是你想在台北開另一家分公司，對嗎？

ARE YOU SAYING ...?

你是說……嗎？

例 Are you saying the <u>chart</u> is not <u>accurate</u>?

你是說圖表不準確嗎？

YOU ARE SAYING ..., RIGHT?

你是說……，對嗎？

例 You are saying the Excel sheet needs to be revised, right?

你是說 Excel 表需要修改，對嗎？

Word List

branch [bræntʃ] *n.* 分公司；分店；分部
chart [tʃɑrt] *n.* 圖；圖表曲；線圖
accurate [ˋækjərɪt] *adj.* 精確的；準確的

3.1d 詢問單字的意思 Asking for Word Meaning

BIZ 必通句型

I DON'T KNOW THAT WORD.
我不認識那個字。

WHAT DOES THAT WORD MEAN?
那個字是什麼意思？

WHAT DOES ... MEAN?
……是什麼意思？
例 What does "conformity" mean?
「conformity」是什麼意思？

WHAT DO YOU MEAN BY "..."?
你所謂的「……」是什麼意思？
例 What do you mean by "internal synergy"?
你所謂的「internal synergy」是什麼意思？

3.1e 詢問拼法 Asking for Spelling

BIZ 必通句型

HOW DO YOU SPELL THAT?
那個字你怎麼拼？

HOW DO YOU SPELL "..."?
「……」你怎麼拼？

Word **List**

conformity [kən`fɔrmətɪ] *n.* 一致；相似　　synergy [`sɪnədʒɪ] *n.* 共同作用；協力

例 How do you spell "<u>curriculum vitae</u>"?

「curriculum vitae」你怎麼拼？

COULD YOU SPELL THAT?

你可不可以把那個字拼出來？

WHAT'S THE SPELLING OF THAT?

那個字要怎麼拼？

◇◇◇ 小心陷阱 ◇◇◇

☹ 錯誤用法

How **to spell** that?

那個字怎麼拼？

☺ 正確用法

How **do you spell** that?

那個字怎麼拼？

3.1f 詢問寫法 Asking for Writing

BIZ 必通句型

COULD YOU WRITE THAT DOWN?

你可不可以把那個寫下來？

COULD YOU SAY THAT SLOWLY SO I CAN WRITE IT DOWN?

你可不可以說慢一點，好讓我把它寫下來？

LET ME WRITE THAT DOWN.

讓我把那個寫下來。

Word List

curriculum vitae [kə`rɪkjələm `vaɪti] *n.* 履歷；簡歷（複數為 curricula vitae）

3.1g 要求再次說明 Asking for Restatement

以下用語是用在只有一句或者少數幾句不清楚時。

BIZ 必通字彙

COULD YOU REPEAT THAT?
你可不可以重複一次？

COULD YOU SAY THAT AGAIN?
你可不可以再說一次？

COULD YOU REPHRASE THAT?
你可不可以換個方式說？

WOULD YOU MIND SAYING THAT AGAIN?
你介不介意再說一次？

WHAT DO YOU MEAN WHEN YOU SAY ...?
你說……是什麼意思？
例 What do you mean when you say, "decreasing the lead time could be a problem"?
你說「decreasing the lead time could be a problem」是什麼意思？

假如還是不了解 If You Still Can't Understand

ONE MORE TIME, PLEASE.
請再說一次。

I STILL CAN'T UNDERSTAND. SORRY.
抱歉，我還是不了解。

Word List

rephrase [rì`frez] v. 改變措辭；換一個方式來表達
lead time 前置時間

COULD YOU REPEAT THAT AGAIN?

你可不可以再重複一次？

3.1h 要求釐清整體 Asking for General Clarification

以下用語用在不了解一個段落的整體意義時，比如說，不了解一個複雜的問題時。

BIZ 必通句型

COULD YOU EXPLAIN THAT AGAIN?

你可不可以再解釋一次？

COULD YOU CLARIFY ...?

你可不可以釐清……？

例 Could you clarify your idea?

你可不可以釐清你的想法？

COULD YOU GO OVER ... AGAIN?

你可不可以再把……說一遍？

例 Could you go over your proposal again?

你可不可以再把你的提案說一遍？

3.1i 尋求更深入的理解 Seeking Deeper Understanding

BIZ 必通句型

COULD YOU BE MORE SPECIFIC?

你可不可以具體一點？

COULD YOU BE MORE PRECISE?

你可不可以更精確一點？

COULD I ASK YOU ...?

我可不可以請教你……?

例 Could I ask you a few questions?

我可不可以請教你幾個問題?

COULD YOU TELL ME ...?

你可不可以告訴我……?

例 Could you tell me the <u>rationale</u> for the decision?

你可不可以告訴我該決定的理論基礎為何?

DO YOU MIND IF I ASK ...?

你介不介意我問……?

例 Do you mind if I ask the reasons?

你介不介意我問原因?

IF YOU DON'T MIND, I'D LIKE TO KNOW ....

假如你不介意,我想知道……。

例 If you don't mind, I'd like to know about the service <u>guarantee</u>.

假如你不介意,我想知道關於服務保證的事。

◇◇ 小心陷阱 ◇◇

☹ 錯誤用法

Could you mind telling me more?

你介不介意告訴我更多?

☺ 正確用法

Would you mind telling me more?

你介不介意告訴我更多?

Word List

rationale [ˌræʃəˋnæl] *n.* 理論基礎;基本原理

guarantee [gærənˋti] *n./v.* 保證;擔保

3.1j 詢問更多訊息 Asking for More Information

BIZ 必通句型

COULD YOU TELL ME MORE ABOUT ...?

你可不可以告訴我更多關於……?

例 Could you tell me more about that company?

你可不可以告訴我更多關於那家公司的事?

COULD YOU GIVE ME MORE INFORMATION ABOUT ...?

你可不可以給我更多關於……的訊息?

例 Could you give me more information about your target market?

你可不可以給我更多關於目標市場的訊息?

COULD YOU EXPAND ON ...?

你可不可以詳加說明……?

例 Could you expand on what you just said?

你可不可以詳加說明你剛才說的話?

COULD YOU GIVE ME MORE DETAILS ABOUT ...?

你可不可以給我更多有關……的細節?

例 Could you give me more details about the special discounts?

你可不可以給我更多有關特惠折扣的細節?

WOULD YOU MIND TELLING ME ...?

你介不介意告訴我……?

例 Would you mind telling me some additional information?

你介不介意告訴我一些額外的訊息?

WHAT ELSE CAN YOU TELL ME ABOUT ...?

關於……,你還有什麼可以告訴我的?

例 What else can you tell me about her plan?

關於她的計畫,你還有什麼可以告訴我的?

I'D LIKE TO KNOW MORE ABOUT ....
我想知道更多關於……。
例 I'd like to know more about the specification changes.
我想知道更多關於規格變更的事。

3.1k 說話者說得太快 Speaker Is Talking Too Quickly

BIZ 必通句型

COULD YOU SLOW DOWN A LITTLE?
你可不可以說慢一點？

COULD YOU SPEAK A LITTLE MORE SLOWLY?
你可不可以講慢一點？

3.2 說話者作的釐清 Clarification for the Speaker track 05

　　聽話者有責任確定說話者是否察覺到有任何不清楚的地方。不過，說話者也可以採取一些步驟來確定聽話者是否清楚而充分地了解，尤其是在談論複雜的事情時。

3.2a 確認聽者理解 Checking the Listener's Comprehension

BIZ 必通句型

IS EVERYTHING CLEAR?
一切都清楚嗎？

DO YOU FOLLOW ME?
你知道我在說什麼嗎？

DOES EVERYTHING MAKE SENSE?
一切都清楚嗎？

DO YOU CATCH MY MEANING?
你懂我的意思嗎？

IS THERE ANYTHING I CAN CLARIFY?
有什麼需要我釐清的嗎？

📎 **Note**

你可以在上述各句後加上「so far」（到目前為止），例如：

Is everything clear so far?

到目前為止，一切都清楚嗎？

3.2b 修正誤解 Correcting Misunderstanding

BIZ 必通句型

I DIDN'T MEAN THAT. I MEAN ....
我不是那個意思。我的意思是說……。

例 I didn't mean that. I mean your offer is fine with me.

我不是那個意思。我的意思是說你的提議我認同。

I THINK I WASN'T CLEAR. I MEAN ....
我想我沒說清楚。我的意思是說……。

例 I think I wasn't clear. I mean the progress is too slow.

我想我沒說清楚。我的意思是說進度太慢了。

THAT'S NOT QUITE WHAT I MEAN. I MEAN ....
我不全然是那個意思。我的意思是說……。

例 That's not quite what I mean. I mean your suggestion is worth further consideration.

我不全然是那個的意思。我的意思是說你的建議值得進一步考慮。

I THINK YOU MISUNDERSTOOD. I MEAN ....

我想你誤會了。我的意思是說……。

例 I think you misunderstood. I mean that we can probably accept your idea.

我想你誤會了。我的意思是說我們也許可以接受你的想法。

MAYBE YOU MISUNDERSTOOD. I MEAN ....

也許你誤會了。我的意思是說……。

例 Maybe you misunderstood. I mean the size of your order is not quite large enough.

也許你誤會了。我的意思是說你訂的量還不夠大。

◇◇ 小心陷阱 ◇◇◇

☹ 錯誤用法

I think I **wasn't clearly**.

我想我沒說清楚。

☺ 正確用法

I think I **wasn't clear**.

我想我沒說清楚。

3.2c 確定訊息充分 Checking for Sufficient Information

BIZ 必通句型

DID I GIVE YOU ENOUGH INFORMATION?

我給你的訊息夠嗎？

DO YOU NEED ANY MORE INFORMATION?
你還需要什麼更多的訊息嗎？

IS THE INFORMATION ENOUGH FOR YOU?
這些訊息對你來說夠了嗎？

3.2d 確定你的意思清楚 Making Sure Your Meaning Is Clear

　　你可以用以下這些用語打斷自己，把話說得更清楚，以確定聽者了解你的想法。
這些用語也可以用來回應聽者要求釐清的問題。

BIZ 必通句型

I'D LIKE TO CLARIFY ...: ....
我想釐清……：……。
例 I'd like to clarify one thing: The deadline can't be <u>postponed</u>.
　　我想釐清一件事：截止期限不能延後。

I WANT TO MAKE ... CLEAR.
我想把……說清楚。
例 I want to make the explanation clear.
　　我想把解釋說清楚。

MAYBE ... ISN'T/AREN'T CLEAR. WHAT I MEAN IS ....
也許……不清楚。我的意思是……。
例 Maybe my <u>recommendation</u> isn't clear. What I mean is we should post-pone the shipment.
　　也許我的建議不清楚。我的意思是我們應該把運貨日期延後。

LET ME REPHRASE THAT: ....
讓我換個方式說：……。

Word **L**ist

postpone [post`pon] *v.* 延後
recommendation [͵rɛkəmɛn`deʃən] *n.* 勸告；建議

27

例 Let me rephrase that: *All* employees are required to attend.

讓我換個方式說：「所有」的員工都必須參加。

LET'S GO OVER ... AGAIN.

我們再重述一次……。

例 Let's go over the <u>mounting</u> instructions again.

我們再重述一次安裝說明。

3.2e 確定答覆是否清楚 Checking If Your Answers Are Clear

BIZ 必通句型

IS MY ANSWER CLEAR?

我的答覆清楚嗎？

DID I ANSWER EVERYTHING CLEARLY?

我一切都回答清楚了嗎？

DOES MY ANSWER MAKE SENSE?

我的答覆清楚嗎？

◇◇ 小心陷阱 ◇◇◇

☹ 錯誤用法

Do I answer everything clearly?

我一切都回答清楚了嗎？

☺ 正確用法

Did I answer everything clearly?

我一切都回答清楚了嗎？

Word List

mountimg [ˋmaʊntɪŋ] *n.* 架設；裝設

3.2f 應付不熟悉的問題 Handling Unfamiliar Questions

BIZ 必通字彙

● 說你不知道 Saying You Don't Know

I AM NOT FAMILIAR WITH ....
我對……不熟。
例 I am not familiar with the import market.
　　我對進口市場不熟。

I'M AFRAID I DON'T KNOW THE ANSWER TO THAT.
恐怕我不知道那個問題的答案。

I DON'T HAVE THAT INFORMATION WITH ME.
我並不知道那則訊息。

● 說你稍晚會提供訊息 Saying You Will Supply Information Later

I WILL GET BACK TO YOU (time).
我會（時間）回覆你。
例 I will get back to you as soon as I can.
　　我會盡快回覆你。

I WILL GET THE INFORMATION TO YOU (time).
（時間）我會給你消息。
例 I will get the information to you by closing time today.
　　今天下班前，我會給你消息。

CAN I GET BACK TO YOU (time)?
我可以（時間）回覆你嗎？
例 Can I get back to you tomorrow?
　　我可以明天回覆你嗎？

29

3.3 結合聽者和說者的用語
Combining Listener's Language and Speaker's Language

track 06

Show Time 1

Two businesspeople are talking about how to improve production efficiency at an industrial plant.
Joyce: Line manager at the production plant
Kenny: A consultant on using technology to improve efficiency

Joyce: Thanks for telling me your ideas for improving our production efficiency.

Kenny: No problem. Is everything clear?

Joyce: I understand what you mean. Do you mind if I ask some questions?

Kenny: Not at all. Go ahead.

Joyce: First, could you clarify the point about training the <u>assembly</u> line workers? We already have detailed written instructions for them.

Kenny: Oh. I better go over that again. [detailed explanation]

Joyce: Thanks. I am clear on that. Could I ask you about the quality controls that you suggested?

Kenny: Sure.

Joyce: Could you give me more information about the <u>RFID</u> tags?

Kenny: Yes. [complete information] Do you catch my meaning?

Joyce: Yeah, it makes sense. Thanks for your explanation.

Kenny: Do you need any more information?

Joyce: I think I understand everything.

Kenny: Oh, I want to make the post-production process clear. [detailed explanation]

Joyce: I got it. Thanks!

Word List

assembly [əˋsɛmbəlɪ] *n.* （零件之）裝配

30　RFID 無線射頻識別（= Radio Frequency Identification）

兩位商務人士在談論要如何改善工廠的生產效率。
喬伊絲是工廠生產線的經理，肯尼是利用科技來改善效率的顧問。

喬伊絲：謝謝你把提高我們生產效率的構想告訴我。

肯　尼：小意思。一切都清楚嗎？

喬伊絲：我了解你的意思。你介意我問一些問題嗎？

肯　尼：一點都不會啊。請問。

喬伊絲：首先，你可以釐清訓練生產線工人的要點嗎？我們已經有詳細的書面說明給他們了。

肯　尼：喔。我最好再重說一次。〔詳細解釋〕

喬伊絲：謝謝。我清楚了。我可以請問一下有關你所建議的品管嗎？

肯　尼：當然。

喬伊絲：你可以給我更多關於無線射頻識別標籤的訊息嗎？

肯　尼：好。〔完整的訊息〕你懂我的意思嗎？

喬伊絲：懂，滿清楚的。謝謝你的解釋。

肯　尼：你還需要什麼訊息嗎？

喬伊絲：我想我一切都了解了。

肯　尼：喔，我想把後製流程說清楚。〔詳細解釋〕

喬伊絲：我懂了。謝謝！

Show Time 2

Two businesspeople are on the phone discussing whether or not to introduce a new series of exercise bikes.

Steve:　Owner of an exercise bike company

Kyra:　A buyer for a large American retailer

Steve:　Did you read my report about the proposed new series of exercise bikes?

Kyra:　Yes. Thanks for preparing that for me. It contained a lot of useful information, especially the section on ...

Steve: Kyra, could you speak a little more slowly? The phone connection is not so good.

Kyra: No problem. Anyway, I was just saying your report was useful for me.

Steve: That's good to hear. Does everything make sense?

Kyra: Maybe I am missing your point in the report. Do you mean that you will definitely introduce the new series of bikes?

Steve: I think I wasn't clear. I mean that we will introduce the new series if most of our customers think it's better than the current series. So, it depends on our survey of our customers.

Kyra: I see. What do you mean by "survey"? Do you have a formal written survey for me to fill out?

Steve: No. It's just informal. I am calling all my customers to get their opinions.

Kyra: Could you say that again? My office is really noisy today.

Steve: Sure. I just said that I will call all my customers and chat with them to find out what they think.

Kyra: Okay. Well, our report says that the new series has more fancy models. Could you be more specific?

Steve: [provides specific details] Is my answer clear?

Kyra: Could you say that more slowly so that I can write it down?

Steve: You mean the last part about the colors?

Kyra: Yes.

Steve: Oh, I can send an email to you today with all the details.

Kyra: Alright, thanks. By the way, would you mind telling me why the new bikes are ten percent more expensive?

Steve: It is because of the special <u>alloy</u> we use. I'm not familiar with the exact <u>composition</u> of the alloy, but I know the higher quality metal is more expensive for us to buy. Can I get back to you about that later today?

Word List

alloy [ˈælɔɪ] *n.* 合金   composition [ˌkɑmpəˈzɪʃən] *n.* 成分；構成

Kyra: Sure. I'd appreciate that.

Steve: Did I give you enough information about the new series?

Kyra: I think so. Everything is <u>crystal clear</u>.

兩位商務人士正透過電話討論要不要引進新系列的運動腳踏車。
史提夫是一家運動腳踏車公司的老闆，奇拉是一家美國大型零售業者的採購人員。

史提夫：妳看了我所提議的新系列運動腳踏車的報告嗎？

奇　拉：看了，謝謝你為我準備的報告。裡面有許多有用的訊息，尤其是……的部分。

史提夫：奇拉，妳可以說慢一點嗎？電話的聲音不是很清楚。

奇　拉：沒問題。反正，我剛才是說你的報告對我很有用。

史提夫：很高興聽到妳這麼說。一切都清楚嗎？

奇　拉：也許我沒有懂你報告上的重點。你是說你一定會引進新系列的腳踏車嗎？

史提夫：我想我沒有說清楚。我的意思是說，假如我們大多數的顧客認為它比目前的系列好，我們就會引進新系列。所以說，這要看我們的顧客調查。

奇　拉：我知道了。你所謂的「調查」是什麼意思？你有正式的書面調查讓我填寫嗎？

史提夫：沒有。只是非正式的。我會打電話給所有的顧客，以得知他們的意見。

奇　拉：你可以再說一次嗎？我辦公室今天真的很吵。

史提夫：當然可以。我剛剛說，我會打電話給我所有的顧客和他們聊聊，以了解他們的想法。

奇　拉：好。呃，我們的報告上說新系列會有更炫的樣式。你可以說得具體一點嗎？

史提夫：〔提供具體的細節〕我的回答清楚嗎？

奇　拉：你可以說慢一點以便讓我寫下來？

史提夫：妳是說有關顏色的最後一部分嗎？

奇　拉：是的。

史提夫：噢，我今天可以用電子郵件把所有的細節寄給妳。

Word List

crystal clear 非常清楚

奇　拉：好，謝謝。對了，你介不介意告訴我為什麼新的腳踏車要貴 10%？

史提夫：那是因為我們用了特別的合金。我對合金的確切成分不熟，不過我知道品質較高的金屬要花較多的錢去買。我可不可以今天稍晚再回覆妳這件事？

奇　拉：當然可以。感激不盡。

史提夫：我給妳的新系列訊息足夠嗎？

奇　拉：我想夠了。一切都非常清楚。

📝 Memo

令人困惑及可笑的英文常見錯誤 Common Confusing and Funny English Usage

本節要談的是可能會令人困惑或發笑的常見英文錯誤。這些錯誤都應該加以避免。相信各位不希望讓顧客覺得困惑，也不希望顧客在跟你說話時心裡暗自竊笑，表面上卻努力裝作沒事。

幾乎所有的商務人士都能在下列發現很多令人驚訝的錯誤。糾正錯誤是改進語言能力最快也最有效的方式。

4.1 單字錯誤 Word Errors

大多數人都認為文法錯誤是最常見的一種錯誤。這完全與事實不符。根據我多年的教學經驗，單字錯誤才是最常見的錯誤。因此，改善英文最好的辦法就是學習更多單字，或是針對你已經粗淺認識的單字學習它的深層意義及正確用法。

☹ I am a sales at my company.

🗣 你值多少錢？這好像是說別人也許可以買下你。當商店的產品在短期內打折時才叫做「sale」。

☺ I am a salesman/saleswoman at my company.
我是我們公司的業務員／女業務員。

☺ I am a salesperson at my company.
我是我們公司的業務員。

☹ Her English is very well.

🗣 台灣有照顧生病英文的特殊醫院嗎？「Well」當形容詞用是指「not sick」（沒生病）或「healty」（健康）。「Not Well」則是「sick」（生病）的意思。

☺ Her English is very good.
她的英文很好。

☺ She speaks English very well.
她英文說得很好。

☹ I am nothing to do today.

🗣 假如你認為自己一無是處，你也許該去看看心理醫生。

☺ I have nothing to do today.
我今天沒有事要做。

☹ I am your contact window.

🗣 你是人，不是窗戶。

☺ I am your contact person.
我是你的聯絡人。

☹ How/what about your weekend?

🗣 "「How about」和「what about」是在做選擇時使用，比方「How about a cup of coffee?」（來杯咖啡如何？）或是「What about going to the beach this weekend?」（這個週末要不要去海邊？）

☺ How was your weekend?
你週末過得如何？

☺ What did you do last weekend?
你上週末做了些什麼？

☺ Did you have a nice weekend?
你週末過得好嗎？

☹ I wish you have a nice flight back home.

🗣 「wish」在這裡是錯誤的用字，聽起來像是你正在施魔咒。要用「hope」，這才是母語人士的講法。

☺ I hope you have a nice flight back home.
希望你返家的旅程愉快。

🗣 願望在特殊的場合可以成真，比方生日、耶誕節、除夕等。在這些場合中，你可以使用「wish」的特殊固定說法：Sb.+ wish + sb. + sth.。注意，「have」不是固定說法的一部分。

☺ I wish you a happy birthday.
祝你生日快樂。

☺ We wish you a merry Christmas.
我們祝你耶誕快樂。

☺ My family wishes you a happy New Year.
我們全家祝你新年快樂。

☹ I will do it as possible as I can.

👤 這個句子並沒有任何意義。句中需要一個明確的副詞。

☺ I will do it as quickly as I can.
我會盡快去做。

☺ I will do it as well as I can.
我會盡我所能把它做好。

☺ I will do it as professionally as I can.
我會盡力以專業的方式來做。

☹ Here is Taiwan.

👤 「Here」用在把你面前的東西展示給別人看時，而且多半是你可以拿在手上的東西。
例如「Here is my passport.」（這是我的護照）。

☺ This is Taiwan.
這是台灣。

☺ This is my office.
這是我的辦公室。

☺ Here is your coffee.
這是你的咖啡。（把咖啡端給顧客。）

☺ Here is the report.
這是報告。（把報告拿給顧客。）

☹ Can you borrow me your pen?

👤 「borrow」指的是「向人借……」；「loan/lend」指的是「借給人……」。

☺ Can you loan me your pen?
你可以把筆借給我嗎？

☺ Can you lend me your pen?
你可以把筆借給我嗎？

☺ Can I borrow your pen?
我可以向你借筆嗎？

☹ Please open the light.

🗣 除非你是玻璃切割器,否則大部分的燈都不可能被你切開。

☺ Please turn on the light.
請把燈打開。

☹ As I know, it is not possible.

🗣 「As I know」的意思是「我知道我知道」。

☺ It is not possible.
那是不可能的。(你「知道」那是不可能的)

☺ As far as I know, it is not possible.
就我所知,那是不可能的。(你「認為」那是不可能的)

☺ As you know, it is not possible.
你知道,那是不可能的。(你在讓別人知道,你知道他們知道那是不可能的)

☹ This presentation will cost me thirty minutes.

🗣 報告的人似乎並不想做報告!

☺ This presentation will take me thirty minutes.
這場報告我將會花三十分鐘。

☹ Late delivery was a popular problem after the typhoon.

🗣 交貨延遲你似乎蠻開心的!

☺ Late delivery was a common problem after the typhoon.
交貨延遲是颱風過後常有的問題。

☹ How are you going? (greeting)

🗣 這麼說所得到的答案可能是:「I am going by train!」(我要搭火車去!)

☺ How are you doing?
你好嗎?

☺ How is it going?
你好嗎?

☹ Listener: Can I have a question?

🗣 既然上帝給了每個人腦袋，我們當然有權問問題。因此，比較好的說法是：

☺ Can I ask a question?

我可以問個問題嗎？

☹ My wife is a good cooker.

🗣 尊夫人似乎是台機器，也許是台電鍋。

☺ My wife is a good cook.

我太太是個好廚師。

☹ Kaohsiung is a funny city.

🗣 這聽起來像是你一到那裡就會開始笑。

☺ Kaohsiung is a fun city.

高雄是個有趣的城市。

☹ Our product has a nice outlook.

🗣 「Outlook」指的是「預測」，而不是東西看起來如何。

☺ Our product has a nice appearance.

我們的產品有不錯的外觀。

☹ I will play with my friend this weekend.

🗣 你可以玩運動、玩遊戲，或是和小孩玩。假如一個成人和另一個成人在「play」，這暗指有性行爲。要小心！

☺ I will go out with my friend this weekend.

這個週末我會和我的朋友出去。

☹ The meatballs in the soup are made by fish.

🗣 台灣的魚似乎很有天分，牠們竟然會做丸子！「By」應用來描述事情如何完成。

☺ The meatballs in the soup are made of fish.

湯裡的肉丸子是用魚肉做的。

☹ Will the waitress service us soon?

🗣 這句話聽起來像是，這家餐廳是違法的理容院！人可以「檢修」機器，但假如一個人「services」另一個人，這暗指「有性行為」。

☺ Will the waitress serve us soon?
女服務生會很快來招呼我們嗎？

☹ I guess the prices will fall down next quarter.

🗣 「Fall down」是指跌倒，摔落在地上。東西和人才會跌倒。

☺ I guess the prices will fall next quarter.
我猜價格下一季會下跌。

☹ I am trying to correct the software bugs. The PDA cannot work.

🗣 假如這台 PDA 沒有用，你幹嘛要浪費時間維修軟體？「Cannot」暗示這台 PDA「永遠」不能用。

☺ The PDA doesn't work.
這台 PDA 壞了。

☺ The PDA isn't working.
這台 PDA 壞了。

☹ My division will grow up in the future.

🗣 你的部門似乎全都是小孩。「Grow up」是指小孩長成大人的過程。

☺ My division will grow in the future.
我的部門將來會成長。

☺ My division will expand in the future.
我的部門將來會擴大。

☹ I told him to stay away from the control panel. He didn't listen to me, so the manager blamed him.

🗣 「Blame」是指「歸咎」。

☺ He didn't listen to me, so the manager scolded him.
他沒有聽我的，所以經理罵了他。

☹ The computer will notice you when the program stops.

🗣 電腦似乎有眼睛可以看你。

☺ The computer will notify you when the program stops.
當程式停止時，電腦會通知你。

☹ Have you met a typhoon in Taiwan?

🗣 這句話聽起來好像你認為台灣的颱風很友善，問問對方是否見過它！

☺ Have you ever encountered a typhoon in Taiwan?
你有沒有在台灣遇到過颱風？

☺ Have you ever experienced a typhoon in Taiwan?
你有沒有在台灣經歷過颱風？

☹ We want to order 1,000 pieces of Intel chips.

🗣 這聽起來像是你希望 Intel 把他們的晶片打碎，然後把小碎片寄給你。

☺ We want to order 1,000 Intel chips.
我們要訂 1000 個 Intel 晶片。

☺ We want to order 1,000 pieces.
我們要訂 1000 片。

☹ I can image that.

🗣 這彷彿是說你是台掃瞄機。

☺ I can imagine that.
那個我可以想像。

☹ Please see this picture.

🗣 這聽來像是你覺得顧客視力不好，應該戴副眼鏡。

☺ Please take a look at this picture.
請看一下這張圖。

☺ Please look at this picture.
請看這張圖。

4.2 文法錯誤 Grammar Errors

　　大部分令人困惑的文法錯誤都跟動詞時態的用法有關。令我非常意外的是，商務人士在基本的動詞時態上會犯那麼多錯。最常見的動詞時態包括：現在簡單式、未來簡單式、過去簡單式、現在完成式以及現在進行式。讀者必須把它們完全搞懂才能清楚地溝通。等你熟悉了這些基本的動詞時態後，就可以開始把重點擺在被動動詞的結構上。一旦精通了基本的動詞時態和被動結構，接著就應該研究 should 、 could 、would 等語態助動詞的用法。你最不需要急著熟練的是形容詞子句。總而言之，你在持續溫習動詞時，優先順序應該是這樣：

- basic verb tenses 基本動詞時態
- passive verb structure 被動動詞結構
- modals 語態助動詞
- adjective clauses 形容詞子句

　　假如你精通了上述的文法要點，接下來就可以溫習一些沒那麼重要的文法重點，比如名詞片語以及主詞和動詞的一致。

　　下面列出了筆者在教授商用英文時所遇到的各種文法錯誤。其中有些屬於基本文法，有些則牽涉到比較複雜的文法要點。

☹ I am boring today.

🗣 假如你讓人無聊，顧客就會覺得無聊！不要讓人覺得無聊！

☺ I am bored today.
我今天很無聊。

☹ How long you come/came to Taiwan?

🗣 從洛杉磯到台北大概要花十三個小時，所以美國人在回應這個問題的答案會是：「十三小時」。「Come」是個動作動詞，「to」則是與動作並用的介系詞。要像這樣問：

☺ How long have you been in Taiwan?
你來台灣多久了？

☹ I have ever been to Japan.

🗣 這句話聽起來令人困惑，好像你不知道自己有沒有去過日本。「Ever」這個字應用在

像這樣的問句中：「Have you ever been to Japan?」（你有沒有去過日本？）

☺ I have been to Japan.
我去過日本。

☹ I see you mean.

🗣 這句話聽起來像你覺得你的顧客不是個好人。

☺ I see your meaning.
我明白你的意思。

☺ I see what you mean.
我明白你的意思是什麼。

☹ The heat test has fail.

🗣 這只是個基本的文法錯誤。注意動詞的變化。

☺ The heat test has failed.
溫度測試已告失敗。

☺ The heat test failed.
溫度測試失敗了。

🗣 現在文法是對了，可是這可能仍然不是你要說的意思。這兩句話是說，測試並未正常
進行，也許是溫度測試的機器壞了。你也許想要說的是：

☺ The product failed the heat test.
產品沒有通過溫度測試。

☹ We will try to cost down.

🗣 「Cost」在這裡並非動詞。試試下面其中一句：

☺ We will try to lower the cost.
我們會試著降低成本。

☺ We will try to reduce the cost.
我們會試著減少成本。

☺ We will try to cut the cost.
我們會試著削減成本。

☹ Today was too tired.

🗣 在這個世界上日子沒辦法感到累。

☺ I was too tired today.
我今天太累了。

☺ Today was too tiring.
今天太累人了。

☹ Do I answer your question?

🗣 這句話聽起來像是你想每天週而復始地回答同樣的問題。這句話要這樣講：

☺ Did I answer your question?
我有沒有回答你的問題？

☹ I suggest that you should attend the meeting.

🗣 「Suggest」表達的是意見，對方不一定要理會它。「Should」則暗指事態較嚴重，而你最好去做。你應該這樣使用：

☺ I suggest that you attend the meeting.
我建議你出席會議。

☺ You should attend the meeting.
你應該出席會議。

☹ I will call you during two weeks.
　I will call you next two weeks.

🗣 這麼說像是你將講兩個星期的電話，或是你會持續撥打兩個星期的電話，因為對方不會接電話。

☺ I will call you within two weeks.
我會在兩星期內打電話給你。（時間不確定）

☺ I will call you sometime in the next two weeks.
我會在接下來兩星期內找時間打電話給你。（時間不確定）

☺ I will call you in two weeks.
我會在兩星期後打電話給你。（時間確定：就是十四天）

☹ Should we have to attend the seminar?

🗣 「Should」暗示嚴重性，但你還是有選擇。「Have to」則指你沒有選擇。它們要分開使用。

☺ Should we attend the seminar?

我們應該參加研討會嗎？

☺ Do we have to attend the seminar?

我們一定得參加研討會嗎？

☹ I like to talk to you next week.

🗣 這句話聽來像是你想每星期都跟某人說話。現在簡單式包含了所有的時間。要表示具體的時間應該這樣說：

☺ I would like to talk to you next week.

我想下星期跟你談談。

☹ I have worked here since two years.

🗣 這是個簡單的文法錯誤。正確的說法有兩種：

☺ I have worked here for two years.

我在這工作已經兩年了。

☺ I have worked here since two years ago.

我從兩年前就在這裡工作了。

☹ I am born in Taiwan.

🗣 這彷彿是說你一而再、再而三地出生。你應該這麼說：

☺ I was born in Taiwan.

我在台灣出生。

☹ Taipei is north of Taiwan.

🗣 這句話聽來像台北並不在台灣。日本才是在台灣北方。

☺ Taipei is in north Taiwan.

台北在台灣北部。

☺ Taipei is in northern Taiwan.

台北在北台灣。

☹ The aluminum pipes almost come from Africa.

🗣 這句話聽起來彷彿運送的船隻沈到海裡去了。

☺ Almost all the aluminum pipes come from Africa.

幾乎所有的鋁管都是從非洲來的。

☹ A: Do you eat yet?

🗣 這是一個簡單的文法錯誤。你應該說：

☺ Did you eat yet?
你吃飯了嗎？

☺ Have you eaten yet?
你吃過飯了嗎？

4.3 情境錯誤 Situational Errors

☹ Nice to meet you again.

🗣 就技術上來說，你只能「遇見」某人「一次」，就是第一次。所以當你遇上已經見過的人時，你應該說：

☺ Nice to see you.
很高興見到你。

☺ Nice to see you again.
很高興又見到你。

☹ I'll go first. See you tomorrow.

🗣 「Go first」是「begin」的意思，比方是「It's time for our presentations. Who will go first?」（我們該報告了。誰先來？）。中文的「我先走了」是宣告某人要離開的禮貌用語，英文並沒有適用這種情境的特殊禮貌用語。在這種情況下，你可以說：

☺ I am leaving now. See you tomorrow.
我現在要離開了。明天見。

☺ I gotta go. See you tomorrow.
我得走了。明天見。

☺ I am out of here. See you tomorrow.
我要閃人了。明天見。

☹ I feel uncomfortable. Can I leave early?

🗣 「Uncomfortable」在英文中是個模糊的字眼。在華語文化中，模糊無傷大雅，但西方文化較講究明確性，尤其是在商業情境中。

☺ I have a headache. Can I leave early?

我頭痛。我可以早點離開嗎？

☺ I feel sick. Can I leave early?

我覺得不舒服。我可以早點離開嗎？

☹ **Have you eaten yet? (greeting)**

假如你這麼說，聽起來像是你想請客戶上餐館，或是你的袋子裡有東西可以請他們吃。「你吃飽了嗎？」純粹是中文的禮貌招呼用語，但是在英文裡「Have you eaten yet?」並不是問候語。問候某人要這麼說：

☺ How are you today?

你今天好嗎？

Memo

5 實戰演練 Partner Practice

當你讀完並複習過本章內容後，找個同伴試試下面的對話練習！

情境 **1**

兩個人在閒聊台北的生活。

練習

角色 A	一家總部設在台灣的貿易公司的業務員
角色 B	角色 A 的外國友人，正在台灣觀光
A	告訴角色 B 一些住在台灣的優點。
B	表示理解。(3.1a)
A	告訴角色 B，台北的交通比台灣的其他城市好，因為警察執法比較嚴格。
B	表示不理解台北的警察比其他城市的警察嚴格。你的邏輯是：台灣是個小國家，所以交通狀況在哪裡應該都差不多。(3.1b)
A	告訴角色 B 你「為什麼」認為台北的警察比其他地方的警察嚴格。舉例說明。
B	要求進一步說明台灣的警察。例如：民眾對警察的看法、台灣的警察有沒有善盡本分。(3.1i)
A	告訴角色 B 你對警察的看法，並詢問角色 B 是否了解你所說的。(3.2a)
B	告訴角色 A 你認為他／她在說什麼，但用一些跟角色 A 的實際用語不一樣的說法來表達。
A	糾正角色 B 的誤解。(3.2b)

情境 **2**

兩個人在正式討論某項產品的品質。

練習

角色 A	角色 B 的美國客戶
角色 B	一家台灣貿易公司的業務員

A	要角色 B 解釋為什麼他／她認為他／她的產品品質很好。選擇一種你想討論且熟悉的產品來談。
B	回答角色 A。談論你的產品的品質。
A	詢問更多與該產品相關的訊息。(3.1j)
B	提供更多你產品的相關訊息。詢問角色 A 你所提供的訊息是否足夠。(3.2c)
A	要角色 B 重申他所說過的某一點。(3.1g)
B	再次說明角色 A 所問的事。
A	向角色 B 詢問有關該產品的一個明確的問題。
B	回答該問題。確定你有把話說清楚。(3.2d) 問角色 A 你的回答是否清楚。(3.2e)
A	檢查是否清楚了，並確定你了解角色 B 所說的話。(3.1c)
B	告訴角色 A，他／她了解你的意思。
A	向角色 B 詢問他／她們公司正在設計的一項新產品。
B	告訴角色 A，你並不知道答案。(3.2f)

Memo

第 2 章

發展話題

Developing Topics

本章所介紹的用語可以幫助你開啟、改變並更深入地探討話題。本章中的片語、句型和字彙將提供你所需要的一切工具，讓你無論在重要的商業議題或純粹閒聊的話題上都能暢所欲言。一旦熟悉了本章內容，你就能自信地和顧客及聯絡人暢談各種他們肯定想要聊的話題。

This chapter provides language to help you open, change, and dive deeper into topics. The phrases, patterns, and vocabulary in this unit give you all the tools you will need in order to talk about the things you want to talk about whether important business issues or just casual topics for chatting. Once you become familiar with the content of this chapter, you will be able to speak with confidence about a range of topics that your customers and contacts will surely want to talk about.

1 開啓及改變話題 Opening and Changing Topics

1.1 開啓眾所皆知的話題 Opening a Generally Known Topic track 07

1.1a 取自任何媒體來源的話題 Topic from Any Media Source

BIZ 必通句型

DID YOU HEAR THAT ...?
你有沒有聽說……？
例 Did you hear that the US dollar is really <u>weak</u>?
　　你有沒有聽說美元非常疲軟？

DID YOU HEAR ABOUT ...?
你有沒有聽說有關……？
例 Did you hear about the high-speed rail delay?
　　你有沒有聽說有關高鐵延宕的消息？

HAVE YOU HEARD THAT ...?
你有沒有聽說過……？
例 Have you heard that China Airlines will change its <u>routes</u>?
　　你有沒有聽說過華航要更改航線？

HAVE YOU HEARD ABOUT ...?
你有沒有聽說過有關……？
例 Have you heard about the bank <u>merger</u>?
　　你有沒有聽說過有關銀行合併的事？

Word List

weak [wik] *adj.* 【商】（市況、行情等）有下跌趨勢的；後勁無力的

route [rut] / [raʊt] *n.* 路線；航線

merger [ˋmɝgɚ] *n.* （公司、企業等）合併

DO YOU KNOW THAT ...?

你知不知道……？

例 Do you know that a typhoon is coming?

你知不知道有颱風要來？

DO YOU KNOW ANYTHING ABOUT ...?

你知不知道有關……？

例 Do you know anything about the recent boat accident in Kaohsiung harbor?

你知不知道有關高雄港最近發生的那起船隻意外？

📎 Note

「Hear」和「heard」不一定是指真的從電視上或收音機裡聽到了什麼，這個字的常見用法基本上就是「知道」的意思。

◇◇◇ 小心陷阱 ◇◇◇

☹ 錯誤用法

Do you hear about the President's trip?

你有沒有聽說有關總統出訪的事？

☺ 正確用法

Have you heard about the President's trip?

你有沒有聽說有關總統出訪的事？

1.1b 取自平面媒體的話題 Topic from Print Media

BIZ 必通句型

DID YOU READ THAT ...?

你有沒有看到……？

例 Did you read that energy prices are expected to rise dramatically?

你有沒有看到能源價格預期會大漲的報導？

DID YOU READ ABOUT ...?

你有沒有看到有關⋯⋯？

例 Did you read about the fire in the <u>industrial park</u>?

　　你有沒有看到有關工業園區火災的報導？

HAVE YOU READ THAT ...?

你有沒有看到過⋯⋯？

例 Have you read that the Electronic Toll Collection system will open soon?

　　你有沒有看到過電子收費系統很快就要啟用的報導？

HAVE YOU READ ABOUT ...?

你有沒有看到過有關⋯⋯？

例 Have you read about the sales of Taiwan fruit in China?

　　你有沒有看到過有關台灣水果在大陸銷售的報導？

Show Time

A: Jack, did you hear about Tiger Wang's winning game?

B: I sure did. Everyone in Taiwan is following his career. Last night I read the sports section in the newspaper. Did you read that some players might be <u>indicted</u> for <u>doping</u>?

A: I didn't read that. Anyway, that won't affect Tiger Wang. He is a clean player <u>for sure</u>!

A：傑克，你有沒有聽說有關王建民勝投那場球的消息？

B：當然有，台灣每個人都在注意他的職涯發展。昨天晚上我看了報紙的體育版。你有沒有看到某些選手可能會因為使用禁藥而遭到起訴的報導？

A：我沒有看到。反正這不會影響到王建民。他絕對是個清清白白的選手！

Word List

industrial park [ɪnˈdʌstrɪəl ˈpɑrk] *n.* 工業園區

indict [ɪnˈdaɪt] *v.* 起訴（控告）某人

dop [dop] *v.* 使用麻醉藥品；吸毒

for sure 確定的；必然的

開啓既定的商業話題 Opening a <u>Predetermined</u> Business Topic

以下用語可用來展開你和顧客見面所要討論的主題。

 track **08**

1.2a 一般的直接開場 General Direct Openings

BIZ 必通句型

SHALL WE TALK ABOUT ...?

我們是不是該談談⋯⋯？

例 Shall we talk about how you plan to <u>finance</u> your loan?

我們是不是該談談你打算如何取得貸款？

WOULD YOU LIKE TO TALK ABOUT ... NOW?

您現在想談談⋯⋯嗎？

例 Would you like to talk about your <u>outsourcing</u> now?

您現在想談談你們外包的事嗎？

I GUESS WE HAD BETTER TALK ABOUT ....

我想我們最好談談⋯⋯。

例 I guess we had better talk about your <u>restocking</u> procedures.

我想我們最好談談你們的補貨程序。

WELL, IT'S TIME TO TALK ABOUT ....

嗯，該來談談⋯⋯了。

例 Well, it's time to talk about the order <u>cancellation</u> fees.

嗯，該來談談取消訂貨的費用了。

Word List

predetermined [ˌpridɪˋtɝmɪnd] *adj.* 業已決定的
finance [faɪˋnæns] *v.* 融資；籌措資金
outsourcing [ˋaʊtˌsɔrsɪŋ] *n.*（工作等）外包

restock [rɪˋstɑk] *v.* 更新進貨；補貨
cancellation [ˌkænsᶅˋeʃən] *n.* 取消；註銷

1.2b 之前聯繫所提及的主題 Topic Mentioned in Previous Communication

BIZ 必通句型

I RECEIVED YOUR ... ABOUT ....

我收到了你⋯⋯有關⋯⋯。

例 I received your e-mail about the department restructuring.

我收到了你那封有關部門重組的電子郵件。

I RECEIVED YOUR ... REGARDING ....

我收到了你⋯⋯關於⋯⋯。

例 I received your letter regarding the tennis <u>racket</u> orders.

我收到了你那封關於訂購網球拍的信。

I READ ABOUT ... IN YOUR E-MAIL.

我在你的電子郵件裡看到了有關⋯⋯。

例 I read about the twisted cables in your e-mail.

我在你的電子郵件裡看到了有關電線纏繞在一起的事。

I READ ABOUT ... IN YOUR LETTER/FAX.

我在你的信／傳真裡看到了有關⋯⋯。

例 I read about the proposed changes in your fax.

我在你的傳真裡看到了有關你所提議的改變。

ON THE PHONE YOU MENTIONED ....

你在電話裡提到了⋯⋯。

例 On the phone you mentioned increasing the <u>dimensions</u> of the <u>ceramic</u> <u>figurines</u>.

你在電話裡提到了要放大陶瓷雕像尺寸的事。

Word List

racket [ˋrækɪt] *n.* （網球、羽球等的）球拍

dimension [dəˋmɛnʃən] *n.* （長、寬、厚、高的）尺寸

ceramic [səˋræmɪk] *adj.* 陶器的；陶瓷的

figurine [͵fɪgjəˋrin] *n.* 小塑（雕）像；小人像

Note

「I received (something)」、「I read about (something)」和「You mentioned (something)」皆指「Let's talk about it.」。這些是間接的開場方式，它們比一般的直接開場要婉轉一點，但不一定比較禮貌。商用英文通常都很直接，只有極少數「禮貌的方式」和「不禮貌的方式」的分別。

1.2c 別人所指定的主題 Topic Mandated by Another Person

BIZ 必通句型

... SAID YOU WANT TO TALK ABOUT ....
……說你想談談……。
例 Your manager said you want to talk about bulk order discounts.
你們經理說你想談談大量訂購的折扣。

... SAID WE SHOULD TALK ABOUT ....
……說我們應該談談……。
例 Lydia said we should talk about the meeting agenda.
莉迪亞說我們應該談談會議的議程。

... TOLD ME WE NEED TO TALK ABOUT ....
……告訴我說，我們必須談談……。
例 My department head told me we need to talk about a factory tour.
我的部門主管告訴我說，我們必須談談參觀工廠的事。

I THINK ... WANTS US TO TALK ABOUT ....
我想……要我們談談……。
例 I think Grant wants us to talk about the overstock issue.
我想葛蘭特要我們談談存貨過剩的問題。

Word List

mandated [ˈmændet] v. 任命進行……
bulk [bʌlk] n./adj. 大量（的）；大批（的）

overstock [ˌovɚˈstɑk] v./ [ˈovɚˈstɑk] n. 存貨過剩

57

◇◇ 小心陷阱 ◇◇

☹ 錯誤用法

The director said we **should need to** talk about two things.

主任說我們應該談兩件事。

☺ 正確用法

The director said we **should** talk about two things.

The director said we **need to** talk about two things.

主任說我們應該談兩件事。

Show Time

A: Thanks for treating me to lunch, Tracy,

B: You're welcome.

A: Well, it's time to talk about your letters of credit.

B: Okay. Where shall we begin?

A: I received your fax regarding the payment amounts. My boss told me we need to talk about using one L/C for all the purchases during a given quarter.

A：崔西，謝謝妳請我吃午餐。

B：不客氣。

A：嗯，該來談談你們的信用狀了。

B：好，我們要從哪開始？

A：我收到了妳那份關於付款金額的傳真。我老闆告訴我說，我們得談談是不是一季購買的全部東西用一張信用狀就好。

Word List

letter of credit 信用狀 (= L/C)

given [ˋɡɪvən] *adj.* 規定的；特定的

1.3 改變主題 Changing the Topic

 track 09

1.3a 詢問目前的主題討論是否已經結束 Asking If the Current Topic Is Finished

BIZ 必通句型

HAVE WE COVERED EVERYTHING?
我們是不是每件事都談到了？

WOULD YOU LIKE TO ADD ANYTHING?
您有任何要補充的嗎？

SHOULD WE TALK ABOUT ... NOW?
我們現在是不是該談談……？
例 Should we talk about the quality policy now?
　　我們現在是不是該談談品管政策？

IS THERE ANYTHING ELSE WE SHOULD SAY ABOUT THIS?
針對這點我們還有沒有什麼應該提出的？

SHALL WE PROCEED TO THE NEXT TOPIC?
我們是不是可以進行下一個主題了？

1.3b 結束目前的話題 Closing the Current Topic

BIZ 必通句型

I GUESS THAT'S ALL FOR THAT TOPIC.
我想那個主題就這樣了。

WELL, THAT FINISHES THAT TOPIC.
嗯，這個主題就此打住。

> **I GUESS IT'S TIME TO DISCUSS THE OTHER TOPIC.**
> 我想該討論另一個主題了。

> **IT SEEMS WE SAID EVERYTHING WE WANTED ABOUT THAT.**
> 關於那件事，我們想說的話似乎都說了。

　　當話題進行得差不多而該另起新話題時，參與對話的人通常都心裡有數。因此，上述的用語並非絕對必要，但這些片語可在想要確認討論的主題真的結束時使用。

1.3c 轉移到全新的主題 Changing to a Completely New Topic

BIZ 必通句型

LET'S TALK ABOUT ... (NOW).
（現在）我們來談談……。
例 Let's talk about the <u>fiber optic</u> cables now.
　　現在我們來談談光纖電纜吧。

I GUESS IT'S TIME TO TALK ABOUT ... (NOW).
我想（現在）該來談談……。
例 I guess it's time to talk about the billing records.
　　我想現在該來談談帳單開列的記錄了。

WE HAD BETTER DISCUSS ... (NOW).
我們（現在）最好來討論……。
例 We had better discuss your price recommendations now.
　　我們現在最好來討論你對價格所提出的建議。

🖉 **Note**
　　「Now」是個關鍵字，它代表接下來的主題跟原本所討論的不一樣。

Word List

fiber optic [ˌfaɪbə ˋɑptɪk] *n.* 光纖

1.3d 轉移到附帶主題 Changing to Someone's Sub-topic

BIZ 必通句型

SPEAKING OF ..., ...

說到……, ……。

例 Speaking of IC <u>chips</u>, we might need to change our supplier.

說到積體電路晶片,我們可能得更換供應商。

THAT REMINDS ME, ...

那提醒了我,……。

例 That reminds me, have you seen the new Motorola phones?

那提醒了我,你有沒有看過摩托羅拉的新電話?

YOU MENTIONED ....

你提到……。

例 You mentioned sunglasses. A new company from Germany is selling them in Taipei 101.

你提到太陽眼鏡。有一家新的德國公司正在台北 101 販售太陽眼鏡。

Show Time

A: Would you like to add anything?

B: Nope. I guess it's time to discuss our other topic.

A: All right. Let's talk about the electronic <u>receipts</u>. Your new electronic ordering system seems to have lost a few.

B: Speaking of electronic ordering, I just received some new orders from your company. I hope the receipts were sent out with no problems.

Word List

chip [tʃɪp] *n.* 【電子】晶片   receipt [rɪ`sit] *n.* 收據

A：你還想補充什麼嗎？

B：不了。我想該討論別的主題了。

A：好，那我們就來談談電子收據吧。你們新的電子下單系統似乎漏掉了幾份。

B：說到電子下單，我剛收到了你們公司的幾份新訂單。我希望寄出去的收據都沒有問題。

◇◇◇ 小心陷阱 ◇◇◇

☹ 錯誤用法

You **had mentioned** something interesting.

你提到了某件有趣的事。

☺ 正確用法

You **mentioned** something interesting.

你提到了某件有趣的事。

★★★ *BIZ* 一點通 ★★★

幾乎每個人都會誤用過去完成式，亦即在該用「過去式」或「現在完成式」的時候使用過去完成式。

✗ I had gone to Taichung yesterday.

✓ I went to Taichung yesterday.

  我昨天去了台中。

✗ I had seen that before.

✓ I have seen that before.

  我以前看過那個。

以英文為母語的人很少使用過去完成式。如果你想要了解它精確的用法，應該參考文法書。一本好的文法書一定會用許多情境式例句來詳細解釋。至於在商業英語方面，則一定要確定自己能夠用對過去式和現在完成式，因為它們常用多了。

2 掌控話題 Navigating Topics

　　對話就像是開車前往特定的目的地，在往目的地的路上，你可以左轉或右轉，可以走快速的大路或緩慢的小路，可以放慢速度輕鬆駕駛，可以加速前進快點到達，甚至可以停下來進站休息。參與對話的人必須知道要如何在對話的道路上馳騁。

2.1 岔題 Digressing

 track 10

2.1a 離開主題 Leaving the Topic

BIZ 必通句型

BY THE WAY, ...
對了，……。
例 By the way, we can eat Japanese food after our meeting.
　　對了，開完會我們可以去吃日本料理。

I WANT TO QUICKLY MENTION ....
我想很快說一下……。
例 I want to quickly mention that Jimmy did some analysis of the market trend.
　　我想很快地說一下，吉米做了一些市場趨勢的分析。

THERE IS A SIDE POINT I WANT TO MENTION.
我想附帶提一點。

Word List

navigate [ˈnævəˌget] v. 操縱；駕駛
digress [daɪˈgrɛs] v. 偏離（主題）

2.1b 回到原來的主題 Coming Back to the Topic

BIZ 必通句型

BACK TO ....
回到……。
例 Back to our topic.
回到我們的主題上。
例 Back to the product <u>description</u>.
回到產品說明書上。

BACK TO WHAT WE WERE TALKING ABOUT.
回到我們之前所談的事情上。

ANYWAY, LET'S GET BACK TO ....
不管怎樣，我們回到……。
例 Anyway, let's get back to the main point.
不管怎樣，我們回到主要的重點上。

◇◇ 小心陷阱 ◇◇

☹ 錯誤用法
Let's **back to** the <u>primary</u> issue.
我們回到主要的議題上。
☺ 正確用法
Let's **go back to** the primary issue.
我們回到主要的議題上。

✎ Note
在上面的正確範例中，「back」並非動詞而是副詞。

Word List

description [dɪˈskrɪpʃən] *n.* （物品、計畫等的）說明書；外貌描述
primary [ˈpraɪ͵mɛrɪ] *adj.* 主要的；首要的

2.1c 忘記主題 Forgetting the Topic

BIZ 必通句型

WHAT WERE WE TALKING ABOUT?
我們剛才在談什麼？

SORRY, I FORGOT OUR TOPIC.
抱歉，我忘了我們的主題。

I LOST TRACK OF OUR ORIGINAL TOPIC.
我忘了我們原本的主題。

Show Time

A: The other thing I want to say about the solar cells is that no other company can beat our price. By the way, the next generation of solar cells will be available soon. The core technology was developed by a Canadian company, and we are working with them. Um, uh, sorry, I forgot our topic.

B: We were discussing the main selling points of your solar cells.

A: Oh, yes. Sorry. Back to what we were talking about.

A：關於太陽能電池我想說的另一件事情是，其他公司在價格上都比不上我們。對了，下一代的太陽能電池很快就會問世。它的核心科技是一家加拿大公司開發的，而我們就是和他們合作。嗯，呃，抱歉，我忘了我們的主題。

B：我們正在討論你們太陽能電池的主要賣點。

A：喔，對。抱歉，回到我們之前所談的事情上。

Word List

lose track of 忘記……
original [əˋrɪdʒən] *adj.* 最早的；最初的
solar cell [ˋsolɚ ˋsɛl] *n.* 太陽（能）電池

available [əˋveləbl] *adj.* 可得到的；可取得的
selling point [ˋsɛlɪŋ ˌpɔɪnt] *n.* 賣點；特點

2.2 提及說話者的話 Referring to the Speaker's Words track 11

BIZ 必通句型

REGARDING WHAT YOU SAID, ...
關於你所說的，……。
例 Regarding what you said, do you really believe it can be accomplished?
關於你所說的，你真的認為有辦法完成嗎?

REGARDING WHAT YOU SAID ABOUT ..., ...
關於你所說的有關……，……。
例 Regarding what you said about the equipment, it seems the vendor in Changhua is the most reliable.
關於你所說的有關設備的部分，彰化的廠商似乎最可靠。

IN LINE WITH WHAT YOU SAID, ...
正如你說的，……。
例 In line with what you said, I think the telecommunication system must be <u>top-notch</u> in order to be useful.
正如你說的，我認為電信系統必須要頂級的才有用。

2.3 評論話題 Commenting on a Topic track 12

BIZ 必通句型

AS FOR ..., ...
至於……，……。
例 As for your idea, I am a little <u>skeptical</u>.
至於你的想法，我有點懷疑。

Word List

in line with 與……一致
top-notch [ˈtɑpˈnɑtʃ] *adj.* 最高級的；第一流的

skeptical [ˈskɛptɪkl] *adj.* 懷疑的；多疑的

REGARDING ..., ...

就……而言，……。

 Regarding the fishing regulations, I don't think China will change its position.

就漁業法規而言，我不認為中國會改變立場。

ABOUT ..., ...

關於……，……。

 About our rework, the assembly is ninety percent finished.

關於我們重做的部分，有九○％已經裝配完成。

2.4 切入重點 Getting to the Point track 13

BIZ 必通句型

SO WHAT IS YOUR CONCLUSION?

所以你的結論是什麼？

WHAT IS YOUR FINAL THOUGHT ABOUT THAT?

你對那件事的最終想法是什麼？

CAN YOU TELL ME YOUR FINAL ANALYSIS?

你能不能告訴我你最後的分析為何？

WHAT EXACTLY IS YOUR POINT?

你的重點到底是什麼？

Show Time

A: As for the tobacco grown in central Taiwan, I think it is perfectly good enough to be <u>exported</u> to any country. The rich soil and the weather conditions both make for a high quality tobacco plant.

B: Regarding what you said, I agree that Taiwanese tobacco is as good as any in Asia, but I don't know how well it can compete with tobacco grown in the American South.

A: Maybe, but that is just a marketing problem. I don't think American tobacco is actually better.

B: So what is your conclusion?

A: I think we should try to market our tobacco all around Asia.

A：至於中台灣所栽種的菸草，我認為它絕對好到足以外銷到任何一個國家。肥沃的土壤加上氣候條件好，所以能種出高品質的菸草。

B：關於你所說的，我同意台灣的菸草跟亞洲各國的一樣好，可是我不知道和美國南部所栽種的菸草比較，它能有多少競爭力。

A：也許，但那只是行銷的問題。我並不認為美洲的菸草真的比較好。

B：所以你的結論是什麼？

A：我想我們應該設法把我們的菸草賣到全亞洲。

2.5 更深入地探討話題 <u>Digging</u> Deeper <u>into</u> a Topic

 track 14

BIZ 必通句型

LET'S GET INTO THIS IN MORE DETAIL.
我們來更仔細地探討這一點。

Word List

export [ɪks`port] *v.* / [`ɛksport] *n.* 輸出（品）　　　dig into 鑽研；探究

WE HAD BETTER DIG INTO THIS MORE.
我們最好更深入地探討這一點。

CAN WE <u>DELVE INTO</u> THIS FURTHER?
我們能進一步研究這件事嗎？

2.6 徵求意見 Seeking Input

 track 15

2.6a 一般意見 General Input

BIZ 必通句型

HOW DO YOU FEEL ABOUT ...?
……你覺得如何？
例 How do you feel about that/the policy?
　　那件事/那項政策你覺得如何？

WHAT DO YOU THINK ABOUT ...?
你對……有什麼想法？
例 What do you think about Kieran's report?
　　你對奇亞倫的報告有什麼想法？

WHAT IS YOUR VIEW OF ...?
你對……有什麼看法？
例 What is your view of the current situation?
　　你對時局有什麼看法？

Word List

delve [dɛlv] into 探究；鑽研

WHAT IS YOUR <u>TAKE</u> ON ...?

你對……有什麼高見？

例 What is your take on the stock market?

　　你對股市有什麼高見？

WHAT IS YOUR POINT OF VIEW?

你的觀點是什麼？

WHAT ARE YOUR THOUGHTS ABOUT ...?

你對……有些什麼想法？

例 What are your thoughts about her proposal?

　　你對她的提案有些什麼想法？

◇◇ 小心陷阱 ◇◇

☹ 錯誤用法

How do you think about that?

你對那點有什麼想法？

☺ 正確用法

What do you think about that?

你對那點有什麼想法？

Note

「How」在英文中有兩種用法：（1）和形容詞或副詞並用；（2）解釋過程。

「What」在英文中有兩種用法：（1）和名詞或動詞並用；（2）解釋想法。

Word List

take [tek] *n.* 見解；想法

2.6b 引出更多細節 Pulling out More Details

BIZ 必通句型

WHAT ELSE CAN YOU TELL ME ABOUT ...?
對於……你還能告訴我什麼？
例 What else can you tell me about the <u>retailer</u>'s complaints?
對於零售商的抱怨，你還能告訴我什麼？

TELL ME MORE ABOUT YOUR THINKING.
多告訴我一些你的想法。

I'D LIKE TO HEAR MORE ABOUT YOUR THINKING.
我想多聽聽你的想法

DO YOU HAVE OTHER IDEAS ABOUT THAT?
你對那件事有別的想法嗎？

2.6c 尋求替代想法 Seeking <u>Alternative</u> Thoughts

BIZ 必通句型

HAVE YOU THOUGHT ABOUT ...?
你有沒有想過……？
例 Have you thought about placing a <u>trial</u> order first?
你有沒有想過先試訂？

Word List

retailer [`ritelɚ] *n.* 零售商                    trial [`traɪəl] *n./adj.* 嘗試（的）；試用（的）
alternative [ɔl`tɝnətɪv] *adj.* 替代的

HAVE YOU CONSIDERED ...?

你有沒有考慮過……？

例 Have you considered changing your methods?

　　你有沒有考慮過改變你的方法？

HAS ... (EVER) ENTERED YOUR THINKING?

你（曾經）想到過……嗎？

例 Has the new import regulation entered your thinking?

　　你曾經想到過新的進口規定嗎？

Show Time

A: What is your take on trying to sell gardening supplies to North America?

B: There are already some Taiwanese companies competing successfully in this market. If we produce high quality products, there is no reason we cannot succeed as well.

A: Let's get into this in more detail.

B: Specifically, I think we can produce very nice hand tools for home gardening.

A: Tell me more about your thinking.

B: Americans and Canadians with houses often have gardens for growing food or flowers. Have you ever thought about how large the gardening sections are at Wal-mart?

Word List

enter [ˈɛntɚ] v. （主意等）在（腦）中浮現

A：你對嘗試把園藝用品賣到北美有什麼高見？

B：有一些台灣公司已經成功地在這個市場上競爭。如果我們能生產高品質的產品，我們沒有理由不能像它們一樣成功。

A：我們來更仔細地探討這點。

B：明確來說，我認為我們可以製造出非常好的家庭園藝手用工具。

A：多告訴我一點你的想法。

B：擁有房子的美國人和加拿大人通常都會有花園來種植作物和花卉。你曾想過沃爾瑪超市的園藝區有多大嗎？

✎ **Memo**

3 結束對話 Finishing a Conversation

3.1 結束訊號 Closing Signal

 track 16

3.1a 討論完成 The Discussion Is Complete

BIZ 必通句型

IT SEEMS WE ARE FINISHED.
看來我們談完了。

I THINK WE COVERED EVERYTHING.
我想我們每件事都談到了。

I GUESS THAT'S ALL WE HAVE TO TALK ABOUT.
我想我們該談的就是那樣了。

I GUESS THERE'S NOTHING ELSE TO DISCUSS.
我想沒有別的事要討論了。

I THINK WE ARE DONE.
我想我們討論完了。

3.1b 討論還沒完成 The Discussion Is Incomplete

BIZ 必通句型

• 因時間不夠必須中斷談話 There Is No More Time

WELL, IT'S TIME TO GO.
嗯,該走了。

I GUESS YOU NEED TO GO.

我想你該走了。

OUR TIME IS UP, SO I SHOULD LET YOU GO.

我們的時間到了，所以我該讓你走了。

I'M SORRY, I HAVE TO GO NOW.

抱歉，我現在得走了。

I'M SORRY, I HAVE TO RUN.

抱歉，我得走人了。

● 因其他原因必須中斷談話 There Is An <u>Interruption</u>

I'M SORRY, I HAVE AN URGENT ....

抱歉，我有要緊的……。

例 I'm sorry, I have an urgent phone call.

　　抱歉，我有通要緊的電話得接。

LET'S PICK THIS UP LATER.

我們稍後再來談這件事。

WE CAN FINISH THIS LATER.

我們可以稍後再把這件事談完。

I'LL <u>GET BACK TO</u> YOU RIGHT AWAY TO FINISH TALKING ABOUT THIS.

我馬上就會回來跟你談完這件事。

LET ME KNOW WHEN WE CAN FINISH DISCUSSING THIS.

讓我知道我們什麼時候可以討論完這件事。

Word **L**ist

interruption [ˌɪntəˋrʌpʃən] *n.* 中斷；阻礙　　　　get back to 再與……說話

3.2 愉快的結語 Pleasant Concluding Remarks

 track **17**

BIZ 必通句型

IT WAS NICE TALKING WITH YOU.
很高興跟你談話。

I ENJOYED TALKING WITH YOU.
和你談話很開心。

I HAD A <u>FRUITFUL</u> DISCUSSION WITH YOU.
跟你討論讓我受益良多。

OUR DISCUSSION WAS QUITE <u>PRODUCTIVE</u>.
我們的討論成果豐碩。

I LOOK FORWARD TO TALKING WITH YOU AGAIN.
期待能再次跟你談話。

3.3 交換聯絡方式 Exchanging Contact Information

 track **18**

BIZ 必通句型

I SHOULD GIVE YOU MY CONTACT INFORMATION.
我應該給你我的聯絡方式。

HERE IS MY ....
這是我的……。

Word List

fruitful [ˋfrutfəl] *adj.* 收穫多的;有益的
productive [prəˋdʌktɪv] *adj.* 有生產力的;豐富的

例 Here is my office phone number.

這是我的辦公室電話號碼。

LET ME GIVE YOU MY ....

讓我給你我的……。

例 Let me give you my email address.

讓我給你我的電子郵件地址。

YOU CAN REACH ME AT ....

你可以撥……跟我聯絡。

例 You can reach me at 09-1234-5678.

你可以撥 09-1234-5678 跟我聯絡。

YOU CAN CONTACT ME AT ....

你可以在……找到我。

例 You can contact me at my office.

你可以在我的辦公室找到我。

◇◇ 小心陷阱 ◇◇◇

☹ 錯誤用法

Here is my contact **informations**.

這是我的聯絡方式。

☺ 正確用法

Here is my contact **information**.

這是我的聯絡方式。

3.4 道別 Saying Goodbye

 track 19

BIZ 必通句型

SEE YOU.
再見。

SEE YOU LATER.
回頭見。

TALK TO YOU LATER.
再聊。

CATCH YOU LATER.
再聯絡。

SEE YOU NEXT TIME.
下次再見。

Show Time 1

A: I think we are done.
B: Yes, I think we covered everything.
A: Well, it was nice talking with you.
B: Thanks. Our discussion was quite productive.
A: If you think of anything else you want to discuss, you can contact me at my home.
B: That's very kind of you.
A: Alright, catch you later.
B: See you!

A：我想我們討論完了。

B：是的，我想我們每件事都談到了。

A：嗯，很高興跟你談話。

B：謝謝。我們的討論成果豐碩。

A：如果你想到其他什麼事要討論，可以在我家找到我。

B：你真好。

A：好了，再聯絡囉。

B：再見！

Show Time 2

A: I'm sorry, I have to run.

B: It's okay. We can finish this later.

A: Yes, good. I look forward to talking with you again.

B: Here is my business card. My contact information is on the front.
You can send me an e-mail or give me a call.

A: Thanks, and here is my business card.

B: Thanks.

A: You're welcome. Talk to you later.

B: Catch you later.

A：抱歉，我得走人了。

B：沒關係，我們可以稍後再把這件事談完。

A：是，很好。期待能再跟你談話。

B：這是我的名片。正面有我的聯絡方式，你可以寄電子郵件或打電話給我。

A：謝謝。這是我的名片。

B：謝謝。

A：不客氣。再聊。

B：再聯絡。

談論他人時所用的字彙 Vocabulary for Talking About People

　　在一般的商業對話中，談論別人、提到別人或者只是提到他人的名字是很稀鬆平常的事。有很多字彙可以用來談論別人，因為畢竟是人類創造了語言。人際關係是商場很重要的一部分，懂得各式各樣談論別人的詞彙，對於維繫各種話題的談話能力將有莫大的幫助。

4.1 十分常用的術語 Very General Terms

 track 20

4.1a 名詞 Nouns

BIZ 必通字彙

> **高頻字彙** Most-frequently used

businessperson/businesspeople *n.* 商務人士

例 I met a nice **businessperson** on the plane.
我在飛機上遇到一位很好的商務人士。

例 **Businesspeople** these days need many computer skills.
現在的商務人士需要具備多種電腦技能。

businessman/businesswoman *n.* 男／女性商務人士

例 He is a **businessman** who does financial consulting work.
他是位從事金融顧問工作的商務人士。

例 Is that **businesswoman** part of your team?
那位女性商務人士是你們團隊的一員嗎？

> **加分字彙** Nice-to-know terms

entrepreneur [ˌɑntrəprəˋnɜ] *n.* 企業家

例 I am an **entrepreneur** based in Taoyuan, Taiwan.
我是個以台灣桃園為據點的企業家。

business-owner *n.* 經營者
例 My cousin is a **business-owner** in Vietnam.
我堂哥在越南是一位企業經營者。

● 其他字彙　Other terms for businesspeople

suit [sut] *n.* 企業主管
例 Look at all the **suits** smoking cigars in the corner of the pub.
你瞧那些群在酒吧角落裡抽著雪茄的企業主管們。

capitalist [ˈkæpətḷɪst] *n.* 資本家
例 He's nothing but a **capitalist** trying to make a fast buck.
他只不過是一位想快速輕鬆賺筆錢的資本家。

4.1b 描述上述用語的形容詞 Adjectives for the Terms Above
注意這些用字的不同。

BIZ 必通字彙

respected [rɪˈspɛktɪd] *adj.* 受敬重的
例 I gather that your boss is a **respected** businessman.
我想你們老闆是位受敬重的商界人士。

leading [ˈlidɪŋ] *adj.* 首屈一指的；最重要的
例 She is a **leading** businesswoman in this field.
她在這個領域是首屈一指的女商界人士。

prominent [ˈprɑmənənt] *adj.* 傑出的；著名的
例 There will be many **prominent** businesspeople at the conference.
有很多傑出的商界人士會參加那場會議。

Word List

buck [bʌk] *n.*【美俚】元　　　gather [ˈgæðɚ] *v.* 推測；猜想

81

successful [sə`ksɛsfəl] *adj.* 成功的；有成就的

例 Everyone <u>surmises</u> that you are quite a **successful** businessperson.
大家都猜想你是位非常成功的商界人士。

4.2 特定用語 Specific Terms

 track 21

4.2a 各種工作人員 Types of Workers

BIZ 必通字彙

• 可數名詞 Countable Nouns

❶ employee [ˌɛmplɔɪ`i] *n.* 員工；受僱者
❷ staff member [`stæf ˌmɛmbə] *n.* 工作人員；職員
❸ office worker [`ɔfɪs ˌwɜkə] *n.* 公司職員
❹ salesperson [`selzˌpɜsn̩] *n.* 業務人員；售貨員
❺ line worker [`laɪn ˌwɜkə] *n.* 線上工人；線上作業人員
❻ foreman [`formən] *n.* 領班；工頭
❼ technician [tɛk`nɪʃən] *n.* 技術人員
❽ guard [gɑrd] *n.* 警衛
❾ clerk [klɜk] *n.* 辦事員；職員
❿ analyst [`æn̩lɪst] *n.* 分析師
⓫ purchaser [`pɜtʃəsə] *n.* 買主

• 不可數名詞 Uncountable Nouns

❶ personnel [ˌpɜsn̩`ɛl] *n.* 全體人員
❷ staff [stæf] *n.* 全體職員

Word List

surmise [sɜ`maɪz] *v.* 揣測；猜想

❸ workforce [`wɜk͵fors] *n.* 全體從業人員

❹ labor [`lebə] *n.* 勞工階級；勞工

❺ management [`mænɪdŋmənt] *n.* 管理階層；資方

❻ sales force [`selz ͵fors] *n.* 全體銷售人員

◇◇ 小心陷阱 ◇◇◇

☹ 錯誤用法

She is a **staff** in my department.

她是我部門的職員。

☺ 正確用法

She is a **staff member** in my department.

She is an **employee** in my department.

她是我部門的職員。

4.2b 職務名稱 Names of Positions

BIZ 必通字彙

● 高階職位 Top Positions

❶ founder [`faʊndə] *n.* 創辦人

❷ president [`prɛzədənt] *n.* 總裁；董事長

❸ director [də`rɛktə] *n.* 董事

❹ managing director [`mænɪdʒɪŋ də`rɛktə] *n.* 常務董事

❺ officer [`ɔfəsə] *n.* 高級職員

❻ chief executive officer [`tʃif ɪg`zɛkjʊtɪv `ɔfəsə] *n.* 執行長 (=CEO)

❼ executive [ɪg`zɛkjʊtɪv] *n.* 主管 (=exec.)

❽ chairperson [`tʃɛr͵pɝsṇ] *n.* 主席

❾ chairwoman [`tʃɛr͵wʊmən] *n.* 女主席

❿ chairman [`tʃɛrmən] *n.* 主席；董事長；理事長

中階職位 Middle Positions

❶ manager [ˋmænɪdʒɚ] *n.* 經理

❷ project manager [ˋprɑdʒkt ˏmænɪdʒɚ] *n.* 專案經理

❸ plant manager [ˋplɑnt ˏmænɪdʒɚ] *n.* 廠長

❹ executive assistant [ɪgˋzɛkjʊtɪv ˋəsɪstənt] *n.* 副理

❺ head [hɛd] *n.* 主管；總經理

❻ supervisor [ˏsupɚˋvaɪzɚ] *n.* 主任；主管

Note

「small potato」這個字可用來形容職位不重要的人。例如：I am a small potato in my company.（我是我們公司裡的小螺絲釘）。

4.2c 特殊修飾用語 Special Modifying Terms

Senior:	Top:	Chief:
executive	executive	executive
manager	manager	manager
officer	researcher	editor

Vice-:	Co:	Assistant:
chairperson	head	manager
president	chairperson	head
director	director	director
	founder	

Note

上述的修飾語可用來形容公司內不同的位階（如：manager、president 等）或工作職務（如：editor、engineer 等）。表中所列出的，是在一般公司較常見到的搭配用法。

4.3 描述商界人士的用語 Describing Businesspeople

 track **22**

4.3a 正面用語 Positive Terms

BIZ 必通字彙

❶ decisive [dɪ`saɪsɪv] *adj.* 果斷的；堅決的

❷ active [`æktɪv] *adj.* 積極的；主動的

❸ responsible [rɪ`spɑnsəbl] *adj.* 負責的

❹ devoted [dɪ`votɪd] *adj.* 專心致力的；投入的

❺ cooperative [ko`ɑpə͵retɪv] *adj.* 合作的

❻ sincere [sɪn`sɪr] *adj.* 誠懇的

❼ committed [kə`mɪtɪd] *adj.* 忠於職守的

❽ competitive [kəm`pɛtətɪv] *adj.* 有競爭力的

❾ patient [`peʃənt] *adj.* 有耐心的

❿ sensitive [`sɛnsətɪv] *adj.* 敏感度高的

⓫ assertive [ə`sɝtɪv] *adj.* 自信的

⓬ reliable [rɪ`laɪəbl] *adj.* 可靠的

⓭ approachable [ə`protʃəbl] *adj.* 易親近的

⓮ ambitious [æm`bɪʃəs] *adj.* 有雄心的；有抱負的

⓯ practical [`præktɪkl] *adj.* 實際的

⓰ industrious [ɪn`dʌstrɪəs] *adj.* 勤勉的

⓱ energetic [͵ɛnə`dʒɛtɪk] *adj.* 精力充沛的

⓲ passionate [`pæʃənɪt] *adj.* 熱情的

⓳ savvy [`sævɪ] *adj.* 精明幹練的

⓴ trusted [`trʌstɪd] *adj.* 被信賴的

㉑ down-to-earth [`daʊntə`ɝθ] *adj.* 實際的

㉒ laid-back [`led`bæk] *adj.* 從容的

㉓ efficient [ɪ`fɪʃənt] *adj.* 有效率的

㉔ talented [`tæləntɪd] *adj.* 有才幹的

㉕ resourceful [rɪ`sorsfəl] *adj.* 富有機智的

4.3b 負面用語 Negative Terms

BIZ 必通字彙

❶ indecisive [ˌɪndɪˋsaɪsɪv] *adj.* 優柔寡斷的
❷ irresponsible [ˌɪrɪˋspɑnsəbl] *adj.* 不負責任的
❸ uncooperative [ˌʌncoˋɑpəˌretɪv] *adj.* 不合作的
❹ over-sensitive [ˋovəˋsɛnsətɪv] *adj.* 過分敏感的
❺ insincere [ˌɪnsɪnˋsɪr] *adj.* 沒有誠意的
❻ passive [ˋpæsɪv] *adj.* 消極的
❼ unreliable [ˌʌnrɪˋlaɪəbl] *adj.* 不可靠的
❽ pretentious [prɪˋtɛnʃəs] *adj.* 矯飾的
❾ greedy [ˋgridɪ] *adj.* 貪心的
❿ impatient [ɪmˋpeʃənt] *adj.* 沒有耐心的
⓫ careless [ˋkɛrlɪs] *adj.* 粗心的；草率的
⓬ ungrateful [ʌnˋgretfəl] *adj.* 忘恩負義的
⓭ unimaginative [ˌʌnɪˋmædʒɪnətɪv] *adj.* 缺乏想像力的
⓮ useless [ˋjusləs] *adj.* 無用的
⓯ arrogant [ˋærəgənt] *adj.* 傲慢的；自大的

4.3c 中性用語 Neutral Terms

BIZ 必通字彙

❶ white-collar [ˋhwaɪtˋkɑlə] *adj.* 白領階級的
❷ blue-collar [ˋbluˋkɑlə] *adj.* 藍領階級的
❸ mid-level [ˋmɪdˌlɛvl] *adj.* 中階的
❹ high-ranking [ˋhaɪˋræŋkɪŋ] *adj.* 高階的
❺ low-ranking [ˋloˋræŋkɪŋ] *adj.* 低階的
❻ former [ˋfɔrmə] *adj.* 前任的
❼ in-coming [ˋɪnˌkʌmɪŋ] *adj.* 新任的
❽ out-going [ˋauˌgoɪŋ] *adj.* 將離職的
❾ current [ˋkɝənt] *adj.* 目前的
❿ temporary [ˋtɛmpərɛrɪ] *adj.* 臨時的；暫時的

5 談論一般話題所用的字彙 Vocabulary for Talking About Common Topics

　　下列各組字彙有助於談論各種最常見的商業話題。懂得這些用字會讓你更有能力和同事、顧客和聯絡人展開有意義的對話。談論一般話題的能力愈好，就愈容易和其他商界人士溝通。此外，懂得各個領域的一些關鍵字則會讓人覺得你既有智慧又精通商業。

5.1 時間的相關用法 Time Metaphors

 track 23

BIZ 必通字彙

❶ spend time 花時間
❷ waste time 浪費時間
❸ kill time 消磨時間
❹ lose time 耗費時間
❺ allocate [ˋæləˌket] time 分配時間
❻ find time 找時間
❼ save time 節省時間
❽ take time 費時
❾ invest time 投入時間

5.2 金錢的相關用字 Money Words

 track 24

5.2a 金錢術語 Money-related Terms

BIZ 必通字彙

❶ income [ˋɪnkʌm] *n.* 收入；所得
❷ salary [ˋsælərɪ] *n.* 薪水
❸ wage [wedʒ] *n.* 工資

❹ deposit [dɪˋpɑzɪt] *n.* 存款

❺ withdrawal [wɪðˋdrɔəl] *n.* 提款

❻ currency [ˋkɝənsɪ] *n.* 貨幣

❼ capital [ˋkɛpətl] *n.* 資本

❽ loan [lon] *n.* 貸款

❾ debt [dɛt] *n.* 債務；負債

5.2b 貨幣名稱 Names of Currencies

Country 國家	Currency 貨幣	Abbreviation 縮寫
Taiwan 台灣	New Taiwan Dollar 新台幣	TWD
China 中國	Yuan/Renminbi 元 / 人民幣	CNY
Japan 日本	Yen 圓	JPY
Australia 澳洲	Dollar 澳幣	AUD
Singapore 新加坡	Dollar 新幣	SGD
Korea 韓國	Won 圜	KRW
Thailand 泰國	Baht 銖	THB
India 印度	Rupee 盧比	INR
United States 美國	Dollar 美元	USD
Britain 英國	Pound 英鎊	GBP
Germany* 德國	Mark 馬克	DEM
France* 法國	Franc 法郎	FRF
Italy* 義大利	Lira 里拉	ITL

註 標有 * 的國家現在都改用歐元（EUR），但原有貨幣的名稱還是很常聽到。

5.2c 使用歐元的國家 Countries That Use the Euro (EUR)

Austria 奧地利	Belgium 比利時	Germany 德國
Spain 西班牙	Finland 芬蘭	France 法國
Greece 希臘	Ireland 愛爾蘭	Italy 義大利
Luxembourg 盧森堡	Netherlands 荷蘭	Portugal 葡萄牙

5.3 國家—名詞和形容詞 Countries — Nouns vs. Adjectives track 25

在提到國家的名稱時，常見的錯誤是把形容詞當成國家的名稱。正確使用詞類是很重要的事，所以商界人士必須熟知以下用字。

國名 Country Name	形容詞 Adjective
Germany 德國	German 德國（人）的；德國人
France 法國	French 法國（人）的；法國人
Britain 英國	British 英國（人）的；英國人
Italy 義大利	Italian 義大利（人）的；義大利人
Australia 澳洲	Australian 澳洲（人）的；澳洲人
America 美國	American 美國（人）的；美國人
Mexico 墨西哥	Mexican 墨西哥（人）的；墨西哥人

◇◇ 小心陷阱 ◇◇◇

☹ 錯誤用法

I just came back from a trade show in **German**.

我剛從德國的商展回來。

☺ 正確用法

I just came back from a trade show in **Germany**.

我剛從德國的商展回來。

5.4 經濟字彙 Economics Words track 26

BIZ 必通字彙

❶ demand [dɪˋmænd] *n./v.* 需求
❷ supply [səˋplaɪ] *n./v.* 供給
❸ money supply 貨幣供應量
❹ recession [rɪˋsɛʃən] *n.* 衰退；不景氣
❺ slowdown [ˋsloˌdaʊn] *n.*（生意等）衰退；怠工；減產

❻ slump [slʌmp] *v.* （物價等）下跌；（經濟等）衰退

❼ depression [dɪ`prɛʃən] *n.* 蕭條；不景氣

❽ downturn [`daʊn͵tɜn] *n.* 下跌；衰退；不振

❾ boom [bum] *n./v.* （景氣）繁榮

5.5 行銷字彙 Marketing Words

 track 27

5.5a 行銷字串 Marketing Word Partnerships

BIZ 必通字彙

❶ marketing trend 行銷趨勢

❷ marketing agency 行銷代理商

❸ marketing campaign [kæm`pen] 行銷活動

❹ market leader 市場領導者

❺ market mix 市場組合

❻ market segmentation [͵sɛgmən`teʃən] 市場區隔

❼ market segment [`sɛgmənt] 市場區塊

❽ market share 市場占有率

❾ target market 目標市場

❿ niche [nɪtʃ]/[nɪʃ] market 利基市場

⑪ market price 市價

⑫ market force 市場力量

⑬ market trend 市場趨勢

⑭ marketplace [`mɑrket͵ples] *n.* 市場

5.5b 描述市場 Describing Markets

BIZ 必通字彙

● 負面的 Negative

❶ sluggish [ˈslʌgɪʃ] *adj.* 不振的；不景氣的
❷ weak [wik] *adj.* 疲軟的
❸ choppy [ˈtʃɑpɪ] *adj.* 起伏的
❹ erratic [əˈrætɪk] *adj.* 不穩定的
❺ bumpy [ˈbʌmpɪ] *adj.* 顛簸的
❻ mixed [mɪkst] *adj.* 混雜的

● 正面的 Positive

❶ brisk [brɪsk] *adj.* 活絡的
❷ booming [ˈbumɪŋ] *adj.* 繁榮的
❸ rebounding [rɪˈbaʊndɪŋ] *adj.* 反彈的
❹ surging [ˈsɜdʒɪŋ] *adj.* 高漲的
❺ stable [ˈstebl̩] *adj.* 穩定的

5.6 「Make」和「Do」的相關片語 Using "Make" and "Do"

Make		Do	
	a profit		business
	a loss		a job
	a deal		a project
	an offer		a presentation
	a proposal		a study
	an appointment		a survey
	a comparison		a test
	a breakthrough		research
	an impact		
	a discovery		

5.7 實用字串 Useful Word Partnerships

 track 28

BIZ 必通字彙

• 「demand」的相關字串 Used with "Demand"

❶ satisfy demand 滿足需求
❷ meet demand 滿足需求
❸ create demand 創造需求
❹ stimulate demand 刺激需求
❺ boost demand 增加需求

• 「offer」的相關字串 Used with "Offer"

❶ generate an offer 出價
❷ withdraw an offer 撤回出價

• 「agreement」的相關字串 Used with "Agreement"

❶ strike an agreement 達成協議
❷ come to an agreement 達成協議
❸ reach an agreement 達成協議

5.8 實用的一般動作字彙 Useful General Action Words

 track 29

BIZ 必通字彙

○ 強力動詞 Power Verbs

❶ minimize [ˋmɪnəˌmaɪz] v. 最小化；使……減至最小
❷ maximize [ˋmæksəˌmaɪz] v. 最大化；使……達至最大
❸ regulate [ˋrɛgjəˌlet] v. 管制；規定

❹ impede [ɪm`pid] *v.* 妨礙

❺ restore [rɪ`stor] 恢復;重建

● 片語動詞 Phrasal Verbs

❶ come up with 提出

❷ come out with 說出

❸ keep up with 趕上

❹ back out of 退出;取消

❺ get on with 著手;繼續

Memo

6 實戰演練 Partner Practice

當你讀完並複習過本章內容後，找個同伴試試下面的對話練習！

情境 1

兩個同事在閒聊食物。

練習 1	
角色 A	美商台灣分公司的台籍員工
角色 B	同公司的美籍員工
A	開啓大家都知道的話題。(1.1a) (1.1b) 告訴角色 B，你最近聽到或看到一個有趣的食物話題，例如新餐廳。
B	對角色 A 表達你對這個話題的想法。
A	離開這個話題討論別的事，然後回到原來話題上。(2.1a) (2.1b)
B	評論話題。(2.3)
A	告訴角色 B 你餓了，並想聊其他的事。(1.3c)
B	問角色 A 對某個話題的意見。(2.6a)
A	告訴角色 B 你對該話題的看法。
B	告訴角色 A，你忘了你要打一通重要的電話，所以你得離開了。(3.1b)

情境 2

兩個行銷主管在會議的休息時間聊到網際網路的事。

練習 2	
角色 A	台灣商務人士
角色 B	外籍商務人士
A	開啓事先決定好的商業話題：網際網路。想像你事先已經打算聊這個話題。(1.2a) (1.2b)
B	告訴角色 A，你對於運用網際網路來做生意的想法，至少舉三個例子。
A	換成談論角色 B 所提到的附帶話題。(1.3d)

B	回到網際網路的主題。(2.1b) 從角色 A 身上引申出更多細節。(2.6b)
A	把你的意見告訴角色 B。
B	看角色 A 有沒有一些其他的想法。(2.6c)
A	把你的想法告訴角色 B。
B	和角色 A 分享你的想法。提到某件角色 A 說過的一些特定事項。(2.2)
A	釋放結束的訊號，因為該回去開會了。(3.1b)
B	說一些愉快的結語。(3.2)

情境 3

談判結束後，兩個商務人士去咖啡店談論各自的老闆。

練習 3	
角色 A	台灣商務人士
角色 B	外國顧客
A	問角色 B 他對他老闆有什麼看法。(2.6a)
B	說明你對你老闆的看法。(4.3a) (4.3b)
A	你的手機響了。告訴角色 B 你要接電話。接聽並告訴電話中的人，你稍後會回他電話。掛斷然後告訴角色 B，你忘了剛才在聊什麼。(2.1c)
B	提醒角色 A，你們剛才在聊什麼。更深入地談論話題。(2.5)
A	告訴角色 B，你對你老闆的想法。(4.3a) (4.3b)
B	要角色 A 說得詳細一點。(2.6b)
A	多解釋一點你覺得怎麼樣。
B	切入重點。(2.4)
A	問角色 B，目前的話題是否結束。(1.3a)
B	結束話題。(3.1a)
AB	交換彼此的聯絡方式。(3.3)
AB	道別。(3.4)

第 **3** 章

接待

Receiving Guests

對很多人來說，接待客人是商場生活中最棒的一環。我們都知道，帶客戶去用餐是做生意很重要的一部分。人人都喜歡品嚐美食和友善的人共度美好時光。本章將介紹許多字彙和用語，來協助你讓外國賓客在本地過得開心，藉此和他們建立穩固的私人關係，並讓他們感受到此地和人的溫馨。

For many people, entertaining a customer is the best part of business life. We all know that taking a customer out for dinner is an important part of doing business. Everybody loves to eat good food and to have a nice time with friendly people. This chapter provides a lot of vocabulary and language that will help you show your foreign guests a great time in you local environment so that you can have smooth personal relations with your customers and give them a warm feeling about this place and the people here.

1 : 與客人碰面 Meeting Customers

1.1 第一次接觸 First Contact

 track 30

1.1a 認出賓客 Identifying a Guest

BIZ 必通句型

EXCUSE ME. ARE YOU (name)?
對不起。請問您是（名字）嗎？
例 Excuse me. Are you Trisha Barnes?
　　對不起。請問您是崔夏‧巴恩斯嗎？

MIGHT YOU BE (name)?
您是（名字）嗎？
例 Might you be Ben Nelson?
　　您是班‧尼爾森嗎？

ARE YOU (name), <u>BY ANY CHANCE</u>?
不知您是否就是（名字）？
例 Are you Gregory Zartman, by any chance?
　　不知您是否就是葛列格里‧札特曼？

PARDON ME. I AM WONDERING IF YOU ARE (name).
對不起。我在想您是不是（名字）。
例 Pardon me. I am wondering if you are Jasper Holmes.
　　對不起。我在想您是不是賈斯伯‧荷姆斯。

Word List

by any chance 也許碰巧

YOU MUST BE (name).

您一定是（名字）。

例 You must be Dilbert Bradley.

　　您一定是戴伯特・布萊得利。

　　不管你是用上述哪句話確認賓客，重點是接下來記得要對客人說：
WELCOME TO TAIWAN!（歡迎來台灣！）

1.1b 詢問原先不認識的賓客 Questioning an Unknown Guest

BIZ 必通句型

HAVE YOU BEEN TO TAIWAN BEFORE?

您以前到過台灣嗎？

IS THIS YOUR FIRST VISIT TO TAIWAN?

這是您第一次來台灣嗎？

I THINK THIS IS YOUR FIRST TRIP TO TAIWAN, RIGHT?

我想這是您第一次到台灣來，對吧？

I THINK YOU HAVE BEEN TO TAIWAN BEFORE, RIGHT?

我想您以前來過台灣，對吧？

🖉 Note

　　可以依照和國外商務賓客見面的地方，自行把上述片語中的「台灣」換成其他地
名，像是「新竹」、「高雄」或「深圳」。

1.1c 給見過面的賓客的溫暖話語 Warm Words for a Guest You Have Met Before

BIZ 必通句型

IT'S NICE TO SEE YOU AGAIN, (name).
（名字），很高興又見到你／妳。
例 It's nice to see you again, Ashley.
艾西莉，很高興又見到妳。

I AM GLAD TO SEE YOU AGAIN, (name).
（名字），很高興又見到你。
例 I am glad to see you again, Brad.
布萊德，很高興又見到你。

IT'S MY PLEASURE TO WELCOME YOU TO TAIWAN AGAIN.
能夠再次迎接你到台灣是我的榮幸。

HOW NICE TO SEE YOU AGAIN!
能再見到你真高興！

1.1d 談論旅途 Commenting on the Trip

BIZ 必通句型

YOU MUST BE TIRED.
您一定累了。

HOW WAS YOUR FLIGHT?
您這趟飛行如何？

HOW WAS YOUR TRIP?
您這趟旅程如何？

I HOPE YOUR TRIP WAS SMOOTH.

希望您旅途還順利。

1.2 自我介紹 Self-Introduction

 track 31

1.2a 示意要做介紹 Introductory Signal

BIZ 必通句型

MAY I INTRODUCE MYSELF?

我可以自我介紹一下嗎？

I'D LIKE TO INTRODUCE MYSELF.

我想自我介紹一下。

ALLOW ME TO INTRODUCE MYSELF.

容我自我介紹。

IT'S MY PLEASURE TO INTRODUCE MYSELF.

能自我介紹是我的榮幸。

1.2b 說出自己的姓名和職務 Stating Your Name and Position

BIZ 必通句型

I AM (name), A/THE (job title).

我是（名字），（職銜）。

例 I am Jason, the project manager for your new product.

我叫傑森，貴公司新產品的專案經理。

例 I am Emily, an assistant in the Business Department.

我叫艾蜜莉，商業部的助理。

> **MY NAME IS (name). I AM A/THE (job title).**
> 我叫（名字）。我是（職銜）。
> 例 My name is Andrew. I am a <u>contract specialist</u> in the Legal Department.
> 　　我叫安卓。我是法律部的約聘專員。
> 例 My name is Jessica. I am the contact person for this project.
> 　　我叫潔西卡。我是這個案子的聯絡人。

　　假如你想要的話，也可以報出公司名稱。不過在大部分的情況下，賓客都已經知道你在哪家公司工作服務（他當然要知道你的公司名稱！），所以公司名稱並不是非說不可，例如：

　　My name is Harriet. I am a product quality assurance engineer at ASUS.
　　我叫哈里特。我是華碩的產品品保工程師。

◇◇ 小心陷阱 ◇◇

☹ 錯誤用法
My name is Josh, a Human Resources specialist.
我叫賈許，人力資源專員。
☺ 正確用法
My name is Josh. **I am** a Human Resources specialist.
I am Josh, a Human Resources specialist.
我叫賈許，人力資源專員。

◇◇ 小心陷阱 ◇◇

☹ 錯誤用法
I am a buyer **in** Tiger Electronics.
我是老虎電子的採購人員。
☺ 正確用法
I am a buyer **at** Tiger Electronics.
我是老虎電子的採購人員。

Word List

contract specialist 約聘專員

1.2c 使用名字 Using Your Given Name

過去幾十年來，商場文化變得愈來愈不拘禮節。現在有許多西方國家的商場人士在工作時常使用名字，而且也希望同事用名字來稱呼他們。根據我的經驗，我發現台灣人也很不拘泥形式而且很隨和（有很多人就經常使用英文名字），這也是台灣人能和太平洋沿岸國家的西方人成為良好商業夥伴的原因之一。

BIZ 必通句型

JUST CALL ME (name).
叫我（名字）就好。
例 Just call me Harry.
　　叫我哈利就好。

PLEASE, CALL ME (name).
請叫我（名字）。
例 Please, call me Pauline.
　　請叫我寶琳。

YOU CAN CALL ME (name).
您可以叫我（名字）。
例 You can call me Rex.
　　您可以叫我瑞克斯。

1.2d 回應自我介紹 Responding to a Self-Introduction

BIZ 必通句型

IT'S NICE TO MEET YOU.
很高興認識您。

HI (Name). NICE TO MEET YOU.
嗨，（名字），很高興認識您。

例 Hi Ethan. Nice to meet you.
嗨，伊森，很高興認識您。

IT'S MY PLEASURE TO MEET YOU.
能夠認識您是我的榮幸。

I AM HAPPY TO MEET YOU.
很高興認識您。

Note

一定要確定自己在聽完客人自我介紹「後」才使用上述用語。中文母語人士常犯的錯誤是，在聽到別人的名字前就先說「Nice to meet you.」。「Meet you」意味已經知道了別人的名字了，所以要等時機對了才能說！

Show Time

Sal: You must be Ruby Walton.
Ruby: Yes, I am Ruby.
Sal: It's my pleasure to meet you. May I introduce myself? I am Sal, the Assistant Manager.
Ruby: It's nice to meet you.
Sal: Welcome to Taiwan, Ms. Walton! Is this your first visit to Taiwan?
Ruby: Yes, it is. Please, call me Ruby.
Sal: Okay. You can call me Sal. How was your trip?
Ruby: <u>Other than</u> the airline losing my luggage, everything went smoothly. Thanks.

薩爾：您一定是茹比‧華頓。
茹比：是，我就是茹比。
薩爾：能夠認識您是我的榮幸。我可以自我介紹一下嗎？我叫薩爾，是公司副理。

Word List

other than 除了……

茹比：很高興認識您。

薩爾：華頓女士，歡迎來台灣！這是您第一次來台灣嗎？

茹比：是的，第一次。請叫我茹比。

薩爾：好，您可以叫我薩爾。您這趟旅程如何？

茹比：除了航空公司搞丟了我的行李外，一切還算順利。謝謝。

1.3 介紹他人 Introducing Someone Else

 track 32

1.3a 示意要做介紹 Introductory Signal

BIZ 必通句型

I'D LIKE TO INTRODUCE (name).

我想介紹（名字）。

例 I'd like to introduce Calvin.

我想介紹卡文。

ALLOW ME TO INTRODUCE (name).

容我介紹（名字）。

例 Allow me to introduce Victor.

容我介紹維特。

LET ME INTRODUCE (name).

我來介紹（名字）。

例 Let me introduce Whitley.

我來介紹惠特利。

I WOULD LIKE YOU TO MEET (name).

我想介紹（名字）給您認識。

例 I would like you to meet Amber.

我想介紹安伯給您認識。

◇◇ 小心陷阱 ◇◇

☹ 錯誤用法

Let me **introducing** Billy.

我來介紹一下比利。

☺ 正確用法

Let me **introduce** Billy.

我來介紹一下比利。

1.3b 說出姓名和職務 Stating Name and Position

BIZ 必通句型

(Name) IS A (job title).

（姓名）是（職銜）。

例 Jasmine is a sales <u>rep</u>.

茉莉是業務代表。

(Name) IS A (job title) at our company.

（姓名）是我們公司的（職銜）

例 Jasmine is a sales rep at our company.

茉莉是我們公司的業務代表。

1.3c 簡單介紹 Quick Introduction

這種介紹方式可以用在雙方已經知道彼此的職位時。當你做這樣的介紹動作時，手應該自然張開，掌心向上，並在指向這個人時說出他／她的名字。

BIZ 必通句型

(Name1), THIS IS (Name2). (Name2), THIS IS (Name1).

（名字 1），這位是（名字 2）。（名字 2），這位是（名字 1）。

Word **List**

rep [rɛp] *n.* 代表（＝ representative）

例 Ernest, this is Phillip. Phillip, this is Ernest.

厄尼斯特，這位是菲利浦。菲利浦，這位是厄尼斯特。

(Name1), MEET (Name2). (Name2), MEET (Name1).

（名字 1），見過（名字 2）。（名字 2），見過（名字 1）。

例 Yvonne, meet Winston. Winston, meet Yvonne.

伊娃，見過溫斯頓。溫斯頓，見過伊娃。

(Name1), (Name2). (Name2), (Name1).

（名字 1），（名字 2）。（名字 2），（名字 1）。

例 Charlotte, Monte. Monte, Charlotte.

夏洛特，蒙堤。蒙堤，夏洛特。

1.4 交換名片 Exchanging Business Cards

 track 33

1.4a 遞名片 Giving a Card

BIZ 必通句型

LET ME GIVE YOU MY (BUSINESS) CARD.

讓我給您我的名片。

HERE IS MY (BUSINESS) CARD.

這是我的名片。

SORRY, I DON'T HAVE ANY CARDS AT THE MOMENT.

抱歉，我目前沒有名片。

1.4b 要名片 Asking for a Card

BIZ 必通句型

COULD I HAVE YOUR BUSINESS CARD?
我可以跟您要張名片嗎？

DO YOU HAVE A CARD?
您有名片嗎？

Show Time

Sal: Ruby, I would like you to meet Ivan. Ivan is the Manager. He will be <u>overseeing</u> your project.

Ruby: Nice to meet you, Ivan. I am Ruby, the project manager at Lion Electrical Company.

Ivan: Hi Ruby. Nice to meet you.

Ruby: Could I have your business card?

Ivan: Sure. Here is my card. Do you have a card?

Ruby: Yes, of course. <u>Here you go.</u>

薩爾：茹比，我介紹艾分給妳認識。艾分是經理，他將負責妳的案子。

茹比：很高興認識您，艾分。我是茹比，獅子電氣公司的專案經理。

艾分：嗨，茹比，很高興認識您。

茹比：我可以跟您要張名片嗎？

艾分：當然可以。這是我的名片。您有名片嗎？

茹比：有的。喏。

Word **List**

oversee [ˌovəˋsi] *v.* 監督（工作或人）

Here you go. 拿去；在這裡

2 邀請賓客外出 Inviting a Guest Out

2.1 詢問賓客的偏好和禁忌
Checking Your Guest's <u>Preferences</u> and <u>Restrictions</u>

track 34

　　要了解賓客喜歡哪種食物，以及有沒有什麼東西是他／她不能吃的。有些人會因為健康因素或宗教信仰而指定特別的飲食，有些人則是為了健康所以對飲食格外小心。不要試圖以自己的想法來建議你的賓客怎麼吃比較好或比較不好。不要拿健康來說教，要尊重賓客所選擇的生活方式。和西方人相處時，貿然向對方提出健康忠告，是一項失禮的行為。

　　要站在賓客的立場設想。假如你是客人，你會希望別人怎麼對待自己？你應該提供給賓客他們喜歡的東西，並盡量讓他們感到舒適。有些人會試圖強迫客人吃一些台灣傳統美食或特別的料理，但來自台灣以外的人多半會覺得這些東西很怪。當然，我指的就是臭豆腐、豬血糕和內臟等美食。如果你的賓客不想吃某種食物，那就尊重他／她的決定。假如你說出「您應該吃吃看，因為您人在台灣」這類的話，那你就同時在人際和商業關係上犯了嚴重錯誤。

　　當然，這並不表示你不可以和賓客去吃本地的食物。儘管帶你的賓客去吃台灣的美食，只要找一些較具傳統性而且你很確定賓客會喜歡的就好。台灣有很多本地料理足以讓任何一個國家的任何一位賓客都覺得很好吃。

2.1a 詢問飲食限制 Checking for <u>Dietary</u> Restrictions

BIZ 必通句型

DO YOU HAVE ANY DIETARY RESTRICTIONS?
您有什麼不吃的東西嗎？

Word List

preference [ˋprɛfrəns] *n.* 喜歡；偏愛
restriction [rɪˋstrɪkʃən] *n.* 限制；約束

dietary [ˋdaɪəˌtɛrɪ] *adj.* 飲食的；規定飲食的

IS THERE ANY FOOD YOU CANNOT EAT?
您有什麼食物不能吃嗎？

IS THERE ANY FOOD YOU PREFER NOT TO EAT?
您有什麼不希望吃的食物嗎？

◇◇◇ 小心陷阱 ◇◇◇

☹ 錯誤用法

Did you have any diet restrictions?

您有什麼不吃的東西嗎？

☺ 正確用法

Do you have any **dietary** restrictions?

您有什麼不吃的東西嗎？

2.1b 詢問偏好 Checking for Preferences

BIZ 必通句型

WHAT KIND OF FOOD DO YOU LIKE?
您喜歡哪種食物？

WHAT KIND OF FOOD DO YOU PREFER?
您偏好哪種食物？

WHAT DO YOU FEEL LIKE EATING?
您想要吃些什麼？

DO YOU HAVE A FAVORITE FOOD?
您有最愛吃的食物嗎？

2.1c 提供選擇 Offering Choices

BIZ 必通句型

DO YOU LIKE ...?

您喜歡……嗎？

例 Do you like <u>leafy</u> vegetables?

您喜歡葉菜類食物嗎？

WHICH DO YOU PREFER: X OR Y?

您比較喜歡哪個：X 或 Y？

例 Which do you prefer: meat or vegetarian food?

您比較喜歡哪個：肉類或蔬菜類食物？

WOULD YOU RATHER EAT/DRINK X OR Y?

您比較想吃／喝 X 還是 Y？

例 Would you rather eat fish or steak?

您比較想吃魚還是牛排？

例 Would you rather drink juice or coffee?

您比較想喝果汁還是咖啡？

WHAT KIND OF FOOD DO YOU LIKE?

您喜歡哪種食物？

WHAT KIND OF FOOD ARE YOU <u>IN THE MOOD FOR</u>?

您想吃哪種食物？

Word List

leafy [ˈlifɪ] *adj.* 多葉的；由葉子組成的

in the mood for 有做……的心情、意向

◇◇ 小心陷阱 ◇◇◇

☹ 錯誤用法

Would you **rather to drink** tea or beer?

您比較想喝茶還是啤酒？

☺ 正確用法

Would you **rather drink** tea or beer?

您比較想喝茶還是啤酒？

2.2 正式邀請 Making an Official Invitation

 track 35

在詢問客人的飲食限制和偏好前後，你都可以提出邀請。如果你已經知道賓客的限制和偏好，可以請他去特定的餐館。如果不知道，可以先提出一般性的邀請，稍後再決定餐廳。

2.2a 確定邀約的種類 Establishing the Kind of Invitation

BIZ 必通句型

I'D LIKE TO TAKE YOU TO ....

我想帶您去……。

例 I'd like to take you to lunch.

　　我想帶您去吃午餐。

WOULD YOU LIKE TO HAVE ... WITH ME/US?

您要不要和我／我們一起……？

例 Would you like to have dinner with me?

　　您要不要和我一起吃晚餐？

I WOULD LIKE TO INVITE YOU TO/FOR ....

我想請您去／吃（或喝）……。

例 I would like to invite you to the hotel's restaurant tonight.

今天晚上我想請您去飯店的餐廳。

例 I would like to invite you for coffee tonight.

今天晚上我想請您喝咖啡。

ARE YOU AVAILABLE FOR ...?

您有空……嗎？

例 Are you available for breakfast tomorrow morning?

明天早上您有空吃早餐嗎？

CAN I TAKE YOU TO ...?

我可以帶您去……嗎？

例 Can I take you to a Chinese restaurant after our meeting?

開完會後，我可以帶您去一家中式餐館嗎？

2.2b 約時間 Setting the Time

BIZ 必通句型

WOULD (time) SUIT YOU?

（時間）您方便嗎？

例 Would 7:00 suit you?

七點鐘您方便嗎？

IS (time) OKAY FOR YOU?

（時間）您可以嗎？

例 Is 6:00 a.m. okay for you?

六點鐘您可以嗎？

HOW ABOUT (time)?

（時間）怎麼樣？

例 How about noon?

中午怎麼樣？

SHALL WE SAY (time)?

我們約（時間）好嗎？

例 Shall we say about 5:30?

我們約五點半左右好嗎？

2.2c 說明人數 Stating the Number of People

BIZ 必通句型

IT WILL JUST BE THE (number) OF US.

就只會有我們（數字）個人。

例 It will just be the three of us.

就只會有我們三個人。

THERE WILL BE (number) OF US.

我們一共會有（數字）個人。

例 There will be five of us.

我們一共會有五個人。

I'VE INVITED A FEW OTHER PEOPLE.

我另外約了一些人。

THERE WILL BE (number) PEOPLE THERE.

到時會有（數字）個人。

例 There will be seven people there.

到時會有七個人。

2.3 確定形式 Establishing the <u>Formality</u>

 track 36

BIZ 必通字彙

❶ formal [ˋfɔrml] *adj.* 正式的（西裝外套加領帶）
❷ semi-formal [ˌsɛmɪˋfɔml] *adj.* 半正式的（領帶，不加西裝外套）
❸ casual [ˋkæʒuəl] *adj.* 非正式的（一般襯衫或馬球衫）
❹ come as you are 隨意（現在穿什麼就把它穿來）

Show Time

A: I would like to invite you for dinner tomorrow evening.

B: That sounds good. I'd be happy to join you.

A: Do you have any dietary restrictions?

B: Well, I have <u>diabetes</u>, so I need to avoid <u>starches</u> as much as possible.

A: I see. That is no problem. What kind of food do you like?

B: I am from the middle of the US, so I like meat. Seafood is okay, too.

A: Would you rather eat beef or chicken?

B: Well, I eat beef so much in the States, so chicken sounds better, actually.

A: Do you like spicy food?

B: Sure.

A: Okay. Then I know a great restaurant you will like. Would six o'clock suit you?

B: Six is fine.

Word List

formality [fɔˋmæləti] *n.* 拘泥形式
diabetes [daɪəˋbitɪs] *n.* 糖尿病

starch [ˋstɑrtʃ] *n.* 澱粉（複數 starches 指澱粉類食物）

A: I've invited a few other people. Some of the sales associates would like to get to know you.

B: Sounds nice. How should I dress?

A: Just **come as you are**. The restaurant is a family-style place. There will be businesspeople in suits and farmers wearing jeans and T-shirts!

A：明天晚上我想請您吃晚餐。

B：聽起來不錯。我就不客氣了。

A：您有什麼不吃的東西嗎？

B：嗯……我有糖尿病，所以我必須盡量避免澱粉類的東西。

A：我知道了。那不成問題。您喜歡哪種食物？

B：我來自美國中部，所以我喜歡肉類。海鮮也可以。

A：您比較想吃牛肉還是雞肉？

B：嗯……我在美國很常吃牛肉，所以雞肉似乎比較好。

A：您喜歡吃辣的食物嗎？

B：當然。

A：好，那我知道一家您會喜歡的好餐廳。六點您方便嗎？

B：六點可以。

A：我另外約了一些人。有幾個業務夥伴想要認識您。

B：聽起來蠻好的。我應該穿什麼？

A：隨意就可以了。那家餐廳是家庭式的。那裡會有穿西裝的商界人士，也會有穿牛仔褲和 T 恤的農夫！

3 餐廳用語 Restaurant Language

3.1 基本餐廳字彙 Basic Restaurant Vocabulary

 track 37

3.1a 人員 People

BIZ 必通字彙

❶ waiter [ˋwetə] *n.* 服務生
❷ waitress [ˋwetrɪs] *n.* 女服務生
❸ cashier [kæˋʃɪr] *n.* 收銀員
❹ cook [kʊk] *n.* 廚師
❺ chef [ʃɛf] *n.* 主廚；廚師
❻ patron [ˋpetrən] *n.* 主顧；老顧客
❼ diner [ˋdaɪnə] *n.* 用餐的人

3.1b 印刷品 Printed Things

BIZ 必通字彙

❶ menu [ˋmɛnju] *n.* 菜單
❷ display board [dɪˋsple͵bord] *n.* 顯示牌
❸ bill [bɪl] *n.* 帳單
❹ receipt [rɪˋsit] *n.* 收據

3.1c 餐具 Table Setting

BIZ 必通字彙

❶ knife [naɪf] *n.* 刀子
❷ fork [fɔrk] *n.* 叉子
❸ spoon [spun] *n.* 湯匙
❹ chopsticks [ˋtʃɑp͵stɪks] *n.* 筷子（複數）
❺ plate [plet] *n.* 盤子
❻ saucer [ˋsɔsə] *n.* 淺碟；茶杯的拖盤

❼ small bowl [ˋsmɔlˋbol] *n.* 小碗

❽ soup bowl [ˋsup͵bol] *n.* 湯碗

❾ tea cup [ˋti͵kʌp] *n.* 茶杯

❿ lazy Susan [ˋlezɪ ˋsuzn̩] *n.* 【美】（餐桌中央的）圓轉盤

⓫ hot plate [ˋhɑt͵plet] *n.* 電磁爐

⓬ toothpick [ˋtuθ͵pɪk] *n.* 牙籤

⓭ napkin [ˋnæpkɪn] *n.* 餐巾

⓮ glass [glæs] *n.* 玻璃杯

3.1d 食物 Food

BIZ 必通字彙

❶ beverage [ˋbɛvərɪdʒ] *n.* 飲料

❷ appetizer [ˋæpə͵taɪzɚ] *n.* 開胃菜

❸ dish [dɪʃ] *n.* 料理；菜餚（食物種類）

❹ main course [ˋmen ˋkors] *n.* 主菜

❺ dessert [dɪˋzɝt] *n.* 甜點

❻ complimentary dish [͵kɑmpləˋmɛtərɪ ˋdɪʃ] *n.* 附贈的菜

3.1e 肉類烹調程度 Cooking Meat

你可以問賓客：How would you like your meat?（您希望肉類如何烹調？）

BIZ 必通字彙

❶ bloody [ˋblʌdɪ] *adj.* 帶血的

❷ raw [rɔ] *adj.* 生的

❸ rare [rɛr] *adj.* 三分熟的

❹ medium-rare [ˋmidɪəm ˋrɛr] *adj.* 四分熟的

❺ medium [ˋmidɪəm] *adj.* 五分熟的

❻ medium-well [ˋmidɪəm ˋwɛl] *adj.* 七分熟的

❼ well-done [ˋwɛl ˋdʌn] *adj.* 全熟的

❽ burnt [bɝnt] *adj.* 燒焦的

3.2 描述食物 Describing Food

track 38

食物和文化密不可分。大多數的料理都沒有直接翻譯，因爲外國並沒有這些料理。你可以在某些書裡或網路上找到許多中式或台式料理的英文翻譯，但對來台灣參訪的外國人來說，這些翻譯大部分都無法理解。這些翻譯多半是爲長期住在台灣的外國人所創造，因爲他們需要特殊的英文詞彙來和其他人談論食物。

精確地描述食物並不容易。食物必須要用看的、聞的、嚐的，有時還得觸摸。不過，讓賓客對中式或台式料理有個大致上的概念倒是不難。你可以用下列詞彙來描述各式各樣的料理，這樣賓客就會知道某道料理是不是他／她可能會喜歡的東西。

3.2a 食物類別 Food Categories

BIZ 必通字彙

❶ meat [mit] *n.* 肉
❷ vegetable [ˈvɛdʒətəbl] *n.* 蔬菜
❸ fruit [frut] *n.* 水果
❹ bread [brɛd] *n.* 麵包
❺ dough [do] *n.* 麵糰
❻ salad [ˈsæləd] *n.* 沙拉

3.2b 各種肉類 Kinds of Meat

BIZ 必通字彙

❶ beef [bif] *n.* 牛肉
❷ chicken [ˈtʃɪkən] *n.* 雞肉
❸ pork [pork] *n.* 豬肉
❹ lamb [læm] *n.* 羊肉
❺ seafood [ˈsiˌfud] *n.* 海鮮
❻ innards [ˈɪnədz] *n.* 內臟

3.2c 各種海鮮 Kinds of Seafood

B/Z 必通字彙

❶ fish [fɪʃ] *n.* 魚
❷ shell fish [ˈʃɛl͵fɪʃ] *n.* 貝類
❸ crab [kræb] *n.* 螃蟹
❹ squid [skwɪd] *n.* 烏賊
❺ octopus [ˈɑktəpəs] *n.* 章魚
❻ clam [klæm] *n.* 蛤蠣
❼ oyster [ˈɔɪstə] *n.* 牡蠣；生蠔

❽ fish meat ball 魚丸
❾ shrimp [ʃrɪmp] *n.* 蝦子
❿ prawn(s) [prɔn] *n.* 對蝦；明蝦
⓫ abalone [͵æbəˈlonɪ] *n.* 鮑魚
⓬ sashimi [sɑˈʃɪmɪ] *n.* 生魚片
⓭ roe [ro] *n.* 魚卵
⓮ lobster [ˈlɑbstə] *n.* 龍蝦

3.2d 常見蔬菜 Common Vegetables

B/Z 必通字彙

❶ garlic [ˈɡɑrlɪk] *n.* 大蒜
❷ cabbage [ˈkæbɪdʒ] *n.* 甘藍菜
❸ greens [grinz] / leafy vegetables [ˈlifɪ ˈvɛdʒətəblz] *n.* 蔬菜／葉菜
❹ mushroom [ˈmʌʃrum] *n.* 蘑菇
❺ green onion [ˈgrin ˈʌnjən] *n.* 青蔥
❻ hot pepper [ˈhɑt ˈpɛpə] *n.* 辣椒
❼ sweet potato [ˈswit pəˈteto] *n.* 蕃薯；地瓜
❽ ginger [ˈdʒɪndʒə] *n.* 薑
❾ carrot [ˈkærət] *n.* 胡蘿蔔
❿ green pepper [ˈgrin ˈpɛpə] *n.* 青椒

3.2e 味道 Flavors

BIZ 必通字彙

❶ sweet [swit] *adj.* 甜的
❷ sour [saʊr] *adj.* 酸的
❸ bitter [ˈbɪtɚ] *adj.* 苦的
❹ spicy [ˈspaɪsɪ] *adj.* 辣的
❺ bland [blænd] *adj.* 淡的；無刺激性的
❻ delicious [dɪˈlɪʃəs] *adj.* 美味的
❼ tasty [ˈtestɪ] *adj.* 好吃的
❽ flavorless [ˈflevəlɪs] *adj.* 無味的

❾ salty [ˈsɔltɪ] *adj.* 鹹的
❿ savory [ˈsevərɪ] *adj.* 美味可口的
⓫ zesty [ˈzɛstɪ] *adj.* 風味十足的
⓬ tart [tɑrt] *adj.* 酸的
⓭ tangy [ˈtæŋɪ] *adj.*（味道）強烈的
⓮ fishy [ˈfɪʃɪ] *adj.* 有魚腥味的
⓯ gamy [ˈgemɪ] *adj.*（肉未烹煮前）有輕微臭味的

3.2f 質地 Textures

BIZ 必通字彙

❶ soft [sɔft] *adj.* 柔軟的
❷ chewy [ˈtʃuɪ] *adj.* 有嚼勁的
❸ crunchy [ˈkrʌntʃɪ] *adj.* 嘎吱作響的；易碎的
❹ crispy [ˈkrɪspɪ] *adj.* 酥脆的
❺ tough [tʌf] *adj.* 老的
❻ tender [ˈtɛndɚ] *adj.* 嫩的；柔軟的
❼ juicy [ˈdʒusɪ] *adj.* 多汁的
❽ springy [ˈsprɪŋɪ] *adj.* 有彈性的
❾ succulent [ˈsʌkjələnt] *adj.* 水分多的
❿ flaky [ˈflekɪ] *adj.* 酥片狀的；薄片狀的
⓫ oily [ˈɔɪlɪ] / greasy [ˈgrisɪ] *adj.* 油膩的；多脂的
⓬ moist [mɔɪst] *adj.* 濕潤的
⓭ creamy [ˈkrimɪ] *adj.* 奶油狀的；含乳脂的
⓮ gooey [ˈguɪ] *adj.* 黏稠的；甜膩的

Word List

texture [ˈtɛkstʃɚ] *n.* 質地；結構

3.2g 料理準備動作 Food Preparation Actions

BIZ 必通字彙

動詞	形容詞
❶ cut [kʌt] *v.* 切	cut [kʌt] *adj.* 切過的
❷ chop [tʃɑp] *v.* 剁	chopped [tʃɑpt] *adj.* 剁碎的
❸ slice [slaɪs] *v.* 切成薄片	sliced [slaɪst] *adj.* 切成薄片的
❹ mince [mɪns] *v.* 切、絞碎	minced [mɪnst] *adj.* 切、絞碎的
❺ shred [ʃrɛd] *v.* 切絲或條狀	shredded [ˈʃrɛdɪd] *adj.* 切絲的
❻ grate [gret] *v.* 磨碎	grated [ˈgretɪd] *adj.* 磨碎的
❼ peel [pil] *v.* 去皮	peeled [pild] *adj.* 去皮的
❽ dice [daɪs] *v.* 切丁	diced [daɪst] *adj.* 切丁的
❾ crush [krʌʃ] *v.* 碾碎	crushed [krʌʃt] *adj.* 碾碎的
❿ mash [mæʃ] *v.* 磨成泥狀或糊狀	mashed [mæʃt] *adj.* 磨成泥的

3.2h 切割的特殊說法 Special Verbs for Cutting

BIZ 必通字彙

❶ cut open 切開
❷ cut in half 對切
❸ cut into pieces 切片
❹ cut down the middle 從中間切成兩半

3.2i 裝盤準備動作 Dish Preparation Actions

BIZ 必通字彙

❶ mix [mɪks] *v.* 混合
❷ blend [blɛnd] *v.* 調和
❸ fold [fold] *v.* 包；對摺
❹ stir [stɜ] *v.* 攪拌
❺ pour [por] *v.* 倒；注
❻ bread [brɛd] *v.* 在……上灑麵包屑

3.2j 烹調器具 Cookery

BIZ 必通字彙

❶ pan [pæn] *n.* 平底鍋
❷ pot [pɑt] *n.* 鍋
❸ baking sheet [ˋbekɪŋ ˏʃit] *n.* 烤盤
❹ bowl [bol] *n.* 碗
❺ blender [ˋblɛndɚ] *n.* 攪拌機

❻ spatula [ˋspætʃələ] *n.* 抹刀
❼ colander [ˋkʌləndɚ] *n.* 濾器
❽ baking dish [ˋbekɪŋ ˏdɪʃ] *n.* 烤碟
❾ wok [wɑk] *n.* 炒菜鍋
❿ deep-fryer [ˋdip ˋfraɪɚ] *n.* 油炸鍋

3.2k 烹調方法 Cooking Methods

BIZ 必通字彙

動詞	形容詞
❶ boil [bɔɪl] *v.* 煮沸	boiled [bɔɪld] *adj.* 煮沸的
❷ fry [fraɪ] *v.* 炸	fried [fraɪd] *adj.* 炸的
❸ stir fry [ˋstɝ ˏfraɪ] *v.* 炒	stir-fried [ˋstɝ ˏfraɪd] *adj.* 炒的
❹ grill [grɪl] *v.* 烤	grilled [grɪld] *adj.* 烤的
❺ steam [stim] *v.* 蒸	steamed [stimd] *adj.* 蒸的
❻ bake [bek] *v.* 烘焙	baked [bekt] *adj.* 烘焙的
❼ dry [draɪ] *v.* 曬乾	dried [draɪd] *adj.* 曬乾的
❽ pan fry [ˋpæn ˏfraɪ] *v.* 油煎	pan-fried [ˋpæn ˏfraɪd] *adj.* 油煎的
❾ deep fry [ˋdip ˋfraɪ] *v.* 油炸	deep-fried [ˋdip ˋfraɪd] *adj.* 油炸的
❿ roast [rost] *v.* 烘烤	roasted [ˋrostɪd] *adj.* 烘烤的
⓫ braise [brez] *v.* 燉煮	braised [brezd] *adj.* 燉煮的
⓬ marinate [ˋmærəˏnet] *v.* 醃泡	marinated [ˋmærəˏnetɪd] *adj.* 醃泡的

3.2I 描述食物範例 Example Food Descriptions

你可以從下面的例子中看到，讓外國人士對一道料理有個大致的概念並沒有那麼難。這個概念如果清楚，他便知道那道菜他喜不喜歡。所以，不要害怕，試著向賓客介紹任何一道菜！

Show Time

Gong Bao Ji Ding 宮保雞丁：
"The dish is made of small chicken pieces, peanuts, and hot peppers. Some cooks add onions. The food is mixed together and stir fried."
「這道菜由小雞塊、花生及辣椒做成，有些廚師會加上洋蔥。先把食材混在一起然後快炒。」

Shui Jiao 水餃：
"Minced pork and chopped vegetables are mixed together and put into a thin piece of dough. The dough is folded. The resulting dumpling can be boiled, steamed, or fried."
「將絞肉和菜絲混在一起，然後放到薄麵皮上，再把麵皮摺起來。包好的餃子可以煮、蒸或煎。」

Zhen Zhu Nai Cha 珍珠奶茶：
"Black tea and milk are mixed together. Many small chewy balls are added to the tea. You can drink the tea and enjoy chewing the balls."
「將紅茶和牛奶混在一起，再加入許多有嚼勁的小粉圓。你可以邊喝茶邊享受咀嚼粉圓的樂趣。」

3.3 點餐 Ordering

3.3a 提議喝飲料 Offering a Drink

BIZ 必通句型

WOULD YOU LIKE A DRINK?
您想喝杯飲料嗎？

WOULD YOU CARE FOR A DRINK?
您想來杯飲料嗎？

CAN I GET A DRINK FOR YOU?
我幫您拿杯飲料好嗎？

THEY HAVE .... WHAT WOULD YOU LIKE?
他們有……。您想要什麼？
例 They have juice, tea, and coffee. What would you like?
他們有果汁、茶和咖啡。您想要什麼？

HERE'S THE DRINK MENU. CHOOSE ANYTHING YOU LIKE.
這是飲料的選單。挑個您喜歡的。

3.3b 看菜單 Perusing the Menu

BIZ 必通句型

HERE IS THE MENU. IT IS IN ENGLISH.
這是菜單，是英文的。

Word List

peruse [pə`ruz] v. 細讀；閱讀

125

TAKE YOUR TIME TO LOOK AT THE MENU.
您慢慢看菜單。

LET ME TRANSLATE THE MENU FOR YOU.
我來替您翻譯菜單。

IS THE MENU CLEAR?
菜單清楚嗎？

ORDER WHATEVER YOU LIKE FROM THE MENU.
您可以點菜單上任何您喜歡的菜。

◇◇ 小心陷阱 ◇◇

☹ 錯誤用法
Please **taking** your time to look at the menu.
請您慢慢看菜單。
☺ 正確用法
Please **take** your time to look at the menu.
請您慢慢看菜單。

3.3c 推薦 Making a Recommendation

BIZ 必通句型

I RECOMMEND ....
我推薦……。
例 I recommend the chicken soup.
我推薦雞湯。

THE ... IS VERY GOOD HERE.
這裡的……很棒。

例 The cabbage is very good here.
這裡的甘藍菜很棒。

THE <u>SPECIALTY</u> OF THIS RESTAURANT IS ....

這家餐廳的招牌菜是……。

例 The specialty of this restaurant is pork <u>ribs</u>.
這家餐廳的招牌菜是排骨。

3.4 用餐時導引賓客 Guiding the Guest Through the Meal

 track 40

3.4a 開始用餐 Beginning the Meal

BIZ 必通句型

SHALL WE EAT?
我們是不是開動了？

SHOULD WE START OUR MEAL NOW?
我們現在是不是可以開動了？

WELL, LET'S EAT!
好，開動吧！

PLEASE, GO AHEAD AND EAT.
請，開始吃吧！

Word List

specialty [ˋspɛʃəltɪ] *n.* 特製品；名產；招牌菜
rib [rɪb] *n.* 肋骨

3.4b 在用餐時觀照賓客 <u>Monitoring</u> the Guest Throughout the Meal

BIZ 必通句型

IS THERE ANYTHING YOU NEED?
您需要什麼嗎？

IS EVERYTHING OKAY?
一切都還好嗎？

IS THE FOOD ACCEPTABLE?
菜吃得慣嗎？

CAN I GET YOU ANYTHING?
我可以幫您點些什麼嗎？

◇◇ 小心陷阱 ◇◇

☹ 錯誤用法
Are you acceptable?
菜吃得慣嗎？
☺ 正確用法
Is the food acceptable?
菜吃得慣嗎？

3.4c 詢問賓客的胃口 Checking the Guest's Stomach

BIZ 必通句型

WOULD YOU LIKE ANYTHING ELSE?
您還要什麼別的嗎？

Word List

monitor [ˋmɑnɪtɚ] v. 監視；監聽

ARE YOU FULL?
您吃飽了嗎？

CAN I GET ANYTHING ELSE FOR YOU?
我可以幫您點些別的嗎？

FEEL FREE TO ORDER SOME MORE IF YOU ARE STILL HUNGRY.
如果您還沒吃飽，可以再多點一些。

3.5 結束用餐 Finishing the Meal track 41

3.5a 結束用餐時間 Time to Go

BIZ 必通句型

SHALL WE GO?
我們可以走了嗎？

WELL, TIME TO GO HOME.
嗯，該回家了。

LET'S HIT THE ROAD.
我們上路吧。

ALRIGHT, I'LL TAKE YOU BACK TO YOUR HOTEL NOW.
好，我現在就帶您回旅館。

Word List

hit the road 出發；上路

3.5b 幫賓客買單 Paying for the Guest's Meal

BIZ 必通句型

THE MEAL IS ON ME.
這餐算我的。

IT'S MY TREAT.
我請客。

I'LL TAKE CARE OF THE BILL.
我來付帳。

THE COMPANY IS PAYING FOR THE MEAL.
這餐公司會付。

3.5c 平分帳單 Splitting the Bill

BIZ 必通句型

IS IT ALRIGHT IF WE GO DUTCH?
我們各付各的好嗎？

SHALL WE SPLIT THE BILL?
我們平分帳單好嗎？

IS IT OKAY IF WE PAY SEPARATELY?
我們各自付帳好嗎？

Word List

split the bill 平分帳單

separately [ˈsɛpərɪtlɪ] adv. 個別地；分別地

4 送禮 Giving Gifts

除了和企業高層主管簽訂大合約這種大事外，送禮已經不合時宜了。其實送禮是維繫人際關係的好方法，關鍵在於要找到不太貴但又具有價值的禮物，這樣看起來才不會像是賄賂。

最好的禮物是能讓客人想起台灣、讓他／她覺得很「酷」，而且會想擺在辦公室或家裡的東西。以下是一些很不錯的點子：

1. 茶具（茶壺和茶杯組）
2. 台灣茶葉
3. 本地特產：例如，台中太陽餅（可以帶上飛機並符合海關規定的東西）
4. 刻有客人名字的印章（可以幫賓客取個中文名字並刻成印章）

許多公司都有招待客戶的預算，卻沒有購買上述小禮物的預算。一件小禮物比整晚喝啤酒或唱 KTV 要持久多了。你可以建議老闆撥出一小筆預算來買禮物。這可是筆聰明的生意！

4.1 送禮 Giving a Gift track 42

 BIZ 必通句型

HERE IS A SMALL GIFT FOR YOU.
這是送給您的小禮物。

THIS IS SOMETHING FOR YOU TO REMEMBER US BY.
這是件可以讓您記得我們的東西。

I'D LIKE TO GIVE YOU THIS SMALL GIFT.
我想送您這個小禮物。

HERE IS SOMETHING FOR YOU TO REMEMBER YOUR TIME IN TAIWAN.
這兒有樣東西可以讓您記得在台灣的時光。

PLEASE ACCEPT THIS <u>TOKEN</u> OF OUR APPRECIATION.
這是我們的一點心意，請笑納。

4.2 詢問賓客是否想買禮物
Asking If the Guest Would Like to Buy a Gift

 track 43

BIZ 必通句型

WOULD YOU LIKE TO BUY SOMETHING TO TAKE BACK TO ...?
您想買些東西回去給……嗎？

例 Would you like to buy something to take back to your wife?
您想買些東西帶回去給尊夫人嗎？

WOULD YOU LIKE TO BUY SOMETHING FOR YOUR ...?
您想幫……買些東西嗎？

例 Would you like to buy something for your family?
您想幫家人買些東西嗎？

IF YOU'D LIKE, I CAN RECOMMEND SOMETHING NICE TO TAKE BACK WITH YOU.
如果您要的話，我可以推薦一些好東西讓您帶回去。

WOULD YOU LIKE ME TO TAKE YOU TO BUY A GIFT OR <u>SOUVENIR</u> TO TAKE HOME?
要不要我帶您去買禮物或紀念品帶回家？

Word List

token [`tokən] *n.* 標記；紀念品　　　　souvenir [͵suvəˋnɪr] *n.* 紀念品；特產

5 為賓客送行 Seeing Guests off

5.1 表達個人感受 Expressing Your Personal Feelings

 track 44

BIZ 必通句型

IT WAS A PLEASURE TO MEET WITH YOU.
很高興能和您見面。

I ENJOYED GETTING TO KNOW YOU.
很高興能認識您。

I APPRECIATE ....
感謝您……。
例 I appreciate all your helpful advice.
　　感謝您一切有益的忠告。

THANKS FOR COMING TO TAIWAN TO TALK WITH US.
謝謝您到台灣來和我們商談。

THANKS FOR EVERYTHING.
謝謝您所做的一切。

Word List

see sb. off 為某人送行

◇◇◇ 小心陷阱 ◇◇◇

☹ 錯誤用法
I **appreciate for** your friendly attitude.
感謝您親切的態度。
☺ 正確用法
I **appreciate** your friendly attitude.
感謝您親切的態度。

5.2 最後的祝福 Final Wishes

 track 45

BIZ 必通句型

HAVE A SAFE TRIP!
一路平安！

I HOPE YOU HAVE A SMOOTH TRIP HOME.
希望您順利返家。

I HOPE YOUR RETURN FLIGHT IS <u>UNEVENTFUL</u>.
希望您回程平安。

MAY YOU HAVE A NICE FLIGHT BACK TO YOUR COUNTRY!
祝您返國旅途愉快！

Word List

uneventful [ˌʌnɪˋvɛntfəl] *adj.* 平靜無事的

6 實戰演練 Partner Practice

當你讀完並複習過本章內容後，找個同伴試試下面的對話練習！

情境 1

一位台灣商務人士和同事去機場接一位未曾謀面的外國客戶。

練習	
角色 A	台灣商務人士
角色 B	外國客戶
A	認出戶人。(1.1a)
B	回應。
A	介紹自己。(1.2a) (1.2b)
B	回應自我介紹，之後再介紹自己。(1.2a) (1.2b)
A	回應自我介紹。(1.2c) 介紹同事（想像你的同事在現場）。(1.3)
B	回應介紹。(1.2c)
A	向對方要名片。(1.4b)
B	回應角色 A。
A	拿名片給角色 B。(1.4a)
A	問客人一些基本問題。(1.1b)
B	回應角色 A。
A	聊聊客戶的旅途。(1.1d)
B	回應。

情境 2

延續情境一，台灣商務人士想邀請外國客戶外出晚餐。

練習	
A	邀請你的客人共進晚餐。(2.2a)
B	問角色 A 要何時用餐。
A	約時間。(2.2b) 說明一起用餐的人數。(2.2c)

B	接受提議，並進一步問角色 A 該穿什麼服裝。
A	確定衣著。(2.3) 確認角色 B 的飲食限制和食物偏好。(2.1a) (2.1b)
B	告訴角色 A，你有沒有任何禁忌或偏好。
A	告訴角色 B，你會去飯店接他。

情境 3

延續情境二，台灣商務人士正在餐廳和外國客戶用餐。

練習	
A	建議飲料。(3.3a)
B	回應。
A	和角色 B 研究菜單。(3.3b) 描述餐廳提供的食物種類。(3.2 all)
A	推薦食物。(3.3c)
	（上菜）
A	開動。(3.4a)
	（想像你們正在用餐）
A	留意角色 B。(3.4b)
A	詢問角色 B 的胃口如何。(3.4c)
B	回應角色 A。
A	送角色 B 一個禮物。(4.1a)
B	用三種不同的方式道謝。
A	結束用餐。(3.5a) 告訴角色 B，這餐你來買單。(3.5b)

✍ **Memo**

_____

_____

_____

_____

Section

TWO

常見商務議題

Common Business Issues

第 4 章

銷售用語

Sales Language

由於任何一家公司的終極目標都是靠產品和服務來獲利，因此所有的員工都必須盡其所能對銷售做出貢獻。本章的目標即提供銷售所須的基本用語；無論你是業務還是接待人員，這些用語皆有助推銷公司的商品。讀者將在文中看到涵蓋價格、產品特色、品質、訂購、運送以及約定各類主題的片語、句型和字彙，讓你能夠和那些想購買貴公司產品的聯絡人做清楚的溝通，並讓你聽起來就像個箇中老手。

In any company, since the ultimate goal is to amass profit from products and services, all employees need to contribute in one way or another to sales. The goal of this chapter is to present the essential language you need to know, whether you're in sales or a receptionist, to help you to move your company's goods. Herein you'll find phrases, patterns, and vocabulary covering a variety of topics — prices, product features, quality, orders, shipping, and appointments — that are perfect for communicating clearly with contacts who want to buy what your company has to offer, and allowing you to sound like a pro doing it.

1 談論價格 Talking About Prices

1.1 價格字彙 Price Vocabulary

 track 46

BIZ 必通字彙

❶ list price 表訂價格
❷ price list 價目表
❸ unit price 單價
❹ wholesale price 批發價
❺ retail price 零售價

❻ special price 特價；特惠價
❼ discount price 折扣價
❽ price quote 報價
❾ total price 總價

Show Time

❶ The **list price** of this unit is NT$22,500.
這一件的表訂價格是新台幣二萬二千五百元。

❷ You can take a look at this **price list**.
你可以看一下這張價目表。

❸ The **unit price** is displayed beside each product.
每樣產品旁邊都有顯示單價。

❹ You will find our **wholesale price** to be quite <u>competitive</u>.
你會發現我們的批發價很具競爭力。

❺ The **retail price** is about thirty percent over the wholesale price.
零售價大概比批發價高三○％。

❻ For you I can offer a **special price**.
我可以給您特惠價。

❼ The **discount price** makes this product a great deal.
折扣價使這樣產品變得很划算。

Word List

competitive [kəm`pɛtətɪv] *adj.* 競爭的；有競爭力的

❽ Let me know if you need a **price quote**.
如果你需要報價，請告訴我一聲。

❾ I will let you know the **total price** when I <u>calculate</u> the freight and tax.
等我計算過運費和稅款後，我會把總價告訴你。

1.2 說明價格 Stating Prices track 47

BIZ 必通句型

... IS/ARE (price) EACH.
……是每個（價格）。

例 Our file <u>cabinets</u> are twenty-four US dollars (US$24.00) each.
我們的檔案櫃是每個二十四美元。

... IS/ARE (price) PER (number).
……是每（數量）（價格）。

例 Standard mosquito killers are ninety dollars ($90.00) per dozen.
標準型捕蚊器是每打九十美元。

THIS ... COSTS (amount).
這……賣（金額）。

例 This item costs four thousand Taiwan dollars (NT$4,000.00).
這一件賣新台幣四千元。

WE CHARGE (amount) FOR ....
……我們賣（金額）。

例 We <u>charge</u> three hundred (300) for this product.
這項產品我們賣三百元。

Word List

calculate [ˋkælkjə‚let] *v.* 計算；估算
cabinet [ˋkæbənɪt] *n.* 櫥；櫃

charge [tʃɑrdʒ] *v.* 索價

THE PRICE RANGE IS (amount) TO (amount).

價位從（金額）到（金額）。

例 The price range is forty US dollars (US$40.00) to sixty US dollars (US$60.00).

價位從四十美元到六十美元。

1.3 回應降價的要求 Giving Answers to Requests for Price <u>Reduction</u>

track 48

1.3a 正面回應 Positive Answer

BIZ 必通句型

I CAN ACCEPT THAT PRICE.

我可以接受那個價格。

WE CAN <u>GO WITH</u> THAT PRICE.

我們可以同意那個價格。

I CAN AGREE TO THAT PRICE.

我可以同意那個價格。

OKAY, BUT THAT'S THE <u>ROCK BOTTOM</u> PRICE.

好吧，不過那是最低價了。

I'LL AGREE TO THAT.

我同意這麼辦。

Word **List**

reduction [rɪˈdʌkʃən] *n.* 減少；削減

go with sth. 同意某事

rock buttom （價格等）最低點

◇◇ 小心陷阱 ◇◇

☹ 錯誤用法

I **agree** that price.

我同意那個價格。

☺ 正確用法

I **agree to** that price.

我同意那個價格。

1.3b 負面回應 Negative Answer

BIZ 必通句型

(price) IS OUR LOWEST PRICE.

（價格）是我們的最低價。

例 That price is our lowest price.

那個價格是我們的最低價。

例 Two seventy-five per box ($275/box) is our lowest price.

每盒二百七十五美元是我們的最低價。

(price) IS AS LOW AS WE CAN GO.

（價格）是我們所能出的最低價。

例 Fifteen hundred ($1,500) is as low as we can go.

一千五百美元是我們所能出的最低價。

WE CAN'T SELL ... AT SUCH A LOW PRICE.

我們沒辦法用這麼低的價格來賣……。

例 We can't sell this particular model at such a low price.

我們沒辦法用那麼低的價格來賣這一型號。

I'M AFRAID I CAN'T DO ANY BETTER THAN THAT.

我恐怕沒辦法再出得更低了。

I CAN'T LOWER THE PRICE ANY MORE THAN I HAVE.
我不能再把價格往下降了。

I'M AFRAID I CAN'T BE MORE <u>FLEXIBLE</u> ABOUT THE PRICE.
我恐怕沒辦法在價格上給你更大的彈性了。

ACTUALLY, THAT PRICE IS BELOW MARKET VALUE.
事實上那個價格已經比市價低了。

◇◇ 小心陷阱 ◇◇

☹ 錯誤用法
I can't **down** the price.
我沒辦法降價。
☺ 正確用法
I can't **lower** the price.
我沒辦法降價。

1.3c 暫時回應 <u>Tentative</u> Answer

BIZ 必通句型

LET ME ASK ... AND GET BACK TO YOU.
讓我問過……再答覆你。
例 Let me ask my boss and get back to you.
　　讓我問過老闆再答覆你。

LET ME THINK ABOUT THAT.
讓我想一想。

Word **L**ist

flexible [ˋflɛksəbl̩] *adj.* 有彈性的；可變通的　　tentative [ˋtɛntətɪv] *adj.* 試驗性的；暫時性的

I NEED TO <u>PONDER</u> THAT A BIT.
我必須考慮一下。

I'LL TALK TO ... AND SEE WHAT I CAN DO.
我會跟……談談，然後看要怎麼處理。

例 I'll talk to Fred and see what I can do.
我會跟弗列得談談，然後看要怎麼處理。

Show Time

Customer: What's the price of this model?
Seller: We charge sixty-five US dollars (US$65.00) for this one.
Customer: Can you sell it for sixty dollars?
Seller: I can agree to that price.
Customer: How about fifty dollars?
Seller: We can't sell this model at such a low price.
Customer: I see. Well, can you accept fifty-five dollars?
Seller: I'll talk to my supervisor and see what I can do.
Customer: Thanks.

顧客：這個型號多少錢？
賣方：這個我們賣六十五美元。
顧客：你可以賣六十元嗎？
賣方：我可以同意那個價格。
顧客：五十元怎麼樣？
賣方：我們沒辦法用那麼低的價格來賣這一型號。
顧客：了解。那，五十五元可以接受嗎？
賣方：我會跟我的主管談談，然後看要怎麼處理。
顧客：謝謝。

Word List

ponder [ˈpɑndə] v. 仔細考慮；衡量

2 ┊ 銷售 Selling

2.1 與「銷售」相關的字彙 Key Words to Use with "Sales"　 track 49

BIZ 必通字彙

❶ sales target 銷售目標
❷ sales volume 銷售量
❸ sales turnover 銷售率；銷售總額
❹ sales figures 銷售數字
❺ sales revenue [ˋrɛvəˏnu] 銷售營收
❻ sales tax 營業稅

Show Time

❶ Our **sales target** for this month is fifteen thousand pieces.
我們這個月的銷售目標是一萬五千件。

❷ The **sales volume** has not been good this <u>quarter</u>.
本季的銷售量一直不好。

❸ It is hard to keep this product in stock because of high **sales turnover**.
這個產品不容易有現貨，因為它的銷售率高。

❹ Let me show you the great **sales figures** for this model.
我來告訴你這個型號奇佳的銷售數字。

❺ Our **sales revenue** report says this model makes more money for us than any other product.
我們的銷售營收報告上顯示，這個型號的獲利比其他任何產品都多。

❻ **Sales tax** must be added to the price of the item.
品項價格都得加上營業稅。

Word List

quarter [ˋkwɔtə] *n.* 季（一年的四分之一，即三個月）；季度

2.2 說明產品銷售量 Describing Product Sales

 track 50

BIZ 必通字彙

❶ hot 搶手 [hɑt] *adj.* 熱門的；搶手的
❷ hot-selling [ˋhɑt ˋsɛlɪŋ] *adj.* 熱賣的；暢銷的
❸ outstanding [ˌaʊtˋstændɪŋ] *adj.* 顯著的；醒目的；突出的
❹ pick up （形勢、成績等）好轉；增加
❺ flat [flæt] *adj.* 停滯的；蕭條的
❻ cold [kold] *adj.* 冷淡的

Show Time

❶ This product is really **hot**!
　這個產品非常搶手！
❷ I envy our competitor's **hot-selling** MP3 players.
　真羨慕競爭對手熱賣的 MP3 播放器。
❸ Sales of this new model are **outstanding**!
　這個新型號的銷售很可觀！
❹ I think sales will **pick up** before Christmas.
　我認為銷售量會在耶誕節前有起色。
❺ After the earthquake, sales became **flat**.
　地震過後，銷售量就停滯了。
❻ Sales have been **cold** since this technology became <u>obsolete</u>.
　自從這項技術過時之後，銷售量就一直很冷淡。

Word List

obsolete [ˋɑbsəˌlit] *adj.* 過時的；落伍的

2.3 買方和賣方 Kinds of Buyers and Sellers

 track 51

BIZ 必通字彙

❶ merchant [ˋmɝtʃənt] *n.* 商家；商人
❷ retailer [ˋritelɚ] *n.* 零售商；零售店
❸ wholesaler [ˋholˌselɚ] *n.* 批發商
❹ dealer [ˋdilɚ] *n.* 經銷商
❺ authorized [ˋɔθəˌraɪzd] dealer 授權經銷商
❻ chain store 連鎖店
❼ end user 最終消費者
❽ agent [ˋedʒənt] *n.* 代理商
❾ broker [ˋbrokɚ] *n.* 經紀人；掮客
❿ middleman [ˋmɪdlˌmæn] *n.* 中間人；掮客

Show Time

❶ Many **merchants** around Taipei sell our products.
台北有很多商家都有賣我們的產品。

❷ Any electronics **retailer** can order this item for you.
任何一家電子零售店都可以幫你訂這項東西。

❸ You can contact a **wholesaler** if you would like to order a large quantity.
如果你想大量訂購，可以跟批發商聯絡。

❹ The **dealer** can make any repairs if you have a problem.
如果有問題，經銷商會提供一切的維修。

❺ We have **authorized dealers** in both America and Europe.
我們在美洲和歐洲都有授權經銷商。

❻ We sell mostly to **chain stores**.
我們多半是賣到連鎖店。

❼ We focus on the <u>expectations</u> of the **end users**, of course.
我們當然會以最終消費者的期望為重。

Word List

expectation [ˌɛkspɛkˋteʃən] *n.* 期望

❽ You can contact our **agent** in Japan if you want items shipped quickly to locations there.
如果你希望東西能很快送到當地的據點，你可以跟我們在日本的代理商聯絡。

❾ Our **broker** can <u>negotiate</u> price discounts for <u>bulk orders</u>.
我們的經紀人可以協商大批訂購的折扣。

❿ Our **middleman** in Mexico serves the entire American market.
我們在墨西哥的中間人負責整個美洲市場。

2.4 軟性推銷用語 Language for Soft Selling

 track **52**

BIZ 必通句型

WOULD YOU BE WILLING TO CONSIDER ...?
你願不願意考慮……?

例 Would you be willing to consider the newer model?
你願不願意考慮較新的型號？

HAVE YOU EVER THOUGHT ABOUT ...?
你有沒有考慮過……?

例 Have you ever thought about the many uses of this product?
你有沒有考慮過這項產品的多種用途？

DID YOU KNOW THAT ...?
你知不知道……?

例 Did you know that this <u>AC</u> <u>adapter</u> will automatically <u>convert</u> <u>voltage</u> in any country?
你知不知道這個變壓器在任何國家都可以自動轉換電壓？

Word List

negotiate [nɪˋgoʃɪ͵et] v. 磋商；協商
bulk order 大量訂購
AC 交流電（＝ alternative current）

adapter [əˋdæptɚ] n.【電學】轉接器
convert [kənˋvɝt] v. 轉換；轉變
voltage [ˋvoltɪdʒ] n.【電學】電壓

CAN I TELL YOU ABOUT ...?

我可以向你介紹……嗎？

例 Can I tell you about all the companies that bought this product?

我可以向你介紹所有買過這項產品的公司嗎？

I CAN INTRODUCE ... IF YOU LIKE.

如果你願意的話，我可以介紹……。

例 I can introduce the top five advantages if you like.

如果你願意的話，我可以介紹五大優點。

◇◇◇ 小心陷阱 ◇◇◇

☹ 錯誤用法

Have you ever **think** about upgrading it?

你有沒有考慮過把它升級？

☺ 正確用法

Have you ever **thought** about upgrading it?

你有沒有考慮過把它升級？

2.5 硬性推銷用語 Language for Hard Selling

 track 53

BIZ 必通句型

WOULDN'T YOU AGREE THAT ...?

你不認為……嗎？

例 Wouldn't you agree that this item is beautiful?

你不認為這項東西很漂亮嗎？

HAVEN'T YOU EVER ...?

你從來沒有……嗎？

例 Haven't you ever heard of this product before?

你以前從來沒有聽說過這項產品嗎？

I STRONGLY SUGGEST THAT YOU ....

我強烈建議你……。

例 I strongly suggest that you <u>give it a try</u>.

我強烈建議你試試看。

I REALLY THINK YOU NEED ....

我真的覺得你需要……。

例 I really think you need to <u>examine</u> the <u>prototype</u>.

我真的覺得你需要檢查一下原型。

I CAN'T EMPHASIZE ENOUGH THAT ....

我要再三地強調……。

例 I can't <u>emphasize</u> enough that your customers will love this product.

我要再二地強調，你的顧客曾愛上這樣產品。

Word List

give sth. a try 試試某事
examine [ɪɡˋzæmɪn] *v.* 檢查
prototype [ˋprotə͵taɪp] *n.* 原型
emphasize [ˋɛmfə͵saɪz] *v.* 強調

3 面對面促銷產品 Face-to-Face Product Promotion

3.1 產品類型 Product Types

 track 54

3.1a 產品類型的字彙 Words for Product Types

BIZ 必通字彙

Multiple Types 多種類型

❶ line [laɪn] *n.* 款式
❷ range [rendʒ] *n.* 批、組、套
❸ selection [sə`lɛkʃən] *n.* 可供選購的同類物品
❹ variety [və`raɪətɪ] *n.* 種類

Single Types 單一類型

❶ model [`mɑdl̩] *n.* 型號　　❷ version [`vɝʒən] *n.* 版本

3.1b 產品類型的銷售用語 Sales Language for Product Types

BIZ 必通句型

WE HAVE A WIDE VARIETY OF ....
我們的……種類很多。
例 We have a wide variety of <u>fluorescent</u> light <u>bulbs</u>.
　　我們日光燈泡的種類很多。

Word List

fluorescent [ˌfluə`rɛsn̩t] *adj.* 螢光的　　　　bulb [bʌlb] *n.* 電燈泡

WE HAVE A FINE SELECTION OF ....

我們有各種精美的……可供選購。

例 We have a fine selection of <u>Persian</u> <u>rugs</u>.

我們有各種精美的波斯地毯可供選購。

THIS LINE OF ... IS VERY POPULAR.

這個款式的……非常受歡迎。

例 This line of products is very popular.

這個款式的產品非常受歡迎。

THIS ... IS AVAILABLE IN ... AND ....

這個……有……和……的。

例 This curtain is available in <u>violet</u> and orange.

這個窗簾有紫色和橘色的。

THIS LINE RANGES FROM ... TO ....

這個款式從……到……都有。

例 This line ranges from small size to large size.

這個款式從小尺寸到大尺寸都有。

WE HAVE AN <u>EXTENSIVE</u> SELECTION OF ....

我們有各種……選擇廣泛。

例 We have an extensive selection of <u>paperweights</u>.

我們有各種紙鎮選擇廣泛。

THIS MODEL COMES IN ....

這個型號有……。

例 This model comes in any color you can imagine.

這樣型號有你能想到的任何顏色。

Word List

Persian [`pɝʒən] *adj.* 波斯的
rug [rʌg] *n.* 地毯
violet [`vaɪəlɪt] *n./adj.* 藍紫色（的）；紫羅蘭（的）

extensive [ɪk`stɛnsɪv] *adj.* 廣泛的；大規模的
paperweight [`pepɚˌwet] *n.* 紙鎮

153

THIS IS THE LATEST VERSION OF ....

這是……的最新版。

例 This is the latest version of our best-selling <u>wireless</u> <u>modem</u>.

這是我們最暢銷無線數據機的最新版。

3.2 特定產品的銷售用語 Sales Language for Specific Products

track 55

BIZ 必通句型

THIS ... IS THE BEST ON THE MARKET.

這個……是市面上最好的。

例 This shoe is the best on the market.

這款鞋是市面上最好的。

THIS ... IS THE ONLY ONE OF ITS KIND.

這個……在同類產品中是獨一無二的。

例 This indoor <u>thermometer</u> is the only one of its kind.

這支室內溫度計在同類產品中是獨一無二的。

THIS ... IS THE HIGHEST QUALITY AVAILABLE.

這是現有最高品質的……。

例 This paint is the highest quality available.

這是現有最高品質的油漆。

THIS ... IS MADE FROM ONLY THE BEST MATERIALS.

這個……只選用最好的材質製造。

例 This speaker set is made from only the best materials.

這組喇叭只選用最好的材質製造。

Word List

wireless [ˋwaɪrlɪs] *adj.* 無線的；無線電信的   thermometer [θəˋmɑmətə] *n.* 溫度計

modem [ˋmodəm] *n.* 數據機

THIS MODEL IS THE BEST ... IN ....

這個型號的……是……最好的。

例 This model is the best electric <u>drill</u> in the world.

　　這個型號的電鑽是全世界最好的。

◇◇ 小心陷阱 ◇◇

☹ 錯誤用法

This model is **best** in Taiwan.

這個型號是台灣最好的。

☺ 正確用法

This model is **the best** in Taiwan.

這個型號是台灣最好的。

3.3 與「產品」相關的字彙 Key Words to Use with "Product" track 56

BIZ 必通字彙

❶ product mix 產品組合

❷ product portfolio [port`folɪo] 產品型錄

❸ product positioning 產品定位

❹ product placement 產品配置

❺ product life cycle 產品生命週期

❻ product line 產品系列；產品款式

Word List

drill [drɪl] *n.* 鑽孔機

Show Time

❶ We have a <u>diverse</u> **product mix**.
我們有多樣的產品組合。

❷ Our **product portfolio** includes more than twenty items.
我們的產品型錄裡有二十多個項目。

❸ **Product positioning** is the key to our success.
產品定位是我們成功的關鍵。

❹ Our marketing department believes that **product placement** should be researched carefully.
我們的行銷部門認為，產品配置應該要仔細地研究。

❺ The **product life cycle** in the <u>automotive</u> <u>components</u> industry is about ten years.
汽車組件業的產品生命週期大約是十年。

❻ We currently offer four **product lines** in Southeast Asia.
目前我們在東南亞有四個產品系列。

3.4 與「產品」相關的重要動詞 Important Action Words for "Product"

track 57

BIZ 必通字彙

❶ introduce [ˌɪntrəˈdjus] *v.* 推出（新產品）；使（新產品）問世
❷ launch [lɔntʃ] *n./v.* 上市；投入市場
❸ release [rɪˈlis] *n./v.* 發行；公開
❹ market [ˈmɑrkɪt] *v.* 銷售
❺ recall [rɪˈkɔl] *v.* 回收
❻ withdraw [wɪðˈdrɔ] *v.* 退出；撤回
❼ bundle [ˈbʌndl] *v.* 搭售

Word List

diverse [daɪˈvɝs] *adj.* 多樣的；多變化的
automotive [ˌɔtəˈmotɪv] *adj.* 汽車的

component [kəmˈponənt] *n.* （機器、設備等的）構成要素；組件

Show Time

❶ We will **introduce** this product at the <u>fair</u> in Los Angeles.
我們會在洛杉磯的展覽會上推出這項產品。

❷ A <u>massive</u> marketing <u>campaign</u> will <u>precede</u> the product **launch/release**.
在產品上市前會有一場大型行銷活動會。

❸ We have **marketed** this product directly to school students.
我們直接向學校的學生銷售這項產品。

❹ Our competitor had to **recall** their <u>defective</u> product.
我們的競爭對手必須回收他們的瑕疵品。

❺ This product was **withdrawn** from the China market due to poor sales.
這項產品因為銷售慘淡而退出了中國市場。

❻ We plan on **bundling** our software with C-Tech's hardware.
我們打算把我們的軟體和 C 科技的硬體一起搭售。

3.5 展現產品 Showing off Products

 track 58

3.5a 展示重要特色 Showing Important Features

BIZ 必通句型

TAKE A LOOK AT THE ....
瞧瞧這……。
例 Take a look at the fine <u>embroidering</u>.
瞧瞧這精細的繡工。

Word List

fair [fɛr] *n.* 展覽會；博覽會
massive [ˋmæsɪv] *adj.* 巨大的；大規模的
campaign [kæmˋpen] *n.* （為特定目進行的）
運動；宣傳活動

precede [priˋsid] *v.* 在……之前發生
defective [dɪˋfɛktɪv] *adj.* 有缺陷的；有瑕疵的
embroidering [ɪmˋbrɔɪdərɪŋ] *n.* 刺（繡）工

FEEL THIS FINE QUALITY ....

摸摸看這個質感絕佳的⋯⋯。

例 Feel this fine quality leather.

摸摸看這個質感絕佳的皮革。

YOU CAN EXAMINE THE ....

你可以檢查一下這⋯⋯。

例 You can examine the many features.

你可以檢查一下這許多的功能。

LET ME SHOW YOU THE ....

我來為你展示這⋯⋯。

例 Let me show you the best part of this product.

我來為你展示這個產品最棒的部分。

YOU CAN TRY OUT THE ....

你可以試用一下這⋯⋯。

例 You can try out the kitchen <u>appliances</u>.

你可以試用一下這些廚房設備。

◇◇◇ 小心陷阱 ◇◇◇

☹ 錯誤用法

See the wonderful colors.

瞧瞧這些美麗的色彩。

☺ 正確用法

Take a look at the wonderful colors.

瞧瞧這些美麗的色彩。

Word List

appliance [əˋplaɪəns] *n.* 設備；器具

3.5b 解釋重要的特性 Explaining Important Characteristics

BIZ 必通字彙

● 名詞 Nouns

❶ capacity [kə`pæsətɪ] *n.* 容量；容積

❷ capability [ˌkepə`bɪlətɪ] *n.* 性能

❸ feature [`fitʃə] *n.* 特色；功能

❹ special feature 特殊功能

❺ unique feature 獨特功能

❻ product life 產品壽命

● 形容詞 Adjectives

❶ lightweight [`laɪtˏwet] *adj.* 輕量的

❷ sturdy [`stɜdɪ] *adj.* 堅固的；耐用的

❸ durable [`djʊrəbl̩] *adj.* 耐用的

❹ solid [`salɪd] *adj.* 堅固的

❺ long-lasting [`lɔŋ`læstɪŋ] *adj.* 持久的

❻ high-performance [`haɪpə`fɔrməns] *adj.* 高性能的

❼ easy-to-use [`izɪtʊ`juz] *adj.* 好用的

❽ portable [`portəbl̩] *adj.* 可攜帶的

❾ versatile [`vɜsətl̩] / [vəsətail] *adj.* 多功能的

❿ heat-resistant [`hit rɪ`zɪstənt] *adj.* 耐熱的

⓫ rustproof [`rʌstˏpruf] *adj.* 防鏽的

⓬ economical [ˌikə`namɪkl̩] *adj.* 經濟的

track 59

3.6 說明尺寸　Specifying Dimensions

3.6a 與尺寸相關的字彙 Dimensions Vocabulary

BIZ 必通字彙

❶ length [lɛŋθ] *n.* 長（度）

❷ width [wɪdθ] *n.* 寬（度）

❸ height [haɪt] *n.* 高（度）

❹ depth [dɛpθ] *n.* 深（度）

❺ thickness [ˋθɪknɪs] *n.* 厚（度）

❻ diameter [daɪˋæmətɚ] *n.* 直徑

3.6b 說明尺寸的用語 Dimensions Sentence Patterns

BIZ 必通句型

... IS/ARE (number + unit) LONG.
……長（數字＋單位）。

例 This side is nine <u>centimeters</u> (9 cm) long.
這一面長九公分。

... IS/ARE (number + unit) WIDE.
……寬（數字＋單位）。

例 Both sides are zero point eight meters (0.8 m) wide.
兩面都是寬零點八公尺。

... IS/ARE (number + unit) HIGH.
……高（數字＋單位）。

例 The <u>antenna</u> is fifteen <u>millimeters</u> (15 mm) high.
天線高十五公釐。

Word List

centimeter [ˋsɛntəˏmitɚ] *n.* 公分

antenna [ænˋtɛnə] *n.*【美】天線

millimeter [ˋmɪləˏmitɚ] *n.* 公釐

... IS/ARE (number + unit) DEEP.

……深（數字＋單位）。

例 Each <u>module</u> is forty-six point five centimeters (46.5 cm) deep.

每個模組深四十六點五公分。

... IS/ARE (number + unit) THICK.

……厚（數字＋單位）。

例 The <u>padding</u> is four millimeters (4 mm) thick.

填料厚四公釐。

... IS/ARE (number + unit) IN DIAMETER.

……的直徑是（數字＋單位）。

例 The hole is two point five centimeters (2.5 cm) in diameter.

洞的直徑是二點五公分。

3.7 解釋結構和成分 Explaining <u>Construction</u> and <u>Composition</u>

 track 60

BIZ 必通句型

... IS/ARE MADE OF (material).

……是（材料）所製成的。

例 The <u>packaging</u> is made of cardboard.

外包裝是卡紙所製成的。

... CONSISTS OF (material).

……是（材料）所組成的。

例 The case consists of hardwood.

箱子是硬木所組成的。

Word List

module [ˋmɑdʒʊl] *n.* 模組

padding [ˋpædɪŋ] *n.* 填料；襯墊

construction [kənˋstrʌkʃən] *n.* 結構

composition [͵kɑmpəˋzɪʃən] *n.* 成分

packaging [ˋpækɪdʒɪŋ] *n.* 包裝

... IS/ARE MADE BY (method).

……是（方法）製作的。

例 The meatballs are made by hand.

肉丸是手工製作的。

例 That clothing is made by machine.

那些衣服是機器製作的。

... IS/ARE MADE BY (process).

……是（程序）所製成的。

例 The base is made by <u>welding</u> the bar onto the steel plate.

基座是把鋼條焊接到鋼板上所製成的。

... <u>FEATURE/FEATURES</u> (material) CONSTRUCTION.

……以（材料）結構為特色。

例 Our <u>patio</u> furniture features stainless steel construction.

我們的中庭家具以不銹鋼的結構為特色。

... IS/ARE COMPOSED OF (material).

……是（材料）所構成的。

例 The cooking pans are composed of <u>nickel</u> and iron.

平底鍋的材質是鎳和鐵所構成的。

◇◇ 小心陷阱 ◇◇

☹ 錯誤用法

The stand is made **from** plastic.

架子是塑膠所製成的。

☺ 正確用法

The stand is made **of** plastic.

架子是塑膠所製成的。

Word List

weld [wɛld] *v.* 焊接；熔接

feature [ˈfitʃɚ] *v.* 以……為特色

patio [ˈpɑtɪˌo] *n.* （西班牙式）內院；中庭

nickel [ˈnɪkl̩] *n.* 鎳

描述產品品質的特殊用語 Special Language to Describe Product Quality

4.1 描述品質的字彙 Words for Expressing Quality

 track **61**

 BIZ 必通字彙

❶ above standard（品質）在標準之上
❷ high-quality [ˋhæˋkwɑlətɪ] *adj.* 高品質的
❸ top-notch [ˋtɑpˋnɑtʃ] *adj.* 頂級的
❹ top-shelf [ˋtɑpˋʃɛlf] 高檔的
❺ superior quality 優異品質

Show Time

❶ The quality is **above standard**.
　品質在標準之上。
❷ All of the internal components are **high-quality**.
　內部所有組件都屬高品質。
❸ This new model is **top-notch**.
　這個新款式是頂級的。
❹ We <u>specialize</u> in **top-shelf** wine.
　我們專賣高檔酒。
❺ The **superior quality** of our products is the reason they sell so well.
　我們產品的優異品質是它們賣得這麼好的原因。

Word **List**

specialize [ˋspɛʃəlˌaɪz] *v.* 專攻；專門從事 (~ in)

4.2 描述生產品質和產能 Describing Production Quality and Capacity

 track 62

BIZ 必通字彙

❶ production standards 生產標準
❷ quality control 品質管理
❸ quality control system 品管系統
❹ quality inspection [ɪŋˋspɛkʃən] certificate [səˋtɪfəkɪt] 品質檢驗證書
❺ defect ratio [ˋreʃo] 瑕疵率
❻ yield [jɪld] rate 出貨率；出產率
❼ production capacity [kəˋpæsətɪ] 生產量；產能
❽ output 產出

Show Time

❶ Our **production standards** are very <u>stringent</u>.
我們的生產標準相當嚴格。

❷ The **quality control** teams carefully monitor all the equipment.
品管團隊仔細監控所有的設備。

❸ You are welcome to examine our **quality control system**.
歡迎來檢視我們的品管系統。

❹ I will show you all of our **quality inspection certificates**.
我會把我們所有的品質檢驗證書都拿給你看。

❺ The **defect ratio** is a very low 0.8%.
瑕疵率是非常低的千分之八。

❻ Our Shanghai plant has a **yield rate** of fifteen hundred pieces per day.
我們上海廠的出貨率是每天一千五百件。

❼ The **production capacity** for this item is half a million per month.
這樣東西的生產量是每個月五十萬件。

❽ The **output** at this <u>facility</u> <u>averages</u> thirty units per hour.
這個工廠平均每小時產出三十件。

Word List

stringent [ˋstrɪndʒənt] *adj.*（規定等）嚴苛地   average [ˋævərɪdʒ] *v.* 平均達到……

facility [fəˋsɪlətɪ] *n.* 場所

4.3 科技相關字彙 Technology-related Words

 track 63

BIZ 必通字彙

❶ innovative [ˈɪnoˌvetɪv] *adj.* 創新的
❷ revolutionary [ˌrɛvəˈluʃənˌɛrɪ] *adj.* 革命的
❸ state-of-the-art *adj.* 先進的
❹ leading-edge *adj.* 領先潮流的
❺ cutting-edge *adj.* 尖端的
❻ artificial intelligence [ˈɑrtəfɪʃəl ɪnˈtɛlədʒəns] 人工智慧 (=AI)

Show Time

❶ This small desktop computer is **innovative** because we added USB slots on both the left and right sides.
這台小型的桌上型電腦很具創意，因為我們在左右兩端都加了 USB 插槽。

❷ The Internet paved the way for a **revolutionary** change in world communication.
網際網路為全球通訊具革命性的變革創造了良好的條件。

❸ Take a look at this **state-of-the-art** digital camera sensor.
瞧瞧這個先進的數位相機感應器。

❹ We are known for our **leading-edge** technology.
我們以領先潮流的科技聞名。

❺ This mini GPS unit is **cutting-edge**.
這台迷你全球定位系統是尖端產品。

❻ We manage an **AI** system to detect credit card fraud.
我們運用人工智慧系統來偵察信用卡的冒用。

Word List

slot [ˈslɑt] *adj.* 長孔；插槽
pave the way for 為……鋪路；為……創造條件

sensor [ˈsɛnsə] *n.* 感應器
fraud [frɔd] *n.* 欺騙（行為）；欺詐；假冒名義的人或物

說明國際認證 Stating International <u>Certifications</u>

 track 64

 必通句型

... HAS ... CERTIFICATION.
……有……認證。

例 This unit has UL certification.
這樣東西有美國 UL 認證。

... HAS/HAVE EARNED ... CERTIFICATION.
……已經獲得……認證。

例 All of our products have earned ISO-9002 certification.
我們的產品都已經獲得 ISO-9002 認證。

... IS ... <u>CERTIFIED</u>.
……是經……認證。

例 This product is CE certified.
這項產品經過 CE 認證。

4.5 解釋可靠程度 Explaining <u>Reliability</u>

track 65

必通句型

YOU CAN DEPEND ON THE ... OF THIS PRODUCT.
你可以信賴這樣產品的……。

例 You can depend on the performance of this product.
你可以信賴這樣產品的性能。

YOU CAN RELY ON THIS PRODUCT'S ....
你可以信賴這樣產品的……。

例 You can rely on this product's <u>marketability</u>.
你可以信賴這樣產品的市場性。

Word List

certification [ˌsɜtɪfəˈkeʃən] *n.* 檢定；保證
certify [ˈsɜtəˌfaɪ] *v.* 發證書（或執照）給……

marketability [ˌmɑrkɪtəˈbɪlətɪ] *n.* 市場性
reliability [rɪˌlaɪəˈbɪlətɪ] *n.* 可靠性

... HAS HIGH RELIABILITY/DEPENDABILITY.

……有很高的可靠度／可靠性。

例 Every model we produce has high reliability.

我們所生產的各種型號都有很高的可靠度。

THE ... OF THIS PRODUCT CAN'T BE BEAT.

這樣產品的……無人能比。

例 The <u>durability</u> of this product can't be beat.

這樣產品的耐久性無人能比。

YOU DON'T NEED TO WORRY ABOUT THIS PRODUCT'S ....

你不用擔心這樣產品的……。

例 You don't need to worry about this product's functionality.

你不用擔心這樣產品的功能性。

YOU CAN <u>REST</u> EASY WHEN YOU ... THIS PRODUCT.

你可以放心地……這樣產品。

例 You can rest easy when you turn on this product.

你可以放心地啟動這樣產品。

◇◇ 小心陷阱 ◇◇◇

☹ 錯誤用法

This product has **a high reliability**.

這項產品非常可靠。

☺ 正確用法

This product has **high reliability**.

這項產品非常可靠。

Word **List**

durability [ˌdjʊrəˋbɪlətɪ] *n.* 耐久性
rest [rɛst] *v.* 安心；放心

5 接單 Taking Orders

5.1 談論有沒有貨 Talking About Availability

 track 66

5.1a 說明有沒有現貨 Saying if Something Is in Stock

BIZ 必通句型

有現貨 In Stock

... IS/ARE IN STOCK.
……有現貨。
例 That item is in stock.
那樣東西有現貨。
例 All the tools are in stock.
所有的工具都有現貨。

WE HAVE THAT/THOSE ... IN STOCK.
我們有那一／些……的現貨。
例 We have that model number in stock.
我們有那一種型號的現貨。

... IS/ARE AVAILABLE.
……有貨。
例 Laser pointers are available.
雷射筆有貨。

沒有現貨 Not in Stock

... IS/ARE NOT IN STOCK RIGHT NOW.
……目前沒有現貨。

168

例 Those old versions are not in stock right now.

那些舊版本目前沒有現貨。

例 ZRT-2000 is not in stock right now.

ZRT-2000 目前沒有現貨。

I'M AFRAID WE DON'T HAVE ... IN STOCK.

恐怕我們沒有……的現貨。

例 I'm afraid we don't have rose-<u>scented</u> soap in stock.

恐怕我們沒有玫瑰花香皂的現貨。

... IS CURRENTLY <u>OUT OF STOCK</u>.

……目前缺貨。

例 That paper cutter is currently out of stock.

那個碎紙機目前缺貨。

5.1b 說明某項貨品何時會有貨 Saying When an Item Will Be Available

BIZ 必通句型

• 會有貨 Will Be Available

... WILL BE IN STOCK (time).

……（時間）會有貨。

例 That product will be in stock next week.

那樣產品下星期會有貨。

... WILL BE BACK IN STOCK SOON.

……很快就會再有貨。

例 Face cream will be back in stock soon.

面霜很快就會再有貨。

Word List

scented [ˋsɛntɪd] *adj.* （加於名詞後）有……香味的

out of stock 無現貨的

WE EXPECT ... TO BE AVAILABLE (time).

我們預計……（時間）會有貨。

例 We expect fish bowls to be available after August 1ˢᵗ.

我們預計魚缸在八月一日以後會有貨。

I'M NOT SURE WHEN THAT WILL BE IN STOCK. I WILL CONTACT YOU AS SOON AS WE HAVE IT.

我不確定什麼時候會有貨。只要一進貨，我就會盡快和你聯絡。

- 不會有貨 Will Not Be Available

WE DON'T STOCK ... ANY LONGER.

……我們不再進貨了。

例 We don't stock that model number any longer.

那個型號我們不再進貨了。

WE NO LONGER SELL ....

我們不賣……了。

例 We no longer sell <u>titanium</u> tools.

我們不賣鈦金屬工具了。

I'M AFRAID ... IS/ARE <u>DISCONTINUED</u>.

……恐怕停賣了。

例 I'm afraid those CDs are discontinued.

那些 CD 恐怕停賣了。

Word List

titanium [taɪˋtenɪəm] *n.* 鈦

discontinued [dɪskənˋtɪnjud] *adj.* 停止的；中斷的

5.2 詢問購買數量 Asking the Number/Amount to Be Purchased

track 67

BIZ 必通句型

HOW MANY ... WOULD YOU LIKE?
你想要多少……?
例 How many cases of chocolate would you like?
你想要多少盒巧克力?

WHAT NUMBER WOULD YOU LIKE?
你要多少數量?

HOW MANY CAN I GET FOR YOU?
我要幫你拿多少個?

WHAT QUANTITY ARE YOU LOOKING AT?
你要的數量是多少?

◇◇◇ 小心陷阱 ◇◇◇

☹ 錯誤用法
How many sets **do** you like?
您想要多少套?
☺ 正確用法
How many sets **would** you like?
您想要多少套?

5.3 詢問運送方式 Asking About Shipping

track 68

BIZ 必通句型

HOW CAN I SHIP THESE TO YOU?
我要怎麼把這些寄給你？

HOW WOULD YOU LIKE ... SHIPPED?
您希望……怎麼運送？
例 How would you like the printers shipped?
　　您希望印表機怎麼運送？

WHAT SHIPPING METHOD DO YOU PREFER?
你想用哪種方式運送？

WHAT ARE YOUR SHIPPING REQUIREMENTS?
你有哪些運送要求？

Show Time

Customer:	I would like to buy several dozen of this version. Do you have that many available now?
Seller:	Sure. We have that model in stock.
Customer:	If I want to order some of the other versions in a couple of days when I go back to my country, how many could I get right away?
Seller:	All the versions are in stock except model Zebra-3. That one will be in stock in a few weeks. We usually have thousands

Word List

requirement [rɪˋkwaɪrmənt] *n.* 要求；必要條件

of the others available at any given time. How many would you like?

Customer: I am thinking of less than one hundred, so it should be no problem.

Seller: Yep, no problem at all. What are your shipping requirements?

Customer: Standard sea shipping is fine. I am in no rush.

顧客：我想買幾打這種版本的。你們現在有這麼多貨嗎？

賣方：當然有，我們有那種型號的現貨。

顧客：假如我想在幾天後回國時訂一些其他的版本，我可以馬上拿到多少個？

賣方：除了 Zebra-3 的款式外，其他所有的版本都有現貨。 Zebra-3 幾週後才會有貨。其他的型號我們通常隨時都有好幾千個。您想要多少個？

顧客：我要的不到一百個，所以應該不成問題。

賣方：是的，完全沒問題。您有哪些運送要求？

顧客：一般的海運就可以了。我不急。

Memo

6 接待用語 Reception Language

　　有很多業務人員都身兼多職，要負責各式各樣的事務。銷售人員經常在外奔波，並擔任公司和其他廠商之間的聯繫窗口。無論你本身是否為業務人員，有些時候也得接待客戶。因此，所有的員工都必須知道一些關鍵的接待用語，以便能恰如其分地招呼來賓及訪客。你可以在以下單元學到這些用語。

6.1 接待商展的訪客 Receiving Visitors at a Trade Show track **69**

6.1a 招呼訪客 Greeting the Visitor

BIZ 必通句型

HOW CAN I HELP YOU?
我可以怎麼幫您？

IS THERE ANYTHING I CAN HELP YOU WITH?
有什麼事我可以幫您的嗎？

HOW CAN I BE OF SERVICE?
我可以怎麼為您服務？

WHAT'S ON YOUR MIND TODAY?
您今天有什麼想法？

WHAT CAN I HELP YOU WITH?
我可以幫您做什麼？

6.1b 與印刷品有關的字彙 Key Words for Printed Materials

BIZ 必通字彙

❶ catalog [`kætəlɔg] *n.* 目錄
❷ brochure [bro`ʃur] *n.* 小冊子
❸ instruction manual [`mænjuəl] *n.* 操作手冊
❹ user manual / user guide 使用手冊 / 使用說明
❺ spec sheet [`spɛk ˌʃit] *n.* 規格表
❻ pamphlet [`pæmflɪt] *n.* 小冊子

6.1c 分發印刷品 Handing out Printed Materials

BIZ 必通句型

HERE IS A ... FOR YOU.
這兒有……給您。
例 Here is a brochure for you.
　　這兒有本小冊子給您。

PLEASE TAKE A LOOK AT THIS ....
請看看這……。
例 Please take a look at this pamphlet.
　　請看看這本小冊子。

THIS ... HAS SOME IMPORTANT INFORMATION.
這……有重要的資訊。
例 This user guide has some important information.
　　這份使用說明有一些重要的資訊。

WOULD YOU LIKE TO LOOK AT ...?
您要不要看一下……？
例 Would you like to look at our catalog?
　　您要不要看一下我們的目錄？

6.2 在辦公室接待客人 Receiving a Guest in an Office

 track 70

約好前來的客人可能會這樣說：

I am Mr. Conner. I have an appointment with Mr. Lin.
我是康納先生。我和林先生有約。

I am Mrs. Langdon. I have an appointment for 2:30.
我是蘭登太太，我約了兩點半。

順道拜訪的人則會這樣說：

Is Mrs. Chen available?
請問陳太太在嗎？

Does Miss Kuo have time to see me?
郭小姐有空見我嗎？

6.2a 釐清重要資訊 Clarifying Important Information

BIZ 必通句型

COULD I HAVE YOUR NAME?
請問貴姓大名？

DO YOU HAVE AN APPOINTMENT?
您有約嗎？

IS ... EXPECTING YOU?
……在等您嗎？
例 Is the manager expecting you?
經理在等您嗎？

WHAT TIME ARE YOU <u>SCHEDULED</u> FOR?
您排定的時間是什麼時候？

Word List

schedule [ˋskɛdʒʊl] v. 安排；預定

COULD YOU TELL ME THE TIME OF YOUR APPOINTMENT?
您能不能告訴我您約的是幾點？

COULD I ASK THE REASON FOR YOUR VISIT?
能不能請問您來訪的原因？

MAY I TELL ... WHAT YOU WANT TO SEE HIM/HER ABOUT?
我可以告訴……您是為了什麼事想見他／她嗎？

例 May I tell Mr. Huang what you want to see him about?
　　我可以告訴黃先生您是為了什麼事想見他嗎？

◇◇ 小心陷阱 ◇◇

☹ 錯誤用法

What time are you **scheduled** ?

您排定的時間是什麼時候？

☺ 正確用法

What time are you **scheduled for**?

您排定的時間是什麼時候？

6.2b 詢問老闆是否有空 Checking If Your Boss Is Available

BIZ 必通句型

LET ME SEE IF ... IS AVAILABLE.
我看一下……有沒有在忙。

例 Let me see if Miss Wang is available.
　　我看看王小姐有沒有在忙。

I WILL SEE IF ... HAS TIME.
我會看看……有沒有時間。

例 I will see if Fanny has time.

我會看看芬妮有沒有時間。

LET ME CHECK (sb.'s) SCHEDULE.

我看一下（某人的）行程表。

例 Let me check Paul's schedule.

我看一下保羅的行程表。

LET ME SEE HOW BUSY ... IS TODAY.

我看一下……今天忙不忙。

例 Let me see how busy Luther is today.

我看一下路瑟今天忙不忙。

6.2c 說明某人無法見客 Saying Someone Cannot Meet with the Guest

BIZ 必通句型

- 太忙 Too Busy

... IS <u>OCCUPIED</u> AT THE MOMENT.

……目前正在忙。

例 Marvin is occupied at the moment.

馬文目前正在忙。

... IS COMPLETELY <u>TIED UP</u>.

……完全抽不了身。

例 The vice president is completely tied up.

副總裁完全抽不了身。

Word List

occupied [ˋɑkjəpaɪd] *adj.* 沒空的
be tied up 脫不了身；忙得不可開交

... IS NOT AVAILABLE NOW.

……現在沒有空。

例 Ms. Donovan is not available now.
唐納文女士現在沒有空。

(Sb.'s) SCHEDULE IS COMPLETELY FULL TODAY.

……的時程今天全滿了。

例 Mr. Lin's schedule is completely full today.
林小姐的時程今天全滿了。

... IS NOT IN HIS/HER OFFICE NOW.

……現在不在他／她的辦公室。

例 Mrs. Tsai is not in her office now.
蔡小姐現在不在她的辦公室。

● 不在公司 Not at the Company

... IS NOT IN TODAY.

……今天不在。

例 The Director is not in today.
總監今天不在。

... IS OUT TODAY.

……今天外出。

例 Kelly is out today.
凱莉今天外出。

... IS OUT OF TOWN.

……出城去了。

例 Walter is out of town.
華特出城去了。

... IS AWAY ON BUSINESS.

……出差去了。

例 Kenny is away on business.
肯尼出差去了。

... HAS TAKEN THE DAY OFF.

……今天請假。

例 Mr. Lee has taken the day off.

李先生今天請假。

... IS ON VACATION.

……在休假。

例 Linda is on vacation.

琳達在休假。

6.2d 說明老闆何時會回來 Stating When Your Boss Will Return

BIZ 必通句型

... WILL BE BACK (date).

……（日期）會回來。

例 Carter will be back tomorrow.

卡特明天會回來。

... WILL BE BACK AT (time).

……（時間）會回來。

例 Jennifer will be back at 9:00.

珍妮佛九點鐘會回來。

... SHOULD BE BACK AROUND (time).

……應該會在（時間）左右回來。

例 Ms. Huang should be back around 4:15.

黃先生應該會在四點十五分左右回來。

... WILL BE BACK SHORTLY.

……很快就會回來。

例 Irma will be back shortly.

艾瑪很快就會回來

... WILL BE RIGHT BACK.

……馬上就會回來。

例 Mr. Harter will be right back.

哈特先生馬上就會回來。

... WON'T BE BACK UNTIL (time).

……要到（時間）才會回來。

例 Sally won't be back until 2:30.

莎莉要到兩點半才會回來。

... WON'T BE BACK TODAY.

……今天不會回來。

例 The manager won't be back today.

經理今天不會回來。

◇◇◇ 小心陷阱 ◇◇◇

☹ 錯誤用法

The president should **return back** around 2:00.

總裁應該會在兩點鐘左右回來。

☺ 正確用法

The president should **be back** around 2:00.

總裁應該會在兩點鐘左右回來。

6.2e 請賓客等候 Asking the Guest to Wait

BIZ 必通句型

... WILL BE RIGHT WITH YOU.
……馬上就來和您見面。
例 Jay will be right with you.
杰馬上就來和您見面。

... WILL BE JUST A MOMENT.
……一會兒就來。
例 Mrs. Chen will be just a moment.
陳太太一會兒就來。

... WILL BE RIGHT OUT.
……馬上就出來。
例 Billy will be right out.
比利馬上就出來。

... IS ON THE WAY.
……已經在路上了。
例 Mr. Hancock is on the way.
韓卡克先生已經在路上了。

PLEASE HAVE A SEAT.
請坐。

6.2f 請客人進來 Telling the Guest to Go in

BIZ 必通句型

GO RIGHT IN.
請直接進去。

PLEASE GO IN.
請進去。

I WILL SHOW YOU IN.
我會帶您進去。

PLEASE FOLLOW ME.
請跟我來。

THIS WAY, PLEASE.
這邊請。

6.3 招呼顧客 Attending to a Customer

 track 71

BIZ 必通句型

○ 上飲料 Offering Refreshment

CAN I GET YOU SOMETHING TO DRINK?
我可以幫您拿點喝的嗎？

CAN I GET YOU A ...?
我可以幫您拿……？
例 Can I get you a cup of coffee?
　　我可以幫您拿杯咖啡嗎？

HOW ABOUT A ...?
……怎麼樣？
例 How about a bottle of water?
　　要不要來瓶水？

查看茶點 Checking the Refreshments

CAN I GET YOU ANYTHING ELSE?
我可以幫您拿點什麼其他的嗎？

CAN I REFILL YOUR ...?
我可以幫您把……加滿嗎？
Can I refill your cup of tea?
> 我可以幫您把茶杯加滿嗎？

WOULD YOU LIKE ANOTHER ...?
您要不要再來……？
Would you like another soda?
> 您要不要再來一杯汽水？

有關咖啡的特別問題 Special Questions for Coffee

HOW DO YOU LIKE YOUR COFFEE?
您的咖啡喜歡怎麼喝？

WOULD YOU LIKE SUGAR OR CREAM WITH YOUR COFFEE?
您的咖啡要加糖或奶精嗎？

Show Time

Guest:　　　Is Mr. Kuo available?
Assistant:　Do you have an appointment?
Guest:　　　No. I am attending the trade show in Kaohsiung and thought I would drop by to say hello.
Assistant:　I see. Let me see if he is available. Could I have your name?

Word List

refreshment [rɪ`frɛʃmənt] *n.* 茶點；點心（常用複數）

refill [rɪ`fil] *v.* 再注滿；再加滿

Guest:　　　 I am Alan Perkins from Sea Systems Company in Boston.

[the sales assistant calls Mr. Kuo's extension]

Assistant:　 Mr. Kuo is occupied at the moment, attending a <u>confer-ence call</u> in his office. He will be available in half an hour. Would you like to wait?

Guest:　　　 Sure.

Assistant:　 Great. Please have a seat and relax. I'll let you know when he is off the phone.

Guest:　　　 Alright, thanks.

Assistant:　 Can I get you something to drink?

Guest:　　　 No, I am fine.

[the sales assistant receives a call from Mr. Kuo]

Assistant:　 Mr. Perkins, Mr. Kuo is free now. Please go right in.

Guest:　　　 Thank you.

來賓：請問郭先生在嗎？

助理：您跟他有約嗎？

來賓：沒有。我來參加高雄的貿易展，順道來打個招呼。

助理：了解。我看一下他有沒有在忙。請問貴姓大名？

來賓：我是波士頓海洋系統公司的艾倫・伯金斯。

〔業務助理撥打郭先生的分機〕

助理：郭先生目前在忙，他正在辦公室裡參加電話會議，半小時後會有空。您要
　　　等他嗎？

來賓：好呀。

助理：好，那您請坐，休息一下。他一掛電話，我就通知您。

來賓：好，謝謝。

助理：我可以幫你拿點喝的嗎？

來賓：不用了，沒關係。

〔業務助理接到郭先生的電話〕

助理：伯金斯先生，郭先生現在有空了。請直接進去。

來賓：謝謝。

Word **List**

conference call 電話會議

7 實戰演練 Partner Practice

當你讀完並複習過本章內容後,找個同伴試試下面的對話練習!

情境 1

一位台灣公司的業務員在商展上正向潛在顧客展示產品。

練習	
角色 A	台灣的業務員。想像你在嘗試銷售某樣產品或系列產品。
角色 B	正在逛商展的國外採購員。
A	招呼角色 B。(6.1a)
B	告訴角色 A,你想更了解他的產品。
A	告訴角色 B 一些產品的事。(3.1) (3.2) 然後介紹產品的優點。(3.5a) (3.5b)
B	向角色 A 詢問產品的尺寸。
A	說明尺寸。(3.6a) (3.6b)
B	要角色 A 解釋,產品是用什麼製造而成的。
A	解釋產品的結構和成分。(3.7)
B	告訴角色 A,你喜歡他的產品,但你也在考慮另外幾家競爭者。
A	嘗試軟性或硬性的推銷方式。(2.4 or 2.5)
B	詢問角色 A,他的產品銷路怎麼樣?
A	回應角色 B。(2.2)
B	向角色 A 詢問產品的價格。
A	說明價格。(1.2)
B	詢問角色 A,如果你大量訂購,可不可以得到折扣。
A	回應角色 B。(1.3a) (1.3b) (1.3c)
B	謝謝角色 A 向你介紹產品。告訴他你會在展覽上到處看看,稍後再決定。
A	拿一些印刷品資料給角色 B。(6.1b) (6.1c)

情境 2

　　國外企業主在找新品牌鞋款的製造商。這位國外商務人士正和一位台灣的業務代表談論台灣公司成為優良製造商的潛力。

練習	
角色 A	台灣公司的代表
角色 B	國外的企業主
B	要角色 A 談談他們公司的生產方式的品質。
A	解釋你們的製造品質及品管系統。(4.1a) (4.2a) (4.4)
B	問角色 A，他們公司有沒有任何比其他公司凸出的優勢。
A	把你們公司的特色告訴角色 B。(4.3a)
	告訴角色 B，他可以靠你們公司把事情做好。(4.5)

情境 3

　　一家外國公司決定和一家生產辦公室設備的台灣公司做生意。外國公司的主管決定造訪台灣公司並和業務經理談談合作的可能。兩個人已是舊識。

練習	
角色 A	台灣的業務經理和業務經理的秘書（一人飾兩角）
角色 B	外國公司主管
B	問角色 A 有沒有空。(6.2)
A	先扮演秘書，詢問角色 B 是哪位。(6.2a)
B	回應角色 A。
A	確認老闆是否有空。(6.2b)
	然後請角色 B 進去老闆的辦公室。(6.2f)
B	招呼角色 A。
A	跟角色 B 打招呼。問角色 B，他要不要喝什麼飲料。(6.3)
B	告訴角色 A，你想要一杯咖啡。
A	問角色 B，他希望咖啡怎麼喝。(6.3)
B	回應角色 A。
B	問角色 A，某樣東西有沒有現貨。
A	告訴角色 B，那樣東西有現貨。(5.1a)
B	問角色 A，另一樣東西有沒有現貨。
A	告訴角色 B，那樣東西沒有現貨。(5.1a)
B	問角色 A，那樣東西什麼時候會有貨。(5.1b)

A	問角色 B，那樣東西他想要多少數量？(5.2)
B	告訴角色 A，你想要買多少。
A	告訴角色 B，那樣東西何時會有貨。(5.1b)
B	告訴角色 A，目前一切都很順利。
A	問角色 B 飲料還可以嗎。(6.3)

Memo

第 5 章

時程安排與物流用語

Scheduling and Logistics Language

本章含括我覺得十分重要，但為中文母語人士所設計的英文教科書卻經常忽略的片語和句型，即時程安排與物流的用語。我們生活在受時間所支配的世界，而國際商務交流十分注重的正是時效性。因此，清楚而正確地使用時程安排與物流用語可說是有效商業溝通的基本環節，而讀者也應該以精通本章的內容為目標。

This unit contains phrases and patterns that I find extremely important, yet often neglected in English language textbooks for Chinese native speakers: scheduling and logistics language. We live in a world governed by time, and the exchanges of international business are highly time sensitive. As such, using the language of scheduling and logistics clearly and correctly is a fundamental part of effective business communication. Your goal now should be mastering this unit.

1 談論時程安排 Talking About Scheduling

1.1 時間的特定用字 Time-specific Words

 track 72

時間是各類商業活動的重要因素，下面列出了在各種商業討論和情境中會一再聽到的常用字詞。

BIZ 必通字彙

• 安排時程 Making Schedules

❶ time commitment 承諾時限
❷ forecast [ˋfor͵kæst] n./v. 預測；預報
❸ timetable [ˋtaɪm͵tebḷ] n. 時間表；時刻表
❹ time frame 時間範圍
❺ time slot [slɑt] 空檔
❻ window [ˋwɪndo] n. 時限

• 調整時程 Adjusting Schedules

❶ extend [ɪkˋstɛnd] v. 延長
❷ pull in 縮短
❸ postpone [postˋpon] v. 使延期；延後
❹ move forward 提前

• 跟上時程 Keeping Schedules

❶ time pressure 時間壓力
❷ ahead of schedule 超前進度
❸ behind schedule 落後進度
❹ on schedule 符合時程
❺ expedite [ˋɛkspɪ͵daɪt] v. 加速；迅速執行

❻ buffer [`bʌfə] *n.* 緩衝；緩衝器

❼ tight [taɪt] *adj.* 緊湊；沒空的

❽ on pace 準時

● 交件 Delivering

❶ delivery time 交期

❷ lead time 前置期

● 形容時程 Describing Schedules

❶ accurate [`ækjərɪt] *adj.* 精確的

❷ precise [prɪ`saɪs] *adj.* 確切的

❸ regularly [`rɛgjələlɪ] *adv.* 定期地

❹ insane [ɪn`sen] *adj.* 荒唐的；瘋狂的

Show Time

● 安排時程 Making Schedules

❶ We have a **time commitment** to this shipping schedule.
這個運送時程我們有一個承諾的時限。

❷ Do you have a **forecast** for the <u>completion</u> time?
你能不能預測完成的時間？

❸ Can you give me a **timetable** of the deliveries?
你能不能給我一份交件的時間表？

❹ Give me a general **time frame** for your decision.
給我你們何時會作決定大致的時間範圍。

❺ We have one **time slot** today at 10:00.
今天十點我們有個空檔。

❻ You have a two-month cancellation **window**.
你有兩個月的取消期。

Word List

completion [kəm`pliʃən] *n.* 完成；結束

調整時程 Adjusting Schedules

❶ I would like to **extend** the schedule a few days.
我想把時程延長幾天。

❷ Can you **pull in** the schedule by one week?
你可不可以把時程縮短一個星期？

❸ We need to **postpone** the meeting and reschedule.
我們得把會議延後並重訂時間。

❹ Let's **move** the meeting **forward** by an hour.
我們把會議提前一小時吧。

跟上時程 Keeping Schedules

❶ I really feel the **time pressure** for this project.
我深深感受到這個案子的時間壓力。

❷ The vendor is three days **ahead of schedule**.
廠商超前進度三天。

❸ We are **behind schedule** again.
我們的進度又落後了。

❹ Blake is **on schedule** as usual.
布雷克一如往常符合時程。

❺ Our customer wants us to **expedite** the order.
我們的顧客要我們加速處理訂單。

❻ Can you give us a one-week **buffer**, in case our vendor is late?
你可不可以給我們一星期的緩衝，以防我們的廠商延誤？

❼ Our schedule is very **tight** because of the Chinese New Year.
因為農曆新年的關係，我們的時程非常緊湊。

❽ I'm **on pace** to make the deadline.
我可準時在截止期限內完成。

Word List

vendor [ˋvɛndɚ] *n.* 賣主；廠商

交件 Delivering

❶ The **delivery time** for this kind of item is at least ten days.
這種品項的交件時間至少要十天。

❷ Is a six-day **lead time** acceptable?
六天的前置期可以接受嗎？

形容時程 Describing Schedules

❶ We need **accurate** shipping schedules.
我們需要精準的運送時程。

❷ Please give us the **precise** order dates.
請給我們確切的下單日期。

❸ We **regularly** send them updated invoices.
我們會定期把最新的發票寄給他們。

❹ My schedule is **insane**. It's going to be a busy month.
我的行程很瘋狂，這將會是忙碌的一個月。

◇◇ 小心陷阱 ◇◇

☹ 錯誤用法
I am your **contact window** for this project.
你這個案子我是的聯絡人。
☺ 正確用法
I am your **contact person** for this project.
你這個案子我是的聯絡人。

1.2 與時程安排相關的字彙 Key Words Related to Scheduling

track 73

BIZ 必通字彙

● 時程 Schedule

❶ critical [ˋkrɪtɪkl̩] *adj.* 緊要的；關鍵性的
❷ flexible [ˋflɛksəbl̩] *adj.* 有彈性的
❸ flexibility [͵flɛksəˋbɪlətɪ] *n.* 彈性

● 庫存 Stock

❶ inventory [ˋɪnvən͵torɪ] *n.* 存貨；存貨清單
❷ availability [ə͵veləˋbɪlətɪ] *n.* 可得性
❸ shortage [ˋʃɔrtɪdʒ] *n.* 短缺；匱乏
❹ surplus [ˋsɝplʌs] *n./adj.* 過剩（的）
❺ capacity [kəˋpæsətɪ] *n.* 容量；生產力

● 訂單 Orders

❶ status [ˋstetəs] *n.* 狀況；狀態
❷ update [ʌpˋdet] *v.* 更新
❸ cancel [ˋkænsl̩] *v.* 取消
❹ cancellation [͵kænsl̩ˋeʃən] *n.* 取消

● 運送 Shipping

❶ freight [fret] *n.* 貨物；運費
❷ via air 用空運
❸ via sea 用海運
❹ via surface mail 用普通郵件
❺ COD 貨到付款 (= cash on delivery)
❻ via FedEx 用聯邦快遞

其他 Miscellaneous

❶ cycle [ˋsaɪkl] *n.* 週期
❷ backup [ˋbækʌp] *n./adj.* 備用品（的）
❸ liability [ˌlaɪəˋbɪlətɪ] *n.* 責任；義務

Show Time

時程特性 Schedule Qualities

❶ The schedule change is **critical**.
時程的變更很要緊。
❷ Can you be more **flexible** about the schedule?
時程方面你可以更有彈性一點嗎？
❸ Ordering **flexibility** is important for us.
下單的彈性對我們很重要。

庫存 Stock

❶ I wonder if the ZPJ959 is in our **inventory**.
我不知道我們的存貨裡是否有 ZP J959。
❷ Please check the **availability** of item 691 again.
請再檢查一次品項 691 有沒有貨。
❸ I am afraid there is a **shortage** of that part.
恐怕那樣零件缺貨。
❹ Our warehouse has a **surplus**.
我們的庫存過剩。
❺ Can you tell me your warehouse **capacity**?
你可以告訴我你們倉庫的容量嗎？

Word List

miscellaneous [ˌmɪslˋenɪəs] *adj.* 混雜的；各種各樣的
warehouse [ˋwɛrˌhaʊs] *n.* 倉庫

● 訂單 Orders

❶ I would like to check the delivery **status** again.
我想要再檢查一下交貨狀況。

❷ The computer will **update** your order automatically.
電腦會自動更新你的訂單。

❸ She asked me to **cancel** the first order.
她要我取消第一筆訂單。

❹ The **cancellation** process is very fast.
取消的流程非常快。

● 運送 Shipping

❶ The **freight** arrives every Friday.
貨每週五到。

❷ The **freight** total is about four hundred US (US$400).
總運費大約是 400 美元。

❸ Would you like us to ship **via air**?
你要我們用空運寄嗎？

❹ We usually ship **via sea**.
我們通常用海運寄。

❺ I can ship the packages **COD** if you want me to.
如果你要的話，我可以用貨到付款的方式運送這些包裹。

❻ The fastest way to ship is **via FedEx**.
用聯邦快遞運送是最快的方式。

● 其他 Miscellaneous

❶ Our procurement **cycle** begins fresh every month.
我們的採購週期每個月都從新起頭。

❷ Do you have a **backup** shipping plan?
你有備用的運送計畫嗎？

❸ Whose **liability** is it if the shipped quantity is wrong?
如果運送的量有錯是誰的責任？

Word List

procurement [prəˋkjʊrmənt] *n.* 取得；採購

quantity [ˋkwɑntətɪ] *n.* 數量

2 ⋮ 詢問及請求 Inquiring and Requesting

2.1 提出一般的詢問 Making a General Inquiry

 track 74

2.1a 常見句型 Common Patterns

以下這些句型經常被誤用，請注意它們的差異。

BIZ 必通句型

WHAT IS THE STATUS OF ...?

……的狀況如何？

例 What is the status of the on-line tracking system?

線上追蹤系統的狀況如何？

HOW IS THE PROGRESS WITH ...?

……的進展如何？

例 How is the progress with the <u>re-routed</u> order?

重新安排訂單的進展如何？

HOW ARE THINGS PROGRESSING WITH ...?

和……的事進展得如何？

例 How are things progressing with the new vendor?

和新廠商的事進展得如何？

WHAT IS THE SITUATION WITH ...?

……的情況如何？

例 What is the situation with the quality control department?

品管部門的情況如何？

Word List

re-routed [rɪˋrutɪd] *adj.* 按新的特定路線運送（或寄發）的

2.1b 常用字彙 Common Vocabulary

這些字彙經常被誤用，請注意它們的差異。

BIZ 必通字彙

CHECK ON 檢查

例 May I **check on** the order?

我可以檢查一下訂單嗎？

DOUBLE CHECK 仔細檢查；複核

例 You had better **double check** the invoice.

你最好再仔細檢查一下發票。

CONFIRM [kən`fɜm] *v.* 確認

例 I'd like to **confirm** the order you placed yesterday.

我想確認你昨天下的那筆訂單。

VERIFY [`vɛrə,faɪ] *v.* 證實

例 Can you **verify** that the contract was signed on time?

你可不可以證實合約有準時簽訂？

2.2 詢問有空的時間 Checking Available Time

 track 75

BIZ 必通句型

○ 詢問建議時間 Asking for a Suggested Time

WHAT IS THE BEST TIME FOR ...?

什麼時候……最好？

例 What is the best time for the meeting?

什麼時候開會最好？

Word List

place an order 下訂單

WHAT IS THE BEST TIME FOR (person) to ...?

（人）什麼時候⋯⋯最好？

例 What is the best time for your manager to meet with us?

你們經理什麼時候和我們見面最好？

WHAT TIME IS GOOD FOR ...?

⋯⋯什麼時間方便？

例 What time is good for you?

你什麼時間方便？

WHEN ARE YOU AVAILABLE TO ...?

你什麼時候有空⋯⋯？

例 When are you available to test the new ordering system?

你什麼時候有空測試新的下單系統？

● 建議時間 Suggesting a Time

IS (time) OKAY FOR YOU?

（時間）你可以嗎？

例 Is 6:00 okay for you?

六點鐘你可以嗎？

CAN WE/YOU ... AT/IN/ON (time/month/date)?

我們／你可以（時間／月份／日期）⋯⋯嗎？

例 Can you finish this at 11:00?

你可以在十一點完成嗎？

例 Can we discuss this in March?

我們可以在三月討論這個嗎？

例 Can you be here on the sixth?

你可以在六號到這裡嗎？

◇◇ 小心陷阱 ◇◇◇

☹ 錯誤用法

What is **a best time** for you?

哪個時間你最方便？

☺ 正確用法

What is **the best time** for you?

哪個時間你最方便？

Show Time

A: I'd like to confirm that you want 500 mountain bikes.

B: Actually, I might change the order to 400.

A: Can you discuss the order with me later this afternoon?

A：我想確認一下你要五百台登山腳踏車。

B：事實上，我可能會把訂單改成四百台。

A：你可不可以今天下午稍後跟我討論這筆訂單？

2.3 要求延期 Requesting Delays

 track 76

BIZ 必通句型

I WOULD LIKE TO REQUEST A ... DELAY.

我想要求延期……。

例 I would like to request a one-month delay.

我想要求延期一個月。

CAN I HAVE A ... EXTENSION?

我可以展延……嗎？

例 Can I have a three-day extension?

我可以展延三天嗎？

IS IT POSSIBLE THAT I CAN DELAY FOR ...?

我有沒有可能可以延期⋯⋯？

例 Is it possible that I can delay for a few days?

我有沒有可能可以延期幾天？

COULD WE POSSIBLY DELAY ...?

我們可不可能可以延後⋯⋯嗎？

例 Could we possibly delay the launch by two weeks?

我們可不可能可以延後兩星期推出嗎？

◇◇◇ 小心陷阱 ◇◇◇

☹ 錯誤用法

Could I **possible to** delay the shipment?

我可不可能可以延後裝運？

☺ 正確用法

Could I **possibly** delay the shipment?

我可不可能可以延後裝運？

2.4 提醒 Giving Reminders

 track 77

BIZ 必通句型

I WANT/NEED TO REMIND YOU TO ....

我想／必須提醒你要⋯⋯。

例 I need to remind you to check your email this afternoon.

我必須提醒你今天下午要看一下電子郵件。

I WANT/NEED TO REMIND YOU THAT ....

我想／必須提醒你⋯⋯。

例 I want to remind you that the presentation is very important.

我想提醒你那場簡報非常重要。

I'D LIKE TO REMIND YOU ABOUT ....

我想要提醒你有關⋯⋯。

例 I'd like to remind you about the conference call.

我想要提醒你有關電話會議的事。

PLEASE REMEMBER TO ....

請記得要⋯⋯。

例 Please remember to bring your notebook computer to the meeting.

請記得要帶你的筆記型電腦來開會。

PLEASE REMEMBER THAT ....

請記得⋯⋯。

例 Please remember that we have to end by noon.

請記得我們必須在中午前結束。

PLEASE KEEP IN MIND THAT ....

請記住⋯⋯。

例 Please keep in mind that deliveries must be received in person.

請記住貨品一定要親自接收。

Show Time

A: Could I possibly delay the next payment by ten days?

B: I need to remind you that current orders will be put on hold if you pay late.

A：我有沒有可能可以把下次的付款延後十天？

B：我必須提醒你，假如你延遲付款，目前的訂單就會暫緩處理。

Word List

in person 親自   on hold 暫緩；擱置

2.5 截止期限 Deadlines

 track 78

2.5a 詢問截止期限 Inquiring About a Deadline

BIZ 必通句型

WHEN IS THE DEADLINE?
截止期限是什麼時候？

WHEN IS THE DEADLINE FOR ...?
……的截止期限是什麼時候？
例 When is the deadline for restocking the warehouse?
倉庫補貨的截止期限是什麼時候？

CAN YOU TELL ME THE DEADLINE FOR ...?
你能不能告訴我……的截止期限？
例 Can you tell me the deadline for Christmas orders?
你能不能告訴我聖誕節訂單的截止期限？

2.5b 要求截止期限 Requesting a Deadline

BIZ 必通句型

I NEED ... BY (time).
（時間）之前，我需要……。
例 I need your suggested timetable by the middle of next week.
下星期中之前，我需要你建議的時間表。

CAN I RECEIVE ... ON (date)?
我可以在（日期）收到……嗎？
例 Can I receive the change requests on the twenty-third?
我可以在二十三號收到變更要求嗎？

203

CAN YOU SEND ... BY (time)?

你可以在（時間）前送出……嗎？

例 Can you send the error list by the end of next week?

你可不可以在下週結束前寄出錯誤表？

WHEN CAN YOU ...?

你什麼時候可以……？

例 When can you e-mail me the updated statistics?

你什麼時候可以用電子郵件把最新的統計資料寄給我？

WHEN CAN I HAVE/RECEIVE ...?

我什麼時候可以拿到／收到……？

例 When can I have the purchase order?

我什麼時候可以拿到採購訂單？

2.5c 訂出截止期限 Giving a Deadline

BIZ 必通句型

THE DEADLINE FOR ... IS ....

……的截止期限是……。

例 The deadline for the project is the end of this month.

案子的截止期限是這個月底。

WE HAVE A DEADLINE OF ....

我們的截止期限為……。

例 We have a deadline of Friday the thirteenth.

我們的截止期限為十三號星期五。

WE HAVE SET THE DEADLINE FOR ....

我們把截止期限訂在……。

例 We have set the deadline for noon on July 4.

我們把截止期限訂在七月四號中午。

◇◇ 小心陷阱 ◇◇

☹ 錯誤用法

We have set the deadline **on** the end of this week.

我們把截止期限定在本週結束前。

☺ 正確用法

We have set the deadline **for** the end of this week.

我們把截止期限定在本週結束前。

Show Time

A: Can you tell me the deadline for requesting order changes?

B: The deadline for order changes is tomorrow, but can you send me your forecasted changes today?

A：你可不可以告訴我要求變更訂單的截止期限？

B：變更訂單的截止期限是明天，但是你能不能今天就把預測的變更寄給我？

2.6 確認時程 Confirming a Schedule

 track 79

BIZ 必通句型

I NEED TO CONFIRM ....

我需要確認……。

例 I need to confirm the restocking time.

　　我需要確認補貨時間。

I'LL CHECK AGAIN ON (day/date).

我（星期／日期）會再檢查一次。

例 I'll check again on next Tuesday, the seventh.

　　我下星期二，七號會再檢查一次。

205

COULD YOU PLEASE CONFIRM ... FOR ME?

可不可以請你幫我確認……？

例 Could you please confirm the order status for me?

可不可以請你幫我確認訂單狀況？

Show Time

A: Is the order still expected to be shipped next week?

B: I'm afraid that's not possible. Can we change the date to the week after next week?

A: I'll see what I can do.

B: Thanks. Could you please confirm the shipping date when you have made a decision?

A：訂貨還是預計下星期運送嗎？

B：恐怕沒辦法。我們可以把日期改到下下週嗎？

A：我會看看可以怎麼辦。

B：謝謝。可以請你在決定好的時候確認一下運送日期嗎？

Memo

3 有無按照時程 On and off Schedule

3.1 準時 On Time

 track 80

以下這些用語的意思差不多。

BIZ 必通字彙

ON SCHEDULE 符合時程

例 The project status update is on schedule.

專案狀況更新符合時程。

ACCORDING TO SCHEDULE 依照時程

例 We expect to finish the <u>specifications</u> according to schedule.

我們希望可以依照時程完成規格說明書。

ON TIME 準時

例 Our deliveries are always on time.

我們一向準時交貨。

Word List

specification [ˌspɛsəfəˋkeʃən] *n.* 規格說明書

3.2 延遲 Late

 track 81

3.2a 表示延遲 Expressing Lateness

BIZ 必通字彙

LATE 延遲
例 The sample run might be a little **late**.
樣品的測試可能會有點延遲。

RUN LATE 遲於預期時間
例 The conference call will **run late**.
電話會議會開到比較晚。

BE DELAYED 延期的
例 I hope the meeting isn't **delayed** again.
希望會議不要又延期了。

BE BEHIND SCHEDULE 進度落後
例 The testing team was **behind schedule** last quarter.
上一季測試團隊的進度落後。

BIZ 必通句型

... NOT ... ON TIME.
……沒有準時……。
例 The test engineer did not arrive on time.
測試工程師沒有準時到達。

... NOT ... ON SCHEDULE.

……沒有按時程……。

例 The assembly machines were not <u>modified</u> on schedule.

裝配機沒有按時程修改。

... NOT ... ACCORDING TO SCHEDULE.

……沒有依照時程……。

例 The catalog mailing is not going according to schedule.

目錄的寄發沒有依照時程。

3.2b 說明延遲的理由 Providing Reasons for Lateness

BIZ 必通句型

BECAUSE OF ... WE .... <u>BEAR WITH US</u>.

因為……，我們……。請見諒。

例 Because of a computer problem, we cannot send you the results yet. Bear with us.

因為電腦出了問題，我們還沒辦法把結果寄給你。請見諒。

THE REASON FOR ... IS ....

……的原因是……。

例 The reason for the delay is a typhoon in Vietnam.

延誤的原因是越南有颱風。

Word List

modify [ˋmɑdəˌfaɪ] v. 更改；修改

bear with sb. 忍受某人；請見諒

BECAUSE (reason), (result).

因為（理由），所以（結果）。

例 Because the factory construction was delayed, our first run will begin later than expected.

因為工廠的建造工程延誤，所以我們首次運轉開始的時間會比預期得要晚。

... HAVE TO ....

……必須……

例 I had to <u>amend</u> the presentation contents before the meeting.

我必須在開會前修改好簡報內容。

... NEED TO ....

……得要……

例 I needed to assist the manager with an urgent request.

我得協助經理處理一件緊急要求。

◇◇ 小心陷阱 ◇◇

☹ 錯誤用法

Because of the holiday, **so** we didn't ship on Friday.

因為放假的關係，所以我們星期五不送貨。

☺ 正確用法

Because of the holiday, we didn't ship on Friday.

因為放假的關係，所以我們星期五不送貨。

Word List

amend [əˋmɛnd] v. 修訂；修改

3.3 更改時程 Schedule Changes

 track 82

3.3a 告知更改時程 Informing of a Schedule Change

BIZ 必通句型

I'M AFRAID WE NEED TO CHANGE THE SCHEDULE.
恐怕我們必須更改時程。

I NEED TO INFORM YOU OF/THAT ....
我必須通知你……。

例 I need to inform you of another change.

　　我必須通知你另一項變更。

例 I need to inform you that the product launch has been changed.

　　我要通知你，產品推出的時間已經改了。

WE NEED TO CHANGE ... FROM ... TO ....
我們必須把……從……改到……。

例 We need to change the seminar from Thursday to Monday.

　　我們必須把研討會從星期四改到星期一。

3.3b 要求更改時程 Requesting a Schedule Change

BIZ 必通句型

IS IT OKAY IF WE ...?
如果我們……可以嗎？

例 Is it okay if we change the reporting dates？

　　如果我們更改報告的日期可以嗎？

IS IT POSSIBLE TO ...?
有沒有可能……？

例 Is it possible to make a couple of modifications?

　　有沒有可能做一些修正？

CAN WE POSSIBLY ...?

我們有沒有可能可以……?

例 Can we possibly move the date forward one week?

我們有沒有可能可以把日期提前一週?

I'M AFRAID THAT'S NOT POSSIBLE. CAN WE ...?

那恐怕不可能。我們可不可以……?

例 I'm afraid that's not possible. Can we move it back three days?

那恐怕不可能。我們可不可以往後挪三天?

THE SCHEDULE IS A PROBLEM FOR US. CAN WE ...?

這個時程對我們而言有困難。我們可不可以……?

例 The schedule is a problem for us. Can we delay it a few more days?

這個時程對我們而言有困難。我們可不可以多延幾天?

THAT MIGHT BE A PROBLEM. CAN WE ...?

那樣可能會有問題。我們可不可以……?

例 That might be a problem. Can we adjust the arrival time?

那樣可能會有問題。我們可不可以調整抵達的時間?

◇◇◇ 小心陷阱 ◇◇◇

☹ 錯誤用法

Can we **possible** to move the dates back?

我們有沒有可能可以把日期延後?

☺ 正確用法

Can we **possibly** move the dates back?

我們有沒有可能可以把日期延後?

或

Is it possible to move the dates back?

有沒有可能把日期延後?

3.4 延期 Postponing

 track 83

BIZ 必通字彙

PUT OFF 延後

例 She asked to **put off** the order inquiry for a few days.

她要求把訂單的查詢時間延後幾天。

DELAY 延期

例 The company wants to **delay** the shipment if possible.

如果可以的話，公司想把運送貨的時間延期。

POSTPONE 延遲

例 We have to **postpone** the submission of the report.

我們不得不延遲提出報告。

Show Time

A: I hope our shipments all arrive on time this month.

B: I heard that some shipments are behind schedule.

A: Perhaps the supplier needed to replace some defective goods again.

B: Maybe, but we really can't delay getting the goods to our customers again and again. That's not good business!

A：希望我們的貨這個月都能準時送達。

B：我聽說有些貨的運送進度落後。

A：或許供應商又需要再把一些瑕疵品換掉。

B：也許吧，但我們實在不能一而再、再而三遲交貨物給顧客。生意不是這樣做的！

Word List

submission [səb`mɪʃən] *n.* 提交；呈遞

3.5 催促別人跟上時程 Pushing People to Keep Schedules track 84

3.5a 禮貌地催促 Polite Pushing

BIZ 必通句型

IT IS IMPORTANT THAT YOU ....

你⋯⋯是很重要的。

例 It is important that you give us the revised schedule soon.

你盡快給我們更正過的時程是很重要的。

（意思是：快點給我們更正過的時程。）

IT IS IMPORTANT THAT I ....

我⋯⋯是很重要的。

例 It is important that I test the sample for you.

我幫你測試樣品是很重要的。

（意思是：你要給我樣品，我才能先測試它。）

I REALLY NEED YOU TO ....

我真的需要你⋯⋯。

例 I really need you to send back the defective component.

我真的需要你把有瑕疵的零件送回來。

（意思是：立刻把有瑕疵的零件送回來。）

I REALLY NEED TO ASK YOU TO ....

我真的必須請你⋯⋯。

例 I really need to ask you to double-check the error today.

我真的必須請你今天把錯誤再檢查一遍。

（意思是：放下你手邊的事，現在就去檢查錯誤。）

I STRONGLY SUGGEST THAT YOU ....

我強烈建議你……。

例 I strongly suggest that you ship the items immediately.

我強烈建議你立刻把那些物件運來。

（意思是：現在就把那些物件運來。）

I'M AFRAID I HAVE TO ASK YOU TO ....

恐怕我必須請你……。

例 I'm afraid I have to ask you to rush the shipment.

恐怕我必須請你儘快把貨送來。

（意思是：抱歉，你現在就得把貨送來。）

◇◇ 小心陷阱 ◇◇◇

☹ 錯誤用法

I strongly **suggest you to** begin soon.

我強烈建議你儘早開始。

☺ 正確用法

I strongly **suggest that you** begin soon.

我強烈建議你儘早開始。

3.5b 提出警告 Giving Warnings

BIZ 必通句型

IF YOU CAN'T ..., WE MIGHT HAVE TO ....

如果你不能……，我們也許就得……。

例 If you can't pay for it now, we might have to cancel all future shipments.

如果你不能現在付款，我們也許就得取消往後所有的運貨。

IF YOU CAN'T ..., WE WILL HAVE TO ....

如果你沒辦法……，我們就只好……。

例 If you can't test the product, we will have to look for another vendor.

如果你沒辦法測試產品，我們就只好去找其他廠商。

THE ONLY WAY WE CAN ... IS IF YOU ....

我們唯一可以……的情況是，你……。

例 The only way we can <u>fund</u> the project is if you provide a lot more details.

我們唯一可以資助這個案子的情況是，你提供更多的細節。

WE CAN'T ... UNLESS ....

除非……，我們沒辦法……。

例 We can't <u>fill the orders</u> on time unless you send us the reports on time.

除非你把報告準時寄給我們，否則我們沒辦法準時完成訂單。

WE WON'T BE ABLE TO ... IF ....

如果……，我們就無法……。

例 We won't be able to complete the deal if you can't agree with the <u>terms</u> today.

如果你不能在今天同意這些條件，我們就無法完成交易。

Show Time

A: I really need you to let us know if there will be any more changes to the schedule.

B: Sometimes our manager changes the schedule and doesn't let us know.

A: Can you inform your manager that we can't have a conference call next week unless we have the correct schedule?

A：我真的需要你告訴我們時程不會再有任何變動。

B：有時候我們經理會更改時程，卻不告訴我們。

A：可不可以告訴你們經理，除非我們得知正確的時程，否則我們下星期沒有辦法舉行電話會議？

Word List

fund [fʌnd] *v.* 提供（事業、活動等）資金　　fill the order　供應訂貨

term [tɜm] *n.* （契約談判等的）條件；條款

時間的用法 Time Usage

由於英文是十分注重時間的語言，所以在討論時程時很容易造成文法和用法上的錯誤。在學習英文時，最容易搞混的就是動詞以及和時間有關的名詞與形容詞。由於商務人士需要在不會引起顧客的焦慮和挫折的情況下有效地處理業務，所以我們現在就討論一下與時間相關的一些用法。

4.1 日期 Dates

 track 85

BIZ 必通句型

... THIS COMING (day/month) ....

……接下來的這個（日／月）……。

例 Can you call back this coming Wednesday?

你可以在接下來的這個星期三回電嗎？

例 There is a trade show this coming October. Can you make it?

接下來的這個十月會有一場商展，你趕得及嗎？

... THIS PAST (day/month) ....

……過去的這個（日／月）……。

例 I met her this past Tudesday.

我過去的這個星期二遇到她。

例 This past March I went to Shenzhen for a training session.

我過去的這個三月去深圳參加了一個訓練講習。

... THIS (day) ....

這（日）……。

例 Will you discuss this with me this (week) Thursday?

這星期四你會跟我討論嗎？

217

... NEXT (day) ....
……下（日）……。

例 The order should arrive next Tuesday.
訂單應該會在下星期二到。

... LAST (day) ....
……上（日）……。

例 He already held a meeting last Wednesday.
他上星期三已經舉行過會議了。

... AT THE BEGINNING OF (month/year) ....
……在（月／年）初……。

例 When we met at the beginning of March, we discussed moving forward with the project.
我們在三月初碰面時，討論了要把案子提前。

例 Please evaluate the procurement system at the beginning of next year.
請在明年初評估採購系統。

... AT THE END OF (week/month) ....
……在（星期／月）末／底……

例 The prototype will arrive at the end of this week.
原型會在這星期末送達。

例 We'll have our part completed at the end of next month.
我們會在下個月底把我們的部分完成。

... IN THE MIDDLE OF (month).
……在（月）中旬……。

例 Let's meet in the middle of September.
我們就約在九月中旬見面。

Word List

evaluate [ɪˋvæljʊˌet] v. 評估；估計

◇◇◇ 小心陷阱 ◇◇◇

☹ 錯誤用法

The **time for** the party is May 11.

派對的日期是五月十一日。

☺ 正確用法

The **date of** the party is May 11.

派對的日期是五月十一日。

4.2 特定時間 Specific Times

 track 86

BIZ 必通句型

... AT (time).

…… （時間）。

例 Mike's flight arrives at 3:30.

　　麥克的班機三點半會到。

... ON (day).

…… （日）。

例 The supervisor would like to begin the project on October 9.

　　主管想要在十月九號開始做這個案子。

... ON (day) AT (time). / ... AT (time) ON (day).

……在（日）的（時間）……。

例 He will arrive on Saturday at 1:30.

　　他會在星期六的一點半抵達。

例 He will arrive at 1:30 on Saturday.

　　他會在星期六的一點半抵達。

... IN (time of day) ....

……在（一天中的時間）……

例 Can you work on this in the evening?

你可以在今天晚上工作嗎？

例 I'll take care of this in the afternoon.

我會在下午處理這件事。

... IN (month) ....

……在（月）……

例 We can have a department meeting in December.

我們可以在十二月開部門會議。

... IN (year / time of year) ....

……在（年／一年中的時間）時……

例 We had a very busy schedule in 1987.

我們在一九八七年時非常忙。

例 Let's take care of this in the spring.

我們在春季時再來處理這件事。

... AROUND (time) ....

……（時間）左右……

例 We will begin around 3:00.

我們會在三點左右開始。

... JUST BEFORE ....

……就在……前

例 Just before I sent the email, I realized I forgot to attach the file.

就在我要寄出電子郵件之前，我發現我忘了附加檔案。

... JUST AFTER ....

……就在……後……

例 Because I got to the meeting just after Jack left, we didn't talk.

因為我就在傑克離開後才去開會，所以我們並未交談。

◇◇◇ 小心陷阱 ◇◇◇

☹ 錯誤用法

We should finish this report **in** the end of this week.

我們應該在這星期末完成這項報告。

☺ 正確用法

We should finish this report **at** the end of this week.

我們應該在這星期末完成這項報告。

Show Time

A: Can I discuss an important issue with you next Thursday?
B: Is it the same issue we discussed this past Wednesday?
A: Yes.
B: Well, let's resolve it as quickly as possible. How about at the end of this week?

A：我可不可以在下星期四跟你討論一個重要的議題？
B：是我們過去的這個星期三討論過的那個問題嗎？
A：是。
B：嗯，我們盡快把它解決吧。這個星期末如何？

4.3 期間 Periods of Time

 track 87

BIZ 必通句型

... BY (specific time).

在（特定時間）前……。

例 Can you send me the documents by closing time today?

你可以在今天下班前把文件交給我嗎？

... BEFORE (specific time).

（特定時間）以前……。

例 We will <u>implement</u> the new plan before October.

十月以前，我們會實施新計劃。

... SINCE (specific time).

打從（特定時間）起……。

例 We have been testing the prototype since last year.

打從去年起，我們就一直在測試原型。

... FOR (time period) ....

……花（期間）……。

例 Let me think about your proposal for a few more days.

讓我多花幾天來考慮你的提案。

... UNTIL (specific time).

……一直到（特定時間）為止。

例 We will test the metal until we are sure it will not break.

我們會測試這個金屬到確定它不會斷裂為止。

◇◇ 小心陷阱 ◇◇◇

☹ 錯誤用法

I have been working on this project **since two years**.

打從兩年前起，我就一直在做這個案子。

☺ 正確用法

I have been working on this project **since two years ago**.

打從兩年前起，我就一直在做這個案子。

Word List

implement [ˋɪmpləˌmənt] *v.* 執行；實施

5 實戰演練 Partner Practice

當你讀完並複習過本章內容後,找個同伴試試下面的對話練習!

情境

你正在開會,討論的議題是:波諾公司必須延期運送一大批電腦螢幕,因為電腦零件的瑕疵率偏高。

練習 1	
角色 A	波諾公司的部門經理
角色 B	波諾公司的採購部門員工
A	詢問貨會多晚到。(2.1)
B	回答。(4.3)
A	問角色 B 他什麼時候可以和零件廠商討論這個問題。
B	回答。(4.1 or 4.2)
A	提醒角色 B 貨有多重要。(2.4)
B	問角色 A 解決這個問題有沒有截止期限。(2.5a)
A	向角色 B 說明截止期限。(2.5b)

練習 2	
角色 A	波諾公司的採購部門員工
角色 B	波諾公司的零件供應商
A	詢問角色 B 零件會不會準時送達。(3.1)
B	告訴角色 A 貨會晚到,並說明理由是他們需要測試所有的零件,以確保其符合國際標準。(3.2a) (3.2b)
A	催促角色 B 跟上預定的時程。(3.5a)
B	要求延期。(2.3)
A	告訴角色 B 你無法接受延期。詢問他們目前零件存貨的狀況。(2.1)
B	告訴角色 A 你不確定狀況是如何。
A	問角色 B 什麼時候可以開會討論這個狀況。(2.2)
B	回答角色 A。(4.1 or 4.2)

第 6 章

討論問題與解決方法
Discussing Problems and Solutions

本章所包含的用語有助於成功對應做生意時最困難的一環，那就是處理問題。由於協調人力本來就不容易，因此商業交涉必然會受一些問題的困擾。成功企業的一個重要特性是，有能妥善處理問題的專業員工。顧客都知道會有問題是自然的事，但公司如何處理這些問題，則決定了顧客是否會對公司不離不棄。因此，有效解決問題就等於維繫了顧客的忠誠度。

This chapter contains language to help you successfully navigate the most challenging part of doing business: handling problems. Because of the implicit difficulty in coordinating labor, business transactions are bound to be plagued with problems. A key trait of a successful company is the presence of a professional staff that handles problems well. Customers know there will be problems; it is how a company handles these problems that will determine if the customers stick with the company or not. In this way, effective problem solving equates to customer loyalty.

1 談論問題及解決方法 Talking About Problems and Solutions

1.1 談論問題 Talking About Problems

 track 88

　　商務人士需要精確地談論問題，因爲唯有清楚了解問題所在，才能找出有效的解決之道。而懂得使用一些明確的字來描述解決之道自然也有所幫助。

1.1a 單字表 Vocabulary

BIZ 必通字彙

○ 人為問題 People Problems

❶ error [ˋɛrə] *n.* 錯誤；失誤
❷ fault [fɔlt] *n.* 過錯；缺點
❸ mistake [mɪˋstek] *n.* 錯誤
❹ miscalculate [mɪsˋkælkjəˌlet] *v.* 算錯
❺ miscalculation [ˌmɪskælkjəˋleʃən] *n.* 算錯
❻ communication breakdown [ˋbrekˌdaun] 溝通破裂
❼ misunderstanding [ˌmɪsʌndəˋstændɪŋ] *n.* 誤會；誤解
❽ miscommunication [ˌmɪskəˌmjunəˋkeʃən] *n.* 溝通不良

○ 非人為問題 Non-people Problems

❶ break down （機器）故障、損壞；拋錨
❷ bug [bʌg] *n.*【口語】故障；毛病
❸ glitch [glɪtʃ] *n.*（設備、機器等的）小故障；失靈
❹ defect [ˋdɪfɛkt] *n.* 缺陷
❺ defective [dɪˋfɛktɪv] *adj.* 有缺陷的
❻ abnormality [ˌæbnɔrˋmælətɪ] *n.* 異常
❼ malfunction [mælˋfʌŋkʃən] *v./n.*（發生）故障；運作失常
❽ failure [ˋfeljə] *n.*（機器的）停止、故障

Show Time

人為問題 People Problems

❶ We made another **error** in the billing statement.
我們在開立帳單上犯了另一個錯誤。

❷ It seems the problem was her **fault**.
這問題看起來是她的錯。

❸ Is this your **mistake**?
這是你犯的錯嗎？

❹ If they **miscalculate** the <u>voltage</u> again, let me know.
如果他們又算錯伏特數，請告訴我。

❺ The **miscalculation** is in the <u>spreadsheet</u>.
算錯的地方在試算表上。

❻ There was a **communication breakdown** between departments.
部門間的溝通出現破裂。

❼ It was just a **misunderstanding**.
那只是個誤會。

❽ Our **miscommunication** created a small problem.
我們的溝通不良造成了一個小問題。

非人為問題 Non-people Problems

❶ The delivery truck **broke down** and the shipment was delayed.
貨車拋錨了，所以運貨延期。

❷ Can you find the **bug** in the software?
你可以找出軟體中的問題嗎？

❸ I found a **glitch** in the <u>circuit board</u>.
我發現電路板上有個小問題。

Word List

voltage [ˋvoltɪdʒ] *n.* 電壓；伏特數

spreadsheet [ˋsprɛd͵ʃit] *n.* 【電腦】空白表格

程式；試算表

circuit [ˋsɝkɪt] board 電路板

❹ The plastic case has a <u>slight</u> **defect**.

塑膠盒有個小瑕疵。

❺ I think the red <u>LED</u>s are **defective**.

我覺得紅色的 LED 有缺陷。

❻ The tool won't work properly due to an **abnormality** in the shape of the metal.

由於金屬的形狀異常，導致工具無法正常使用。

❼ The telephone <u>volume</u> button has a **malfunction**.

電話音量鈕有毛病。

❽ The **failure** was caused by a low quality power supply unit.

未能運轉的狀況是因劣質的電源供應器所引起。

◇◇ 小心陷阱 ◇◇

☹ 錯誤用法

This product is **defect**.

這樣產品有瑕疵。

☺ 正確用法

This product is **defective**.

這樣產品有瑕疵。

 **1.2** 談論成功和失敗 Talking About Success and Failure

 track **89**

BIZ 必通字彙

• 失敗 Failure

❶ fail [fɛl] *v.* 失敗

❷ failure [ˈfeljə] *n.* 失敗

❸ unsuccessful [ˌʌnsəkˈsɛsfəl] *adj.* 不成功的

Word List

slight [slaɪt] *adj.* 輕微的；微小的；小量的

LED 發光二極管 (Light-Emitting Diode)

volume [ˈvɑljəm] *n.* 音量

❹ screwup [`skru͵ʌp] *n.*【口語】失敗的事；把事情搞砸的人

　screw up【口語】搞砸；失敗

❺ blow sth.【口語】將……搞砸

❻ setback [`set͵bæk] *n.* 挫敗

● 成功 Success

❶ succeed [sək`sid] *v.* 成功

❷ success [sək`sɛs] *n.* 成功

❸ accomplish [ə`kɑmplɪʃ] *v.* 完成

❹ accomplishment [ə`kɑmplɪʃmənt] *n.* 成就

❺ achieve [ə`tʃiv] *v.* 完成；達到

❻ achievement [ə`tʃivmənt] *n.* 完成；成就

❼ attain [ə`ten] *v.* 達到

❽ attainment [ə`tenmənt] *n.* 達到；成就

❾ resolve [rɪ`zɑlv] *v.* 解決

❿ resolution [͵rɛzə`luʃən] *n.* 解決

Show Time

● 失敗 Failure

❶ The new designs **failed** to please our customer.

　新設計沒能取悅我們的顧客。

❷ The test of the prototype was a **failure**.

　原型的測試失敗了。

❸ He was **unsuccessful** in his attempt to modify the cable.

　他試圖修改纜線的努力沒有成功。

❹ There was a major **screwup** with the order.

　訂單出了大錯。

　The team **screwed up** and lost the case.

　那個團隊搞砸了並丟掉了案子。

❺ If you **blow it** again like that, you'll lose your job!
如果你再像那樣搞砸了，就會丟掉飯碗！

❻ Losing that <u>account</u> was a major **setback**.
失去那個客戶是項很大的挫敗。

● 成功 Success

❶ We can **succeed** if we try every option.
假如我們嘗試每個選項，我們就會成功！

❷ The **success** of the project depends on her <u>expertise</u>.
案子成功與否要看她的專業知識。

❸ I will **accomplish** the task before the deadline.
我會在截止期限前完成任務。

❹ Her **accomplishment** is <u>enviable</u>.
她的成就令人羨慕。

❺ Try to **achieve** the best result you can.
試著盡你所能獲得最好的結果。

❻ This **achievement** makes our company very proud.
這項成就使我們公司非常引以為傲。

❼ If we can **attain** the goal, we might <u>get a raise</u>.
如果我們能達到目標，也許就能加薪。

❽ **Attainment** of the company mission is the first priority.
達成公司的使命是第一要務。

❾ They will **resolve** the issue tomorrow.
他們明天會解決這個問題。

❿ We need a **resolution** before we can move forward.
我們需要一個解決方案，才能往下進行。

Word List

account [ə`kaʊnt] *n.* 客戶
expertise [ˌɛkspɚ`tiz] *n.* 專門知識；專門技術

enviable [`ɛnvɪəb!] *adj.* 令人羨慕的
get a raise 加薪

1.3 採取行動 Taking Action

 track 90

BIZ 必通字彙

針對問題採取行動 Taking Action on Problems

❶ solve [sɑlv] v. 解決
❷ take care of 處理、負責
❸ fix [fɪks] v. 處理；解決
❹ tackle [ˋtækl] v. 應付；處理
❺ face [fes] v. 面對
❻ clear up 澄清
❼ take corrective action 採取補救行動
❽ contain [kənˋten] v. 控制

針對解決方法採取行動 Taking Action on Solutions

❶ implement [ˋɪmpləmənt] v. 實施
❷ carry out 執行；實行；完成
❸ generate [ˋdʒɛnəˌret] v. 產生
❹ come up with 想出
❺ execute [ˋɛksɪˌkjut] v. 執行
❻ correct [kəˋrɛkt] v. 改正；修正

Show Time

針對問題採取行動 Taking Action on Problems

❶ Did you **solve** the problem yet?
你問題解決了沒？
❷ He should **take care of** the problem himself.
他應該自己處理問題。

❸ John can **fix** the errors <u>in no time</u>!
約翰可以馬上把錯誤處理掉。

❹ That is a difficult problem to **tackle**.
那是個難以應付的問題。

❺ We need to **face** this problem directly.
我們必須直接面對這個問題。

❻ **Clear up** the issue as soon as you can.
盡快澄清這個問題。

❼ Will Janice **take** any **corrective action** on the missing <u>crates</u>?
珍妮絲會對條板箱遺失的事採取任何補救行動嗎？

❽ Do you think we can **contain** this mistake so it doesn't cost us a lot of money?
你認為我們可以控制這個差錯，使它不致於花費太多錢嗎？

針對解決方法採取行動 Taking Action on Solutions

❶ The manager would like to **implement** Roger's plan.
經理想實施羅傑的計畫。

❷ **Carry out** all the repair work by next week, please.
請在下星期前完成所有的修復工作。

❸ Can you **generate** a solution by tomorrow?
你能在明天以前想出解決辦法嗎？

❹ We had better **come up with** at least two good ideas to fix the error.
我們最好提出至少兩個好主意來修正錯誤。

❺ Ask Anne to **execute** her proposal immediately.
要安妮立刻執行她的提案。

❻ Susan would like us to **correct** the mistake before we go home today.
蘇姍希望我們能在今天回家之前修正錯誤。

Word List

in no time 立即
crate [kret] *n.* 條板箱

1.4 描述決定 Describing Decisions

 track 91

BIZ 必通字彙

❶ final [ˈfaɪnl] *adj.* 最終的

❷ hasty [ˈhestɪ] *adj.* 倉促的；草率的

❸ crucial [ˈkruʃəl] *adj.* 極重要的；決定性的

❹ major [ˈmedʒɚ] *adj.* 主要的；重大的

❺ last-minute [ˈlæstˈmɪnɪt] *adj.* 最後的一刻的；最後關頭的

❻ clear-cut [ˈklɪrˈkʌt] *adj.* 一清二楚的；明確的

❼ arbitrary [ˈɑrbəˌtrɛrɪ] *adj.* 武斷的

❽ tough [tʌf] *adj.* 棘手的；困難的

Show Time

❶ This is the **final** decision.
這是最終決定。

❷ Her decision was a bit **hasty**.
她的決定有點倉促。

❸ This decision is **crucial** to the success of the project.
這個決定對案子的成敗至關重要。

❹ The boss's idea to change all the styles is a **major** decision.
老闆打算變更所有的樣式是項重大的決定。

❺ It's time to go home, so we need a **last-minute** decision.
該回家了，所以我們需要做一個最後的決定。

❻ Come on! This decision is **clear-cut**.
拜託！這個決定一清二楚的。

❼ If we make an **arbitrary** decision again, we will have trouble.
如果我們又武斷做決定，就會有麻煩。

❽ It was a **tough** decision, but we had to make it.
那是個困難的決定，但是我們還是得下。

2 通知問題 Notification of Problems

2.1 告知問題 Informing of a Problem

 track 92

BIZ 必通句型

WE HAVE A/AN ... PROBLEM.
我們有個⋯⋯問題。
例 We have a <u>spiny</u> problem.
　　我們有個傷腦筋的問題。
例 We have an extremely sensitive problem.
　　我們有個極為敏感的問題。

I'M AFRAID WE HAVE A PROBLEM.
恐怕我們有個問題。

I NEED TO TELL YOU ABOUT A PROBLEM.
我必須跟你說個問題。

I NEED TO INFORM YOU OF A PROBLEM.
我必須告知你一個問題。

THERE IS A PROBLEM I NEED TO TELL YOU ABOUT.
有個問題我必須跟你說。

Word List

spiny [spaɪnɪ] *adj.* 困難的；麻煩的；刺手的

◇◇ 小心陷阱 ◇◇

☹ 錯誤用法

I need to **tell** you a mistake.

我必須跟你說一個錯誤。

☺ 正確用法

I need to **tell** you **about** a mistake.

我必須跟你說一個錯誤。

2.2 界定問題的重要性 Defining the Importance of a Problem track 93

2.2a 說明要給問題多少注意力 Stating How Much Attention to Place on a Problem
注意以下這些用字的異同。

BIZ 必通字彙

● 最低程度 Lowest Level

ROUTINE [ru`tɪn] *adj.* 例行的；一般的
例 That kind of problem is **routine**. We see it several times a week.
那種問題是一般性的問題。我們一星期會看到好幾次。

STANDARD [`stændəd] *adj.* 普通的；正常的
例 This is a **standard** problem. We'll take care of it right away.
這是正常的問題。我們會馬上處理。

TYPICAL [`tɪpɪkl] *adj.* 有代表性的；一向如此的
例 It's very **typical** for this to happen at this stage. Nothing to worry about.
在這個階段發生這種情形很平常。不用擔心。

● 中等程度 Middle Level

MODERATE [`mɑdərɪt] *adj.* 不很大的；中等的
It is probably a **moderate** problem; check it tomorrow.
這大概不是個大問題。明天檢查一下。

235

SMALL [smɔl] *adj.* 小的

例 We have a **small** problem <u>brewing</u>. Let's see what we can do about it.

我們有個小問題正在形成。咱們來看看該怎麼辦。

REOCCURRING [ˌriəˋkɝɪŋ] *adj.* 一再發生的

例 It's a **reoccurring** problem. It's not serious, but it is annoying.

這是個一再發生的問題。不嚴重但很煩人。

● 最高程度 Highest Level

SERIOUS [ˋsɪrɪəs] *adj.* 嚴重的;危急的

例 This problem is rather **serious**.

這個問題頗為嚴重。

CRITICAL [ˋkrɪtɪkl̩] *adj.* 要緊的;關鍵性的

例 If it is a **critical** problem, tell me now.

如果是個要緊的問題,現在就告訴我。

SEVERE [səˋvɪr] *adj.* 嚴重的;劇烈的

例 This seems like **a severe** problem. It might take a while to fix.

這看起來是個嚴重的問題。可能要花一點時間來處理。

2.2b 說明問題需要多快解決 Stating How Soon the Problem Needs to be Solved

BIZ 必通句型

● 最低程度 Lowest Level

PLEASE ... AS SOON AS POSSIBLE.

請盡快……。

例 Please notify us as soon as possible.

請盡快通知我們。

Word List

brew [bru] *v.* 醞釀;正在形成

I/WE/YOU NEED TO ... AS SOON AS POSSIBLE.

我／我們／你們必須盡快……。

例 We need to inform them as soon as possible.

我們必須盡快通知他們。

I/WE HOPE YOU CAN ... AS SOON AS POSSIBLE.

我／我們希望你能盡快……。

例 I hope you can supply the information as soon as possible.

我希望你能盡快提供消息。

● 中等程度 Middle Level

PLEASE ... QUICKLY.

請趕緊……。

例 Please make your decision quickly.

請趕緊做決定。

I/WE/YOU NEED TO ... QUICKLY.

我／我們／你們必須趕緊……。

例 You need to come to an agreement quickly.

你們必須趕緊達成協議。

I/WE HOPE YOU CAN ... QUICKLY.

我/我們希望你能趕緊……。

例 I hope you can process the paperwork quickly.

我希望你能趕緊處理文書作業。

PLEASE ... RIGHT AWAY.

請馬上……。

例 Please finish it right away.

請馬上完成它。

I/WE/YOU NEED TO ... RIGHT AWAY.

我／我們／你們必須馬上……。

例 We need to make the arrangements right away.

我們必須馬上做安排。

I/WE HOPE YOU CAN ... RIGHT AWAY.

我／我們希望你能馬上……。

例 We hope you can finalize the proposal right away.

我們希望你能馬上把提案定下來。

最高程度 Highest Level

PLEASE ... IMMEDIATELY.

請立刻……。

例 Please fix the problem immediately.

請立刻解決問題。

I/WE/YOU NEED TO ... IMMEDIATELY.

我／我們／你們必須立刻……。

例 You need to head to the branch office immediately.

你必須立刻前往分公司。

I/WE HOPE YOU CAN ... IMMEDIATELY.

我／我們希望你能立刻……。

例 I hope you can settle the dispute immediately.

我希望你能立刻弭平爭端。

I URGENTLY NEED TO ....

我迫切需要……。

例 I urgently need to fax these details to her.

我迫切需要傳真這些細節給她。

Word List

settle [ˋsɛtl] v. 解決（問題、紛爭等）

238　dispute [dɪˋspjut] n./v. 爭論；爭執；爭端

I/WE NEED ... YESTERDAY. GET A MOVE ON!

我／我們昨天就需要……。快點行動！

例 We need those <u>papers</u> yesterday. <u>Get a move on</u>!

我們昨天就需要那些文件了。快點行動！

Show Time

A: Jim, I'm afraid we have a problem.

B: Let me guess. It's about the <u>deluxe</u> wooden pens.

A: It's a routine problem. We have taken care of this kind of problem many times.

B: Alright. Well, please <u>iron it out</u> as soon as possible.

A：吉姆，恐怕我們有個問題。

B：讓我猜猜看。是關於高級木製筆的問題。

A：是個一般性的問題。我們處理過這類問題很多次了。

B：好吧。嗯，請盡快把它搞定。

2.3 指派問題的責任 Assigning Responsibility for a Problem track 94

BIZ 必通句型

I/WE WILL TAKE CARE OF ....

我／我們將會處理……。

例 We will take care of the fourth item.

我們將會處理第四項。

Word List

papers [ˋpepəz] *n.* 文件；證件
get a move on 趕快；趕緊行動（常用祈使語氣）

deluxe [dɪˋlʌks] *adj.* 豪華的；高級的
iron out 解決（問題、困難等）

... WILL TAKE CARE OF ....

……將會負責處理……。

 George will take care of <u>debugging</u> the program.

喬治會負責處理移去程式中的錯誤。

(I THINK/BELIEVE) I AM RESPONSIBLE FOR ....

（我認為）我該為……負責。

 I think I am responsible for that part of the project.

我認為我該為案子的那個部分負責。

(I THINK/BELIEVE)... IS/ARE RESPONSIBLE FOR ....

（我認為）……該為……負責。

 I believe Susan is responsible for the vendor communication.

我認為蘇珊該為與廠商聯繫負責。

◇◇ 小心陷阱 ◇◇

☹ 錯誤用法

I think you are responsible **to** it.

我認為事情該由你負責。

☺ 正確用法

I think you are responsible **for** it.

我認為事情該由你負責。

2.4 歸咎問題的原因 Assigning Blame for a Problem

 track 95

BIZ 必通句型

IT SEEMS THE REASON FOR (problem) IS THAT ....

看來（問題）的原因是……。

Word **L**ist

debug [di`bʌg] *v.* 移去故障；除去（程式中的）錯誤

例 It seems the reason for the malfunction is that your engineer used the wrong component.
看來故障的原因是你們的工程師用錯了零件。

IT SEEMS THE (problem) IS BECAUSE ....
看來（問題）是因為……。
例 It seems the damage to the product is because of how you opened the package.
看來產品的損壞是因為你拆封的方式不對。

WE THINK THAT MAYBE ....
我們認為或許是……。
例 We think that maybe you forgot to <u>install</u> the new version of the software.
我們認為或許是你忘了安裝新版的軟體。

2.5 作決定 Making Decisions

 track 96

BIZ 必通句型

YOU/WE NEED TO MAKE A DECISION.
你們／我們必須做個決定。

YOU/WE NEED TO MAKE A DECISION ABOUT ....
你們／我們必須對……做出決定。
例 We need to make a decision about the malfunction report.
我們必須對故障報告做出決定。

Word List

install [ɪnˋstɔl] v. 安裝；設置

YOU/WE NEED TO MAKE A DECISION BY (day/time).

你們／我們必須在（日／時間）前做出決定。

例 We need to make a decision by Friday afternoon at the latest.

我們最晚必須在星期五下午前做出決定。

例 You need to make a decision by 4:30.

你們必須在四點三十分前做出決定。

Show Time

A: I need to inform you of a problem, Betty.

B: What problem?

A: A problem with the <u>pottery</u> made in Yingge. I'm afraid it's a serious problem. About one-third of the cups and vases are <u>cracked</u>.

B: What caused that?

A: We think that maybe the goods were not packaged carefully.

B: I see. I believe the <u>shipper</u> is responsible for that, then.

A: Yes, I think so. We need to make a decision about how to obtain replacement goods.

A：貝蒂，我得告訴妳一個問題。

B：什麼問題？

A：是鶯歌製造的陶器出了問題。這恐怕是個嚴重的問題。大約有三分之一的杯子和花瓶破了。

B：是什麼原因造成的？

A：我們認為或許是貨品沒有小心包裝。

B：了解。我認為貨運商要為這件事負責。

A：是啊，我也這麼認為。我們得做出決定，看要怎麼取得替換品。

Word List

pottery [ˈpɑtərɪ] *n.* 陶器；陶瓷

cracked [krækt] *adj.* 破裂的

shipper [ˈʃɪpɚ] *n.* 貨運商、公司

3 詢問問題 Inquiring About Problems

3.1 詢問問題的重要性 Asking the Importance of a Problem track 97

BIZ 必通句型

IS THIS PROBLEM ...?
這個問題……嗎？
例 Is this problem urgent?
這問題急迫嗎？

IS THIS A ... PROBLEM?
這是個……的問題嗎？
例 Is this a big, serious problem?
這是個嚴重的大問題嗎？

HOW SERIOUS IS THIS PROBLEM?
這個問題有多嚴重？

WHAT IS THE PRIORITY OF THIS ...?
這個……有多緊要？
例 What is the priority of this defect adjustment?
這個缺陷調整有多緊要？

 ◇◇ 小心陷阱 ◇◇◇

☹ 錯誤用法

How is the priority of this problem?

這個問題有多緊要？

☺ 正確用法

What is the priority of this problem?

這個問題有多緊要？

Word List

priority [praɪˋɔrətɪ] *n.* 優先；優先考慮的事

3.2 詢問問題的責任歸屬 Asking About Responsibility for a Problem

track 98

BIZ 必通句型

AM I RESPONSIBLE FOR ...?

……是我負責的嗎？

例 Am I responsible for the analysis of the defects?

分析缺點是我負責的嗎？

ARE YOU RESPONSIBLE FOR ...?

……是你負責的嗎？

例 Are you responsible for this?

這個是你負責的嗎？

SHOULD I TAKE CARE OF ...?

我應該處理……嗎？

例 Should I take care of the software development?

我應該處理軟體的開發嗎？

WILL YOU TAKE CARE OF ...?

你會處理……嗎？

例 Will you take care of the problems?

你會處理那些問題嗎？

WHO IS RESPONSIBLE FOR ...?

……是誰負責的？

例 Who is responsible for the change?

那項變革是誰負責的？

WHO SHOULD BE RESPONSIBLE FOR ...?

……應該由誰負責？

例 Who should be responsible for the testing?

測試應該由誰負責？

WHO WILL TAKE CARE OF ...?

……誰會處理？

例 Who will take care of the order <u>clearances</u>?

訂單的簽結誰會處理？

WHO SHOULD TAKE CARE OF ...?

……誰應該處理？

例 Who should take care of this?

這個誰應該處理？

3.3 釐清問題 Clarifying a Problem

track 99

3.3a 獲得更多問題的相關資訊 Obtaining More Information About a Problem

BIZ 必通句型

CAN YOU GIVE ME MORE DETAILS ABOUT THE ...?

你可不可以告訴我更多有關……的細節？

例 Can you give me more details about the mistake?

你可不可以告訴我更多有關那項錯誤的細節？

COULD YOU TELL ME MORE ABOUT THE ...?

你可不可以告訴我更多有關……的事？

例 Could you tell me more about the defect?

你可不可以告訴我更多有關那項瑕疵的事？

I NEED MORE INFORMATION ABOUT THE ....

我需要更多關於……的訊息。

例 I need more information about the product failure.

我需要更多關於產品故障的訊息。

Word List

clearance [`klɪrəns] *n.* 清除；出空；結關（手續）

245

CAN YOU SEND ME SOME MORE INFORMATION ABOUT THE ...?
你可不可以多寄給我一些關於……的訊息？
例 Can you send me some more information about the <u>misplaced</u> orders?
　你可不可以多寄給我一些關於下錯訂單的訊息？

◇◇◇ 小心陷阱 ◇◇◇

☹ 錯誤用法
I need more **informations** about the problem.
我需要更多關於那個問題的訊息。
☺ 正確用法
I need more **information** about the problem.
我需要更多關於那個問題的訊息。

3.3b 釐清問題 Clarifying a Problem

BIZ 必通句型

CAN YOU TELL ME THE <u>SYMPTOMS</u> OF THE ...?
你能不能告訴我……的症狀？
例 Can you tell me the symptoms of the error?
　你能不能告訴我那個錯誤的症狀？

CAN YOU DESCRIBE THE ... IN MORE DETAIL?
你能不能更詳細地描述……？
例 Can you describe the problem in more detail?
　你能不能更詳細地描述問題？

Word List

misplace [mɪs`ples] *v.* 誤置；誤給
symptom [`sɪmptəm] *n.* 症狀；徵兆

WHAT IS/WAS THE SITUATION WHEN THE ... OCCURS/OCCURRED?

當……發生的時候是什麼狀況？

例 What is the situation when the problem occurs?

當問題發生的時候是什麼狀況？

例 What was the situation when the failure occurred?

當故障發生的時候是什麼狀況？

WHAT WERE/ARE THE OPERATING CONDITIONS WHEN THE ... OCCURS/OCCURRED?

當……出現的時候是在什麼樣的操作狀態下？

例 What are the operating conditions when the error occurs?

當錯誤出現的時候是在什麼樣的操作狀態下？

例 What were the operating conditions when the glitch occurred?

當故障出現的時候是在什麼樣的操作狀態下？

3.3c 釐清預期結果 Clarifying Expected Results

BIZ 必通句型

WHAT RESULTS DO YOU WANT?

你想要什麼樣的結果？

WHAT RESULTS DO YOU NEED?

你需要什麼樣的結果？

WHAT KIND OF RESULTS DO YOU EXPECT?

你期待哪種結果？

CAN YOU TELL ME THE EXACT PROBLEM WITH THE CURRENT RESULTS?

你可不可以告訴我目前的結果究竟有什麼問題？

◇◇◇ 小心陷阱 ◇◇◇

☹ 錯誤用法

The results are better than I **expect**.

結果比我預期的要好。

☺ 正確用法

The results are better than I **expected**.

結果比我預期的要好。

3.4 詢問決定 Asking About Decision-making

 track 100

BIZ 必通句型

◉ 誰？ Who?

WHO WILL DECIDE ...?

誰會決定……？

例 Who will decide the way to proceed?

誰會決定進行的方式？

WHO WILL MAKE THE DECISION?

誰會做決定？

ARE YOU THE ONE TO MAKE THE DECISION?

你是那個做決定的人嗎？

IS ... THE ONE TO MAKE THE DECISION?

……是那個做決定的人嗎？

例 Is Bart the one to make the decision?

伯特是那個做決定的人嗎？

◉ 怎麼作？ How?

HOW CAN WE SOLVE THIS?

這個問題我們可以怎麼解決？

HOW DO YOU WANT TO HANDLE THIS?
這個問題你要怎麼處理？

WHAT IS THE BEST WAY TO SOLVE THIS?
解決這個問題最好的辦法是什麼？

HOW DO YOU SUGGEST WE TAKE CARE OF THIS?
這個問題你會建議我們怎麼處理？

◉ 什麼時候？ When?

WHEN WILL YOU/WE MAKE A DECISION?
你們／我們什麼時候會做決定？

WHEN WILL YOU/WE DECIDE ...?
你們／我們什麼時候會決定……？
例 When will you decide the <u>wording</u> on the e-mail notices?
你們什麼時候會決定電子郵件公告上的用字？

WHEN SHOULD I/YOU/WE MAKE A DECISION?
我／你們／我們什麼時候該做決定？

Show Time

A: Hi, Fanny. We have a moderate problem.
B: Okay. Tell me about it.
A: The eyeglass frames are the wrong color.
B: Oh, my! Is this a moderate problem? It seems like a critical problem. Can you give me more details about the frame color?

Word List

wording [ˋwɝdɪŋ] *n.* 措辭；用字

A: The frames should be coffee brown, but they are very light, something like <u>khaki</u>.

B: That is <u>rather</u> serious, actually. Who is responsible for handling this sort of error?

A: I am.

B: Okay. Then let's find a solution right away, okay?

A: How can we solve this?

B: I expect the incorrect frames to be replaced by frames in the correct color.

A：嗨，芬妮。我們有個不大不小的問題。

B：好，告訴我吧。

A：眼鏡框的顏色弄錯了。

B：噢，天哪！這是不大不小的問題嗎？似乎是個很緊要的問題。你可以告訴我更多有關鏡框顏色的細節嗎？

A：鏡框應該是咖啡色的，可是它們很淡，有點像是卡其色。

B：那真的是頗嚴重。這類的錯誤誰負責處理？

A：我。

B：好。那我們馬上找出一個解決的辦法，好嗎？

A：這個問題我們可以怎麼解決？

B：我期望錯的鏡框都換成正確顏色的鏡框。

◇◇ 小心陷阱 ◇◇

☹ 錯誤用法

What is **a** best way to solve this?

解決這個問題最好的辦法是什麼？

☺ 正確用法

What is **the** best way to solve this?

解決這個問題最好的辦法是什麼？

Word List

khaki [ˋkɑkɪ] *n./adj.* 卡其色（的）　　　　rather [ˋræðɚ] *adv.* 相當；頗

4 : 後續談話 Follow-up Talk

4.1 一般的詢問 Making General Inquiries

track 101

BIZ 必通句型

HOW IS THE PROGRESS WITH ...?
……的進展如何？
例 How is the progress with last week's supply issue?
　　上週供貨問題的進展如何？

WHAT IS THE SITUATION WITH ...?
……是什麼狀況？
例 What is the situation with the contract?
　　合約是什麼狀況？

HOW ARE THINGS PROGRESSING WITH ...?
……事情進展得怎麼樣？
例 How are things progressing with the vendor problem?
　　廠商問題的事情進展得怎麼樣？

4.2 請求 Making Requests

track 102

4.2a 一般的請求 General Requests

BIZ 必通句型

I NEED .... CAN YOU HELP?
我需要……。你能不能幫忙？

例 I need a new error checklist. Can you help?

我需要一份新的戢誤表。你能不能幫忙？

CAN I HAVE ...?

我能不能知道……？

例 Can I have the exact numbers to be shipped next month?

我能不能知道下個月要運送的確切數量？

COULD YOU ASK ... FOR ...?

你能不能向……要……？

例 Could you ask the engineer for an update of the drop-test results?

你能不能向工程師要一份落下測試的最新結果？

COULD YOU PROVIDE ...?

你能不能提供……？

例 Could you provide the details of the spec changes?

你能不能提供變更規格的細節？

4.2b 困難的請求 Difficult Requests

BIZ 必通句型

I'M SORRY, BUT I HAVE TO ASK IF ....

對不起，但是我必須問一下……。

例 I'm sorry, but I have to ask if you can let us make a few more changes.

對不起，但是我必須問一下你是否能讓我們多作一些變更。

I KNOW THIS SITUATION IS DIFFICULT, BUT ....

我知道這個情形很難，但是……。

例 I know this situation is difficult, but I would like to ask for a five-day extension.

我知道這個情形很難，但是我想要請求五天的延展。

I KNOW THIS IS A LOT TO ASK, BUT ....

我知道我要求得很多，但是……。

例 I know this is a lot to ask, but can you get me an <u>up-to-date</u> copy?

我知道我要求得很多，但是你能不能給我一份最新的副本？

YOU HAVE BEEN VERY HELPFUL IN THE PAST AND NOW ....

你過去一直很幫忙，現在……。

例 You have been very helpful in the past and now I have another urgent request.

你過去一直很幫忙，現在我又有一個緊急的請求。

4.2c 請求協助 Requesting Assistance

BIZ 必通句型

COULD YOU HELP ME WITH ...?

你能不能幫忙我……？

例 Could you help me with the <u>fabric</u> selection?

你能不能幫忙我選擇布料？

CAN YOU GIVE ME SOME ASSISTANCE WITH ...?

你能不能在……上幫我一點忙？

例 Can you give me some assistance with the defect analysis?

你能不能在缺陷分析上幫我一點忙？

We HAVE FOUND A PROBLEM. I NEED YOUR HELP ....

我們發現了一個問題。我需要你幫忙……。

例 We have found a problem. I need your help to solve it.

我們發現了一個問題。我需要你幫忙解決它。

Word List

up-to-date [ˋʌptəˋdet] *adj.* 最新的；包含最新訊息的

fabric [ˋfæbrɪk] *n.* 織品；布料

I COULD USE A HAND ....

我用得上人幫忙……。

例 I could use a hand forwarding this report.

我用的上人幫忙轉交這份報告。

PLEASE ADVISE ....

請指點我……。

例 Please advise how you want to solve the vendor shortage problem.

請指點我你想怎麼解決廠商不足的問題。

Show Time

A: Ashley, how is the progress with the bill corrections?

B: I need your help to find the old billing records.

A: That should be easy. I know where they are.

B: There is one more thing.

A: Yes, what is it?

B: I know this is a lot to ask, but I need you to resend all the bills for last month. The computer printed all the receipts with the wrong dates.

A：艾胥莉，訂正帳單的進展如何？

B：我需要你幫忙找出舊的帳單記錄。

A：那應該不難。我知道它們在哪裡。

B：還有一件事。

A：是，什麼事？

B：我知道我要求得很多，但是我需要你重寄上個月所有的帳單。電腦列印的所有收據都弄錯了日期。

◇◇ 小心陷阱 ◇◇

☹ 錯誤用法

I **find** a problem.

我發現了一個問題。

☺ 正確用法

I **have found** a problem.

我發現了一個問題。

4.3 未解決的問題 Unsolved Problems

 track 103

4.3a 提及某人的職責 Referring to Someone's Responsibility

以下這個句型可用來詢問不論你是否已經知道答案的問題。仔細看下面的例子。

BIZ 必通句型

... WAS/WERE SUPPOSED TO ....

……應該……。

• 已知道 Know

例 We were supposed to examine the invoices by noon. Why didn't you complete your analysis?

我們應該在中午前就檢查好發票。你為什麼沒有完成你的分析？

• 不知道 Don't Know

例 A: Did Jim go to the warehouse to examine the molds?

B: I haven't seen him today. He was supposed to examine them this afternoon.

A：吉米有沒有去倉庫檢查模子？

B：我今天沒見到他。他今天下午應該就檢查了。

以下這個句型可用在不論你是否知道答案的問題上。仔細看下面的例子。

BIZ 必通句型

... SHOULD HAVE ....
……就應該……。

已知道 Know

例 You should have told me the manufacturer's request yesterday. What happened?

你昨天就應該把製造商的要求告訴我。發生了什麼事？

不知道 Don't Know

例 A: Did your customer examine the samples yet?

B: I don't know. He should have examined them yesterday.

A：你的客戶檢查樣品了沒？

B：不知道。他昨天就應該檢查完了。

4.3b 詢問問題為何沒有解決 Asking Why a Problem Is Not Solved

BIZ 必通句型

WHY DIDN'T YOU ...?
你為什麼沒有……？

例 Why didn't you notify me of the failure?

你為什麼沒有通知我故障的事？

WHY CAN'T YOU ...?
你為什麼不能……？

例 Why can't you fix it now？

你為什麼不能現在修理？

WHY ISN'T THE PROBLEM ...?
問題為什麼沒有……？
例 Why isn't the problem resolved?
問題為什麼沒有解決？

WHAT IS THE REASON FOR ...?
……的原因是什麼？
例 What is the reason for the delay?
延期的原因是什麼？

4.4 談論承諾與保證 Talking Promises and Guarantees track 104

4.4a 要求承諾／保證 Asking for a Promise/Guarantee

BIZ 必通句型

CAN YOU GUARANTEE/PROMISE THAT?
那個你能不能保證／承諾？

CAN YOU GUARANTEE THAT ...?
你能不能保證／承諾……？
例 Can you guarantee that the problem will be completely fixed before the first assembly run?
你能不能保證問題會在首次裝配運轉前完全解決？

CAN YOU GIVE ME A GUARANTEE?
你能不能給我一個保證？

CAN YOU PROMISE THAT ...?
你能不能承諾……？
例 Can you promise that the mistake won't happen again?
你能不能承諾錯誤不會再發生？

CAN I <u>HAVE YOUR WORD</u>?
我能不能得到你的保證？

4.4b 給予承諾／保證 Giving a Promise/Guarantee

BIZ 必通句型

I CAN GUARANTEE/PROMISE THAT.
那個我能保證／承諾。

I CAN GUARANTEE THAT ....
我能保證……。
例 I can guarantee that the new models won't have a similar problem.
　　我能保證新模型不會有類似的問題。

I GIVE YOU MY PROMISE.
我向你承諾。

I CAN PROMISE THAT ....
我可以承諾……。
例 I can promise that this solution will work.
　　我可以承諾這個解決方案會有效。

I GIVE YOU MY WORD.
我向你保證。

Word **List**

have one's word 得到某人的承諾

4.4c 拒絕承諾／保證 Declining to Give a Promise/Guarantee

BIZ 必通句型

I CAN'T PROMISE/GUARANTEE THAT.
那個我不能承諾／保證。

I CAN'T PROMISE THAT ....
我不能承諾……。
例 I can't promise that it won't happen again.
我不能承諾它不會再發生。

I AM NOT ABLE TO GUARANTEE THAT ....
我沒辦法保證……。
例 I am not able to guarantee that the stability will improve.
我沒辦法保證穩定性會改善。

I CAN'T GIVE YOU MY WORD.
我不能向你保證。

4.4d 給個暫時的答案 Giving a Tentative Answer

BIZ 必通句型

I NEED TO ... FIRST.
我必須先……。
例 I need to check with my boss first.
我必須先跟老闆確定一下。

I SHOULD ... FIRST.
我應該先……。

Word List

decline [dɪ`klaɪn] v. 婉拒；謝絕          stability [stə`bɪlətɪ] n. 穩定性   259

例 I should ask our supervisor first.

我應該先問一下我們主管。

IS IT ALRIGHT IF I ... FIRST?

我先……可以嗎？

例 Is it alright if I double-check the data first?

我先把資料再檢查一遍可以嗎？

I BETTER ... BEFORE I MAKE ANY PROMISES.

在我作出任何承諾前，我最好先……。

例 I better confirm the schedule before I make any promises.

在我作出任何承諾前，我最好先確認一下時程。

Show Time

A: You were supposed to fix this bug last week. Why didn't you fix it?

B: I tried to fix it, but it is too difficult to solve by myself.

A: Can you promise that it will be fixed tomorrow?

B: I can't guarantee that.

A：你應該要在上星期就修好程式的錯誤。你為什麼沒修？

B：我有試著修，可是太困難了，我一個人搞不定。

A：你能不能承諾明天把它修好？

B：那我不能保證。

4.5 表達遺憾 Expressing Regret

 track 105

BIZ 必通句型

• 不是你的錯 It Is NOT Your Fault

I REGRET ....

很遺憾……。

例 I regret there was some trouble with the furniture deliveries.

很遺憾家具交貨出了一些麻煩。

I AM SORRY TO HEAR ....

很遺憾聽到……。

例 I am sorry to hear that the workers <u>went on strike</u>.

很遺憾聽到工人罷工。

• 是你的錯 It is Your Fault

I APOLOGIZE FOR ....

我為……道歉。

例 I apologize for the malfunction.

我為故障道歉。

I AM SORRY THAT ....

……我很抱歉。

例 I am sorry that the product was delayed.

產品延誤我很抱歉。

I AM SORRY ABOUT ....

對於……，我很抱歉。

例 I am sorry about the defects.

對於那些瑕疵，我很抱歉。

Word List

go on strike 罷工

◇◇ 小心陷阱 ◇◇

☹ 錯誤用法

I can't give you my **words**.

我不能向你保證。

☺ 正確用法

I can't give you my **word**.

我不能向你保證。

4.6 表達謝意 Expressing Gratitude

 track 106

BIZ 必通句型

THANKS FOR ....

謝謝……

例 Thanks for your help with the <u>consignment</u>.

謝謝你幫忙託運。

I APPRECIATE YOUR EFFORTS.

感謝您的努力。

I APPRECIATE YOUR UNDERSTANDING.

感謝您的體諒。

WE APPRECIATE YOUR HELP ....

我們感謝您幫忙……。

例 We appreciate your help with the <u>backorders</u>.

我們感謝您幫忙處理延期交貨單的問題。

Word List

consignment [kən`saınmənt] *n.* 委託（販賣）；託運；交付

backorder [`bæk`ɔrdə] *n.* 延期交貨單 (=back order)

YOUR HELP WITH ... IS REALLY APPRECIATED.

非常感謝您幫忙……。

例 Your help with the cardboard box shortage last month is really appreciated.

非常感謝您幫忙處理上個月紙箱短缺的問題。

Show Time

A: I am sorry to hear the sales for the latest model have really <u>fallen off</u>.

B: Oh, thanks for your kind words. You did your best. I appreciate your efforts.

A：我很遺憾聽到最新型號的銷售量的確已經銳減了。

B：噢，謝謝你的貼心的話語，你盡了力，謝謝你的努力。

Word List

fall off（數量等）減少

5 回答常見問題 Answering Common Questions

　　問題經常可以靠巧妙的回應帶過去。一些具創意的思維可以幫助你想到許多好答案，來回答顧客可能提出的常見問題。以下是一些相當適切的基本回應。當然，你也可以想到更多種適合特定情況的回答。

5.1 回答短缺問題 Answering Shortage Questions

 track 107

BIZ 必通句型

尋找其他貨源 Finding Other Sources

I WILL LOOK FOR ....

我會找找其他……。

例 I will look for another source.

　　我會找找其他貨源。

I WILL TRY TO FIND ....

我會試著尋找……。

例 I will try to find an alternative supplier.

　　我會試著尋找替代的供應商。

催促廠商 Pushing Vendors

I WILL PUSH ....

我會催促……。

例 I will push our vendor to speed up the deliveries.

　　我會催促我們的廠商加速交貨。

I WILL INFORM ....

我會通知……。

例 I will inform our vendor that we need the shipments immediately.
我會通知我們的廠商，我們即刻需要那批貨。

I WILL TELL ....
我會吩咐……。
例 I will tell the vendor to increase their <u>output</u>.
我會吩咐廠商增加他們的產量。

5.2 回答價格問題 Answering Price Questions

 track 108

BIZ 必通句型

OUR PRICES ARE REASONABLE FOR THE HIGH QUALITY PRODUCT WE OFFER.
以我們所賣的高品質產品而言，我們的價格很合理。

OUR PRODUCT IS A GOOD VALUE AT THIS PRICE.
以這個價錢買我們的產品很划算。

OUR PRICES ARE ACTUALLY MID-RANGE FOR THIS TYPE OF PRODUCT.
就這類產品而言，我們的價格其實是中等價位。

YOU CAN FIND THAT OUR PRICE IS <u>ON A PAR WITH</u> OTHER COMPANIES' PRICES.
你可以發現我們的價格跟其他公司的相同。

Word **List**

output [ˋaʊtˏpʊt] *n.* 產量
on a par with 與……同等（同樣、同價）

5.3 回答設計／品質問題 Answering Design/Quality Questions

track 109

BIZ 必通句型

WE WOULD BE GLAD TO <u>CUSTOMIZE</u> AN ORDER FOR YOU.
我們很樂意為您特製訂貨。

WE ARE HAPPY TO HEAR YOUR SUGGESTIONS ON HOW WE CAN IMPROVE OUR DESIGNS.
我們很高興聽到您對我們該如何改進設計的建議。

WE PERFORM 100% QUALITY INSPECTION ON ALL OUR PRODUCTS.
我們對我們所有的產品都做一○○%的品質檢測。

WE ARE ... CERTIFIED.
我們經過……認證。
例 We are ISO 9002 certified.
　　我們經過 ISO9002 認證。

WE HAVE ... CERTIFICATION.
我們有……的認證。
例 We have UL certification.
　　我們有 UL 的認證。

OUR QUALITY CONTROL SECTION MAINTAINS <u>RIGOROUS</u> QUALITY CONTROLS.
我們的品管部維持嚴格的品管。

I CAN PROVIDE YOU WITH <u>REFERENCE</u> LETTERS FROM OUR SATISFIED CUSTOMERS.
我可以提供您對我們滿意的顧客的推薦函。

Word **L**ist

customize [ˈkʌstəˌmaɪz] v. 訂作；客製化
rigorous [ˈrɪgərəs] adj. 嚴格的；嚴屬的

reference [ˈrɛfərəns] n. 推薦（函）；推薦人

◇◇ 小心陷阱 ◇◇◇

☹ 錯誤用法

We **have** ISO 9002 **certified**.

我們有 ISO 9002 的認證。

☺ 正確用法

We **have** ISO 9002 **certification**.

我們有 ISO 9002 的認證。

We **are** ISO 9002 **certified**.

我們經過 ISO 9002 認證。

5.4 回答交貨緩慢的問題 Answering Slow-Delivery Questions

 track 110

BIZ 必通句型

OUR PRODUCT IS IN GREAT DEMAND NOW BECAUSE OF ITS HIGH QUALITY. WE WILL INCREASE PRODUCTION SO THAT WE CAN MAKE FUTURE DELIVERIES ON TIME.

因為品質好,我們的產品現在需求很大。我們會增加產量,以便在未來能準時交貨。

WE CHANGED TO A NEW SHIPPER AND THEY ARE NOT USED TO OUR SHIPPING REQUIREMENTS. I AM SURE THAT SHIP-MENTS WILL BE BACK TO NORMAL SOON.

我們換了一家新的運貨商,但他們還不習慣我們的運送要求。我確定貨物運送很快就會恢復正常。

I WILL CHECK WITH THE PRODUCTION CONTROL DEPART-MENT AND GET BACK TO YOU IMMEDIATELY.

我會和生產控管部確認,並立刻回覆你。

5.5 安撫生氣的顧客 Calming an Angry Customer

 track 111

BIZ 必通句型

I WILL DO MY BEST TO ....
我會盡最大努力……。
例 I will do my best to resolve the issue <u>satisfactorily</u>.
我會盡最大努力把問題解決得令您滿意。

I UNDERSTAND HOW YOU FEEL.
我了解您的感受。

IF I WERE YOU, I WOULD FEEL THE SAME WAY.
如果我是您，我也會這麼覺得。

IF YOU HAVE ANY OTHER PROBLEMS, PLEASE LET ME KNOW.
如果您有任何其他的問題，請通知我一聲。

Word **L**ist

satisfactorily [ˌsætɪsˈfæktərəlɪ] *adv.* 令人滿意地

6 實戰演練 Partner Practice

當你讀完並複習過本章內容後，找個同伴試試下面的對話練習！

情境 1

一家台灣公司寄給外國客戶的產品有瑕疵，外國客戶於是退回了這些商品。之後台灣公司把運貨帳單寄給外國客戶，但外國客戶認為台灣公司應該付這筆錢。兩家公司的代表正透過電話討論這個問題。

練習	
角色 A	台灣商務人士
角色 B	外國客戶
B	把問題告訴角色 A。(2.1) 告訴角色 A，這個問題有多重要。(2.2a)
A	詢問問題的責任。(3.2)
B	告訴角色 A，你認為他們公司要負責。
A	詢問角色 B，這次他們公司可不可以付這筆錢，即使不是他們公司的錯。(4.2b)
B	告訴角色 A，你不能那麼做。
A	告訴角色 B，他／她沒有仔細看合約，他們公司應該要付運費。(2.4)
B	告訴角色 A，那個答案你無法接受。詢問角色 A，這個問題誰可以做決定。(3.4)
A	告訴角色 B，你的經理可以做決定。
B	告訴角色 A，付運費是他們公司的責任。(4.3a)
A	告訴角色 B，你願意負責出運費，但你要先跟你的主管討論。(4.4d)
B	告訴角色 A，他／她可以明天回電給你，說明他／她的決定。

情境 2

兩位商務人士正透過電話討論問題。一家台灣公司的廠商所運送的電子零件瑕疵率偏高。這是第二批瑕疵率偏高的零件。

練習	
角色 A	台灣商務人士
角色 B	外國供應商
A	把問題告訴角色 B。(2.1) 詢問第二批零件為什麼有這麼多瑕疵品。(4.3b)
B	表達你的遺憾，但堅稱你認為問題錯不在你。(4.5) 告訴角色 A，你測試過零件，而且瑕疵率在可接受的範圍內。 試著獲得更多問題的相關訊息。(3.3a)
A	更仔細地解釋問題。(1.1a)
B	詢問角色 A，問題有多嚴重。(3.1)
A	告訴角色 B 問題有多嚴重。(2.2a) 說明問題需要多快解決。(2.2b)
B	詢問角色 A，你能不能明天回電給他／她。
A	告訴角色 B，你要他／她現在就決定該怎麼辦。(2.5)
B	告訴角色 A，你會處理這個問題。(2.3) 釐清角色 A 想要什麼樣的結果。(3.3c)
A	要角色 B 保證下批貨不會有任何瑕疵。(4.4a)
B	拒絕給予保證。(4.4c) 告訴角色 A，你想進一步了解問題。要角色 A 釐清問題。(3.3b)
A	告訴角色 B，有太多零件明顯有瑕疵，必須做出決定。(1.4a)
B	要角色 A 提供瑕疵零件的分析報告。(4.2a)
A	告訴角色 B，你會盡力提供報告。
B	向角色 A 表達謝意。(4.6)

✏ **Memo**

Section

THREE

商務 Email 寫作

E-Writing

第 7 章

Email 的標點、段落與格式

Making E-mail Clear

本章將說明讓電子郵件清楚呈現的基本要素,包括精簡的寫作和恰當的格式。寫出清晰的英文有賴使用簡潔的語言和正確的標點,並能夠把句子組織成段落。電子郵件的格式和正式寫作的格式有點不同,因為電子郵件是獨特且相當新穎的溝通媒介。不過,它也是格式最簡單的媒介,各位應該會樂於學習。只要跟著我研讀本章,你就會發現它有多簡單。

This chapter explains the basic elements of making e-mail clear: Concise writing and proper formatting. Writing clear English demands using simple language, correct punctuation, and organizing sentences into paragraphs. E-mail formatting is a little different than the formats used in formal writing because e-mail is a distinct and relatively new medium of communication. However, as you will be pleased to learn, it is the easiest medium to format. Follow me through this chapter and you'll see just how easy it is.

1 標點 Punctuation

　　語言主要是由字彙和文法所組成。如果你在看這本書，那你一定有運用單字和文法的基本能力，所以這不是我想要花時間探討的重點。既然本章要談的是電子郵件寫作，所以我想討論英文寫作兩個重要的特點，一旦你學會熟練地運用它們，將有助於你把東西寫清楚。這兩個特點就是標點和段落。

　　我們首先看標點，因為它是句子層次的課題。如果你能把句子的標點弄對，接著就可以專注在把這些句子組織成段落。本章的第二單元將討論段落組織的問題。

1.1 標點符號 Punctuation Marks

符號	名稱	作用
.	句號 period	1. 結束句子。 2. 形成縮寫。
?	問號 question mark	結束問題。
!	驚嘆號 exclamation mark	以強烈的情感結束句子。
,	逗號 comma	1. 把片段的訊息連貫起來。 2. 配合連結副詞結合句子。
;	分號 semicolon	1. 結合密切相關的句子。 2. 配合連結副詞結合句子。
:	冒號 colon	1. 介紹東西。 2. 用來表達時間。
-	連字號 hyphen	結合事物以產生整體的新意義。
—	破折號 dash	用來表示句子裡出現中斷，或是在逗號、冒號或括號看起來令人困惑時來代替這類標點。

( )	括號 parenthesis (parentheses)	把非必要的文字和句子中的其他部分隔開。
[ ]	方括號 bracket(s)	1. 在句子中插入資訊，但此資訊不一定重要或必需，端視是誰在看這個句子而定。 2. 在直接引述中加入其他文字。
/	斜線 slash	當不知道哪個對讀者適用時，用來區隔選項。
" "	引號 quotation mark(s)	1. 指出他人所說或所寫的確切字語，或是單字本身。 2. 指出某人所說或所寫的事情不是事實；指出矛盾或諷刺。 3. 用於某些書目的引述。
'	撇號 apostrophe	1. 指出有些字母或數字被省略。 2. 指出所有權。
...	刪節號 ellipses	1. 指出時間的停頓。 2. 指出有些資訊已經被省略。

1.2 標點用法 Punctuation Usage

○ 句號 Period

例 This sentence ends with a period.

這個句子以句號結尾。

○ 問號 Question Mark

例 Is this a question? Yes. It ends with a question mark.

這是個疑問句嗎？是的，它以問號結尾。

○ 驚嘆號 Exclamation Mark

例 I need your assistance right away! That's why I'm yelling!

我現在就需要你幫忙！所以我才會大叫！

● 逗號 Comma

例 My colleague speaks Japanese, German, and Spanish.
我同事會說日語、德語和西班牙語。

例 We will discuss the budget tomorrow, and Tom will bring some important data.
我們明天會討論預算,而湯姆會帶一些重要的資料來。

● 分號 Semicolon

例 The material is very soft; careful handling is important.
這材質很柔軟;小心處理很重要。

例 The parts arrived on time; everything is okay.
那些零件準時到達;一切都沒問題。

例 I think your proposal has some good ideas; however, I need to check it with my supervisor first.
我覺得你的提案有些構想不錯;然而我必須先和我的主管商量一下。

● 冒號 Colon

例 There are two solutions: fix the broken piece or send the item back to the factory.
有兩個解決辦法:把損壞的部分修好或是把該物件寄回工廠。

例 There is only one problem: the cover is a little too tight.
只有一個問題:蓋子太緊了一點。

例 We will begin the meeting at 11:30.
我們會在 11:30 開始開會。

● 連字號 Hyphen

例 That is an out-of-date model.
那是個過時的型號。

Word List

part [pɑrt] *n.* (機器、器具的)零件

例 Can you ask your manager if we can have twenty-five copies of the meeting <u>minutes</u>?

你可不可以問問你們經理，我們是否可以拿二十五份會議記錄？

例 The company name is spelled S-U-P-E-R-S-T-A-R.

公司名稱的拼法是 S-U-P-E-R-S-T-A-R。

例 You might want to read pages 4-7.

你可能會想看第四到七頁。

破折號 Dash

例 Some of the faxes you sent yesterday — the ones addressed to Ivy — have incorrect calculations.

你昨天寄出的傳真——給艾薇的那些——有些算錯的地方。

例 There is no other way to make the deadline — or is there?

沒別的辦法可以在截止期限內完成——還是有呢？

括號 Parentheses

例 We recommend that you order mostly purple packaging (my favorite color) for products <u>aimed</u> at the young people.

以青少年為目標的產品，我們建議您以訂購紫色（我個人最喜歡的顏色）的包裝為主。

方括號 Brackets

例 The new software is easy to <u>incorporate</u> into your current ordering system. [Users with very old operating systems can consult our technical support team.]

新軟體可以輕易融入您現有的訂購系統。〔老舊作業系統的使用者可洽詢我們的技術支援小組。〕

Word List

minutes [ˈmɪnɪts] *n.* 會議記錄（minute 備忘錄、筆記）

aim [em] *v.* 瞄準；以……為目標

incorporate [ɪnˈkɔrpəˌret] *v.* 使……合併；結合

例 "Never give a [circus-going] <u>sucker</u> a break." — P.T. Barnum
「千萬別對〔去看馬戲團的〕笨蛋客氣。」—— P.T. 巴南

斜線 Slash

例 After you have purchased the <u>spare</u> parts, please send me the receipt/invoice.
在您買了備用零件後，請把收據／發票寄給我。

引號 Quotation Marks

例 Did your customer really say, "I will never buy your products again"?
你的顧客真的說過：「我再也不會買你的產品了」？
〔注意：問號在最後的引號外面，這代表整句話是一個問題〕

例 My customer asked me, "Do you think I will ever buy your products again?"
我的顧客問我說：「你想我還會再買你的產品嗎？」
〔注意：問號在最後的引號裡面，這代表整個句子是陳述句，引述是問句〕

例 Maybe you should check the section of the <u>manual</u> <u>labeled</u> "<u>troubleshooting</u> questions."
也許你該查一下使用手冊中標示「疑難排解」的部分。

例 We changed vendors because our previous one charged two times the market value and told us we should stop asking for discounts. It is a relief to not have to deal with such a "customer-friendly" company.
我們換了廠商，因為之前那家的收費是市價的兩倍，還跟我們說我們應該停止要求折扣。不必和這種「對顧客友善」的公司打交道真是一種解脫。

例 I just read an interesting article entitled "Strategic Marketing Techniques" in *The Wall Street Journal*.
我剛在《華爾街日報》上看了一篇有趣的文章，叫做「策略性行銷技巧」。
〔注意：刊物名用斜體，文章名用引號〕

Word List

sucker [ˋsʌkɚ] *n.* 易受騙的人
spare [spɛr] *adj.* 備用的
manual [ˋmænjʊəl] *n.*（使用）手冊

label [ˋlebl] *v.* 用標籤標明
troubleshooting [ˋtrʌblˌʃutɪŋ] *n.* 疑難排解

撇號 Apostrophe

例 What has he been doin' recently?

他最近都在做什麼？

例 Don't sign the contract until you read it thoroughly.

在沒徹底看過合約之前不要簽約。

例 I received Mike's e-mail yesterday.

我昨天收到邁克的電子郵件。

Note

「it」的所有格不用撇號，因為「it」加撇號（it's）表示「it is」。

例 Can you tell me its <u>expiration</u> date?

你能不能告訴我它的有效期限？

例 It's a nice day today in Tainan.

台南今天的天氣很好。

例 Can you check the records from '98?

你可不可以查一下九八年開始的記錄？

刪節號 Ellipses

例 Let me think ... is it possible to change the current marketing strategy?

讓我想想……有可能更改現行的行銷策略嗎？

例 Your last e-mail said "The shipment was received ... everything is okay."

你上一封電子郵件說：「貨已經收到……一切都沒問題。」

Word List

expiration [ˌɛkspəˈreʃən] *n.* 終止；期滿（～ date 有效期限）

2 : 清楚分段 Clear Paragraphing

　　段落由一群屬於同一主題的句子組合而成。每一個段落各自傳達一個重點。比方說，如果你的電子郵件有三個重點，那就應該有三段。

　　下列的電子郵件不易閱讀，因為它沒有組織成段落。實際上，它的寫法是每句話都自成一段。如此一來，當眼睛往下掃瞄訊息時，大腦就會把這封電子郵件詮釋成有八個重點。它需要重新組織。

✗ 錯誤範例

Hi Winona,

How are you?
I just want to ask one question.
Did you receive the fax that I sent yesterday?
The fax contained some price tables.
The tables contain the information you need.
If you have any questions, let me know.
Thanks.
By the way, new price tables will be available in January.

Bobby

下面是把該電子郵件依重點分段的正確方式。

✔ 正確範例

Hi Winona,

How are you?

I just want to ask one question. Did you receive the fax that I sent yesterday? The fax contained some price tables. The tables contain the information you need. If you have any questions about tables, let me know. Thanks.

By the way, new price tables will be available in January.

Bobby

☐ 翻譯

嗨，薇諾娜：

妳好嗎？

我只想問個問題。妳有沒有收到我昨天寄的傳真？傳真裡有一些價目表。價目表中有妳需要的資訊。如果妳有任何問題，請告訴我。謝謝。

對了，新的價目表將可在一月時提供。

巴比

　　以這種方式組織，電子郵件就容易閱讀多了，大腦也可以輕易理解主要的訊息。這封電子郵件主要有兩段。第一段有一個主題，那就是傳真。這段的重點在提出一個問題：「妳有沒有收到傳真？」第二段有關新的價目表。雖然只有一句話卻無妨。電子郵件每一段的長度並無特別限制，但愈短愈好！

3 清楚的格式 Clear Formatting

3.1 以空行來分段 Separate Paragraphs with Blank Lines

清楚區隔段落的唯一辦法就是空行。以下兩個例子因爲分段方式錯誤而難以閱讀。其後則是正確的範例。

✗ 錯誤範例 1

> Hi Ethan,
> I examined the sales figures again, as you requested. I came to the same conclusion: we shouldn't introduce the new product line yet. The current products are selling well.
> Would you like me to analyze the sales figures some more? I can check them again and tell you if I change my mind.
> Gina

以上這封電子郵件有兩個重點，可是段落之間缺乏清楚的區別。「Hi Ethan,」後面有一些空白，可是並不夠。雖然「The current products are selling well.」後面有一些空白，但那也不足以表示段落。首先，在稱呼語「Hi Ethan,」和電子郵件的正文之間就要空一行。再來，訊息的正文和結尾的「Gina」之間也要空一行來區隔。然而要做的還不只如此，不過我們先來看看這兩個改變如何改善這封電子郵件。

✗ 錯誤範例 2

> Hi Ethan,
>
> I examined the sales figures again, as you requested. I came to the same conclusion: we shouldn't introduce the new product line yet. The current product line is selling very well.

> Would you like me to analyze the sales figures some more? I can check them again and tell you if I change my mind.
>
> Gina

　　相信各位都會同意第二個範例已有所改善。稱呼語「Hi Ethan,」後面及「Gina」前面各空了一行。此外，這個範例用了縮排來表示分段。這樣做蠻好的，不過電子郵件必須要能輕易瀏覽；也就是說，讀者要一眼掃過電子郵件就能立刻知道其中有多少個重點（有幾段）。空行比縮排更能讓大腦有效地瀏覽電子郵件。我們再改一次。

☑ 正確範例

> Hi Ethan,
>
> I examined the sales figures again, as you requested. I came to the same conclusion: we shouldn't introduce the new product line yet. The current product line is selling very well.
>
> Would you like me to analyze the sales figures some more? I can check them again and tell you if I change my mind.
>
> Gina

☐ 翻譯

> 嗨，伊森：
>
> 我照你的要求把銷售數字再檢查了一次。我的結論還是一樣：我們還不應該引進新的產品系列，目前的系列銷售得很好。
>
> 你要我再分析一下銷售數字嗎？我可以再檢查一次，如果有改變想法再告訴你。
>
> 吉娜

在上面的電子郵件中有兩個清楚的段落。每一段的前後都空了一整行，而沒有任何一行用縮排。其實縮排並不是非要不可，用空行就能清楚地分段。如此不但對讀的人清楚，對寫電子郵件的人而言也比較簡單：寫完一段後就按兩次「enter/return」鍵，而不必按「tab」鍵或忙著縮排。

👁 **Tips**

1. 電子郵件的每一行都應該從最左邊開始。
2. 段與段之間一定要空一行間距，段落中的句子都息息相關，只要句子間無空行，就會對大腦清楚傳達出這個訊息。段落間的空行數只能是一行，而不是一點五行或兩行。

3.2 盡可能利用編號 Use Numbering Whenever Possible

如果可能，要盡量把電子郵件中的訊息編號，好讓讀者知道你有多少個重點、訊息或問題。對需要回覆的電子郵件來說，這點尤其重要。如果電子郵件裡有編號，回覆起來就簡單得多。再者，編號可以幫助讀者避免遺漏任何重點。

✗ 錯誤範例 1

Hi Lynette,

I have three questions about the product design.
1. Can we use blue instead of green?

2. Did you approve the final <u>draft</u> for the packaging style?
3. When can we tell the plant to begin production?

George

Word **List**

draft [dræft] *n.* 草稿；草圖

284

上面的電子郵件有兩段，但卻沒有理由分成兩段。它的寫法會讓讀者懷疑分成兩段是不是有特殊的理由。第一個問題和後面兩個問題是否有本質上的不同？其實並沒有，正因如此這封電子郵件令人覺得困惑，需要修改一下。

☒ 錯誤範例 2

Hi Lynette,

I have three questions about the product design. 1. Can we use blue instead of green? 2. Did you approve the final draft for the packaging style? 3. When can we tell the plant to begin production?

George

上面的電子郵件只有一段，這是正確的，但編號方式卻難以閱讀。每個編號都應該出現在最左邊，以便讓讀者容易瀏覽，也方便他們回覆。

☑ 正確範例 1

Hi Lynette,

I have three questions about the product design.
1. Can we use blue instead of green?
2. Did you approve the final draft for the packaging style?
3. When can we tell the plant to begin production?

George

這封電子郵件很清楚。它只有一段，重點是「我有問題」，而且問題也有清楚的編號。

Tips

1. 每個編號的後面都有空一格。

2. 每一行後面向右延伸的空格並不重要，它們不具任何意義，所以各位不必擔心。別忘了，代表分段的是空行，而不是其他任何一種空格。上例中段落前後都有空行，非常清楚！

☑ 正確範例 2

Hi Lynette,

I have three questions about the product design.

1. Can we use blue instead of green?
2. Did you approve the final draft for the packaging style?
3. When can we tell the plant to begin production?

George

☐ 翻譯

嗨，琳內特：

我有三個關於產品設計的問題。
1. 我們可不可以用藍色代替綠色？
2. 妳是否同意包裝樣式的最後定稿？
3. 我們什麼時候可以叫工廠開始生產？

喬治

這則範例電子郵件也可以接受。它有兩段，而不是一段。第二段只有問題，所以比其他例子更有強調的作用。

3.3 回覆格式 Formatting for Replies

現代的電子郵件系統全都可以設定回覆格式，只要利用電子郵件功能選單上的「reply」（回覆），它就會自動把電子郵件的原始內容放進回覆的電子郵件中。這些內容會以某種方式表示，通常是在每行最左邊出現「>」符號。你應該利用這個功能和這個符號讓你回覆的電子郵件更清楚。此外，這也能替你省下解釋你到底在回覆哪些要點的時間。

以下的例子示範了如何有效使用回覆功能。

來信範例

> Hi Quinn,
>
> How's it going? I haven't seen you around town for a while.
>
> Well, I just need some product specifications. My boss lost the original copy you sent us. Sorry.
>
> First, I need to know the exact dimensions. If you can provide them in <u>metric</u>, that would be great. I know some American companies still don't use metric even on the international market.
> Second, I need to know the location of the power button for each model.
>
> Sorry for all the trouble. See you soon, I hope.
>
> Kandy

Word List

metric [ˈmɛtrɪk] *adj.* 公尺（制）的；公制的

☐ 翻譯

嗨，昆恩：

你好嗎？有一陣子沒在城裡見到你了。

嗯，我只是需要一些產品說明書。我老闆把你寄給我們的原稿弄丟了。抱歉。

首先，我需要知道確切的尺寸。假如你能提供公制，那會很理想。我知道有些美國公司就連在國際市場上也還是不使用公制。

其次，我需要知道每種型號的電源按鈕位置。

抱歉，這麼麻煩你。希望很快能再見面。

甘蒂

回覆範例 1

Hi Kandy,

No problem. Below are the answers to your questions.

>First, I need to know the exact dimensions.

14.2 inches x 10.5 inches x 5.7 inches

>Second, I need to know the location of the power button for each model.

Model A -- upper right
Model B -- middle
Model C -- center top

Quinn

☐ 翻譯

嗨，甘蒂：

沒問題。妳的問題回覆如下。

> 首先，我需要知道確切的尺寸。

14.2 英寸 x 10.5 英寸 x 5.7 英寸

> 其次，我需要知道每種型號的電源按鈕位置。

A 款：右上方
B 款：中間
C 款：中上方

昆恩

　　注意原始電子郵件和回覆電子郵件的內容之間有空行來區隔。還要注意的是，原始電子郵件中不必要的部分被刪掉了。這使回覆電子郵件變得更容易閱讀。

回覆範例 2

Hi Kandy,

No problem. Below are the answers to your questions.

>First, I need to know the exact dimensions.
Answer: 14.2 inches x 10.5 inches x 5.7 inches

>Second, I need to know the location of the power button for each model.
Answer:
Model A: upper right
Model B: middle

Model C: center top

Quinn

☐ 翻譯

嗨，甘蒂：

沒問題。妳的問題回覆如下。

> 首先，我需要知道確切的尺寸。
答：14.2 英寸 x 10.5 英寸 x 5.7 英寸

> 其次，我需要知道每種型號的電源按鈕位置。
答：
A 款：右上方
B 款：中間
C 款：中上方

昆恩

　　在這第二個例子中，原始內容和回覆內容之間沒有空行，而是用「Answer」這個字來釐清回覆電子郵件中哪些內容是新的。有些人偏好這種方式，因為電子郵件的螢幕長度會比較短。和第一個例子一樣的是，原始電子郵件中不必要的部分被刪掉了。

3.4 用 HTML 格式製作欄位和表格 Use HTML for Columns and Tables

　　每種電子郵件的系統都不盡相同，假如你想要把標準的純文字電子郵件（而不是 HTML 格式的電子郵件）做出欄位或表格，收件人所看到的電子郵件可能就不會正確地顯示格式。那是因為由空白鍵所產生的間隔和由 tab 或縮排鍵所產生的縮排，不同的電子郵件系統對兩者的處理方式不一樣。

　　舉例來說，在寫下列電子郵件時，你可以用空白鍵和縮排把部分資訊排列成欄跟列的形式。

☑ 正確範例

Hi Tiffany,

Here is your bank account information.

	June	July	August
Deposit	20,000	15,000	5,000
Withdrawal	7,000	6,000	0

Wendy

☐ 翻譯

嗨，蒂芬妮：

這是您的銀行帳戶資料。

	六月	七月	八月
存款	20,000	15,000	5,000
提款	7,000	6,000	0

溫蒂

不過，收件人看到的電子郵件可能會變成這樣：

✗ 錯誤範例 1

> Hi Tiffany,
>
> Here is your bank account information.
>
> | | June | July | August |
> |---|---|---|---|
> | Deposit | 20,000 | 15,000 | 5,000 |
> | Withdrawal | 7,000 | 6,000 | 0 |
>
> Wendy

甚至可能變成這樣：

✗ 錯誤範例 2

> Hi Tiffany,
>
> Here is your bank account information.
>
> | | June | July | August | |
> |---|---|---|---|---|
> | Deposit | 20,000 | 15,000 | 5,000 | Withdrawal 7,000 |
> | | 6,000 | 0 | | |
>
> Wendy

　　因此，最好把欄位和表格放在可以附加在電子郵件的檔案裡。此外，用 Word 或 Excel 來製作這類資訊的格式通常會比較簡單。假如你選擇把欄位或表格放在電子郵件的本文裡，則一定要用 HTML 格式。

4 常見的 E-mail 錯誤 Common Mistakes

4.1 標點錯誤 Punctuation Mistakes

4.1a 濫用驚嘆號 Overusing Exclamation Marks

　　驚嘆號是用來表示強烈的感受，比如快樂或憤怒。它代表句子應該以比正常更大與更強的聲音唸出來。雖然表達情緒有時是可被接受甚至很管用，但商場溝通仍應盡量保持客觀，不應過於情緒化。和面對面溝通比較起來，讀者通常難以百分之百確定寫電子郵件的人所要傳達的情緒。因此，使用驚嘆號常會引發問題，最好加以避免。

✗ Hi! How are you!! I received your e-mail a little late! Please forgive my late reply!!
　嗨！你好嗎！！我比較晚收到你的電子郵件！回覆遲了請見諒！！

　　這樣的電子郵件很令人困惑。讀者會覺得奇怪，為什麼這麼平常的句子裡會有這麼多的情緒。更糟的是，讀者可能會覺得寫者在為某事生氣。

✓ Hi! How are you? I received your e-mail a little late. Please forgive my late reply.
　嗨！你好嗎？我比較晚收到你的電子郵件。回覆遲了請見諒。

　　這裡只有第一個字加了情緒。這顯然是封友善的電子郵件。句子的意義都很清楚，而且語調很客氣，沒有必要藉驚嘆號來強調情緒。意義比情緒重要，尤其是在寫商業電子郵件時，所以把驚嘆號留到跟朋友寫信時再用吧。

4.1b 用引號來強調 Using Quotation Marks for Emphasis

　　引號是用來指出某人說過或寫過的確切用語、某些原文中的特殊用字，以及在本質上不真實或具諷刺性的一些字語。引號也適用於某些類型的參考書目引述。除此以外，引號就沒有其他用途了。

✗ We hope you can send the packages "immediately."
　我們希望你能「立即」寄出包裹。

正確的做法是使用斜體字來表示強調：

✓ We hope you can send the packages *immediately*.
我們希望你可以立即寄出包裹。

你也可以用星號來表示強調：

✓ We hope you can send the packages *immediately*.
我們希望你可以 * 立即 * 寄出包裹。

假如你是用 HTML 的電子郵件，你可以用粗體或顏色來強調：

✓ We hope you can send the packages **immediately**.
我們希望你可以立即寄出包裹。

✓ We hope you can send the packages immediately.
我們希望你可以立即寄出包裹。

4.1c 標點的不當間隔 Incorrect Spacing in Punctuation
• 句子結尾的標點要緊接著最後一個字。
　　正確使用標點間隔很重要。原因有兩點：
1. 標點間隔在英文用法和文體中是很基本的觀念，所以用錯會讓人覺得你不專業。
2. 恰當的標點間隔可以使句子更容易閱讀。

✗ I received it . 我收到了 。
✓ I received it. 我收到了。

✗ What is her request ？她的要求是什麼 ？
✓ What is her request? 她的要求是什麼？

✗ It is perfect ! 太完美了 ！
✓ It is perfect! 太完美了！

- **逗號及分號的前面不需要空格，後面則要空一格。**

✗ If you have a question , please ask me.
假如你有問題 ，請問我。

✓ If you have a question, please ask me.
假如你有問題，請問我。

✗ I received your e-mail ; your point is clear.
我收到了你的電子郵件 ；你的論點很清楚。

✓ I received your e-mail; your point is clear.
我收到了你的電子郵件；你的論點很清楚。

- **冒號的前面不空格，後面通常空兩格。**

✗ Here are the product numbers : AZ5, AZ6, AZ7.
產品編號是： AZ5, AZ6, AZ7 。

✗ Here are the product numbers: AZ5, AZ6, AZ7.
產品編號是： AZ5, AZ6, AZ7 。

✓ Here are the product numbers: AZ5, AZ6, AZ7.
產品編號是： AZ5, AZ6, AZ7 。

- **中斷句子的標點應該仿照下列範例：**

✗ Daphne sent the data(I forgot how much)yesterday.
黛芬妮昨天寄出了資料(我忘了有多少)。

✓ Daphne sent the data (I forgot how much) yesterday.
黛芬妮昨天寄出了資料（我忘了有多少）。

✗ The new product — OP55 — is the best one.
新產品 — OP55 — 是最好的。

✓ The new product—OP55—is the best one.
新產品— OP55 —是最好的。

✗ Jason said the spec sheet[section A4.3]requires that we use Intel chips.
傑生說規格說明表上〔第 A4.3 節〕要求們必須使用英特爾的晶片。

✔ Jason said the spec sheet [section A4.3] requires that we use Intel chips.
傑生說規格說明表上〔第 A4.3 節〕要求們必須使用英特爾的晶片。

4.2 用字錯誤 Word Usage Mistakes

4.2a 祝好運 Good Luck
「Good luck」只能在某人想要達成特定目標時使用。它不像「best wishes」和「take care」那麼平常且可用在任何一種電子郵件中。

舉例來說，假如某人正要參加多益考試以獲得升遷，你便可以寫：

例 Good luck!
祝好運！
例 Good luck on your test!
祝考試好運。

4.2b 因為及由於 Because, Due to, and Because of
「Because」要接含主詞和動詞的完整子句。

例 Because he forgot to send the file, I couldn't complete the work.
由於他忘了寄檔案，所以我無法完成工作。

「Due to」和「Because of」則接名詞或名詞片語，不接動詞。

例 Due to the holiday, we need to postpone the delivery one day.
由於放假的關係，所以我們必須延後一天送貨。
例 Because of the increase in profits, our yearly bonus will be larger this year.
由於獲利增加的關係，所以我們今年的年終紅利會比較多。

4.3 其他錯誤 Miscellaneous Mistakes

4.3a 上午和下午 a.m. vs. p.m.

✗ A.M.　P.M.

✗ AM　PM

✓ a.m.　p.m.

> 例 See you tomorrow at 8:00 p.m.
> 明天晚上八點見。

　　上述這些錯誤的形式會出現在專有名詞的縮寫中，像是公司名（A.M. 塑膠有限公司, AM PM 迷你超市）、人名（P.M. 瓊斯）或職稱（PM = Project Manager 專案經理）。

4.3b 濫用全大寫字母 Overuse of All-<u>capital</u> Letters
　　全部使用大寫字母表示十分強調，且可能表示強烈的情緒，尤其是憤怒。

✗ Please send me the UPDATED DOCUMENTS when you have completed them.
請你一完成「更新的文件」就寄給我。

　　這也許會使讀者覺得作者在生氣。我建議用星號來表達一般、非情緒性的強調。

✓ Please send me the *updated documents* when you have completed them.
請你一完成 * 更新的文件 * 就寄給我。

Word List

capital [ˋkæpətḷ] *adj.* 大寫字母的

5 特殊 E 用語 Special E-English

有一些特殊的英文是為了在網路上使用而存在，像是收發電子郵件和線上聊天。我們已經討論過電子郵件，所以現在繼續來討論在網路上聊天所用的英文。

工作上需要收發電子郵件的人經常也會上網聊天，因為兩者都是透過網路進行。徹底了解這種特殊的 E 用語可以幫助商場人士以這兩種形式來溝通。

5.1 常見的混淆錯誤 Common Confusing Mistakes

5.1a 「哈」與「哈哈」"Ha" vs. "Ha ha"

「Ha」的意思是「我不相信你」或「那真可笑！」。

例 You got a raise? Ha.

你加薪了？哈。

例 Ha. That deadline is impossible.

哈，那個截止期限是不可能的。

「Ha ha」的意思是「那很好笑」。

例 Ha ha. That's the best joke I've heard all week.

哈哈，那是我這整個星期所聽到最棒的笑話。

5.1b 「嗯」與「唔」"Mmm" vs. "Hmm"

「Mmm」（嗯）表示你正在考慮某件事，還沒準備好要回答。

「Hmm」（唔）的意思是「我不知道耶！」、「哇，那真讓我意外」或「那真有趣」。

「Mmm」（嗯）和「Hmm」（唔）並「不」代表「是」。我有些學生犯過這個錯，因為「m」的音對說中文的人來說可以用來代表「是」。例如：

A: Will you tell me which music you prefer?

B: Mmm. [B means "yes"]

A: Come on, tell me. [because "Mmm" means "I am thinking"]

B: I said I will tell you. [because B thinks "Mmm" means "yes"]

A: Huh?

A：能不能告訴我你偏好哪種音樂？

B：嗯。〔B 的意思是「會」〕

A：說吧，告訴我。〔因為「嗯」的意思是「我正在想」〕

B：我說了我會告訴你。〔因為 B 認為「嗯」的意思是「會」〕

A：嘎？

5.2 常見的表情符號 Common Smileys

下列的符號英文皆稱為「smileys」（微笑符號），甚至包括那些看起來不快樂的表情。微笑符號這個詞源自簡單的笑臉（☺），過去在一九七〇年代的各種平面媒體和廣告上都可以看得到。這個符號就叫做微笑符號。當網際網路被創造出來後，大家開始設計各式各樣的微笑符號，不過所有的樣式仍保有微笑符號的原始稱呼。其中有快樂的微笑符號、悲傷的微笑符號，以及生氣的微笑符號。微笑符號只是這些可以顯示各種表情臉孔的名稱。由於這可能會造成困惑，所以這些符號後來就統一被稱為「表情符號」（emotions）。

5.2a 開心的表情符號 Happy Smileys

:-)	"I am happy," "I agree"「我開心」、「我同意」
:)	"I am happy," "I agree" 「我開心」、「我同意」
:-]	a unique happy face 獨特的開心表情
:-D	"I am very happy," "I am excited"「我很開心」、「我很興奮」
:^D	"I am very happy," "I am excited" 「我很開心」、「我很興奮」
:-P	silly happy ─ tongue hanging out 傻笑──伸出舌頭
;-)	a clever or seductive wink 慧黠的或誘惑的眨眼
^_*	a sweet wink 甜蜜的眨眼
:'-)	"I am crying because I am so happy"「我喜極而泣」
:^)	a unique smiling face 獨特的笑臉
^_^	a charming smiling face 迷人的笑臉

5.2b 難過的表情符號 Unhappy Smileys

:-(	"I am sad"「我難過」
:(	"I am sad"「我難過」
:-[	unique sad face 獨特的悲傷表情
:-<	"I am sad and unhappy"「我既悲傷又難過」
:'-(	"I am crying because I am sad"「我在哭，因為我難過」

5.2c 驚訝的表情符號 Surprised Smileys

:-o	"Wow, I am surprised!"「哇，我好驚訝！」
:-O	"Wow, I am super surprised!"「哇，我太驚訝了！」

5.3 E 縮寫 E-Abbreviations

5.3a 網路聊天的縮寫 Abbreviations for Online Chat

儘管網路聊天是以書寫文字進行，但其中所用的字彙和用語跟面對面口頭溝通完全相同。口語溝通比信件、報告、甚至是電子郵件等文字溝通簡單得多，因此，網路聊天是文字溝通裡最簡單的形式。

以下是一些有助於進行網路聊天的常用縮寫。有些人會在電子郵件中使用這些縮寫，但各位不該這麼做。E 縮寫是非常不正式的用語。雖然電子郵件不像書面信件那麼正式，但它絕對比網路聊天正式。由於商務電子郵件必須專業，所以不要使用網路聊天時所用的 e 縮寫。另一個不要用這些縮寫的原因是，縮寫在商業寫作中經常用來代表商業名詞。假如電子郵件裡突然冒出 E 縮寫，讀者會感到困惑，因爲對方可能會以爲你指的是什麼商業術語。

A/S/L	=age, sex, location 年齡、性別、地點
BTW	=by the way 對了
BRB	=be right back 馬上回來
BF	=boyfriend 男友

（續下頁）

BFN	=bye for now 暫時聊到這裡
B4	=before 之前
CU	=see you [later]（待會）再見
EZ	=easy 簡單
F2F	=face to face 面對面
GF	=girlfriend 女友
HTH	=hope this helps 希望這有幫助
IC	=I see 我知道
IM	=immediate message 即時訊息
IMO	=in my opinion 在我看來
LOL	=laugh out loud 大聲笑
OIC	=oh, I see 喔，我懂了
POC	=piece of cake 小事一件
PDA	=public display of affection 公開表示親暱
SOL	=shit out of luck 真衰
SYS	=see you soon 希望很快再見
TKS	=thanks 謝謝
THX	=thanks 謝謝
TTYL	=talk to you later 稍後再聊
WTG	=way to go! 做得好！

5.3b 常用的商業縮寫 Common Business Abbreviations

下列縮寫是正式的商用縮寫，所以在電子郵件和網路聊天中都適用。根據許多傳統的寫作原則，大多數的縮寫通常是以句號「.」結尾。不過，省掉句號已經變得很普遍。假如你不確定能不能在縮寫中省略掉句號，那就注意顧客的寫作方式並照著做，或是親自查閱一本好的英文字典。

acct.	=account 帳戶
add.	=address 地址
AFC	=asking for correction 要求更正
agmt.	=agreement 協議
agt.	=agent 代理商
amt.	=amount 數量
A.R.	=accounts receivable 應收帳款
ASAP	=as soon as possible 愈快愈好
asst.	=assistant 助理
bal.	=balance 結餘
B.O.	=branch office 分公司
bx.	=box 信箱
cat.	=catalog; category 目錄；分類
co.	=company 公司
corp.	=corporation 企業
dept.	=department 部門
doc.	=document 文件
ea.	=each 每個
ex.	=example 範例
FAQ	=frequently asked questions 常見問題
frt.	=freight 運費
ft.	=feet 呎
fwd.	=forward 轉寄
FYI	=for your information 僅供參考
gds.	=goods 商品
gr.	=gross 總量
hrs.	=hours 時數
ht.	=height 高
in.	=inches 吋
incl.	=included 包含

（續下頁）

inc.	=incorporated 合併的
ins.	=insurance 保險
inv.	=invoice 發票
kg.	=kilogram 公斤
km.	kilometer 公里
LOC	=letter of credit 信用狀
Ltd.	=limited (company) 有限（公司）
max.	=maximum 最大
med.	=medium 中等
min.	=minimum 最小
mm.	=millimeter 公釐
N/A	=not applicable 不適用
orig.	=original 原始的
pcs.	=pieces 件（複數）
pct.	=percent 百分比
pd.	=paid 已付
Pls	=Please 請
qr.	=quarter 季
qty.	=quantity 數量
qlty.	=quality 品質
sig.	=signature 簽名
shpt.	=shipment 裝運
TTL.	=total 總計
val.	=value 價值
wt.	=weight 重量

Word List

applicable [ˈæplɪkəbl] *adj.* 適用的；適合的

6 實戰演練 Practice

1. 圈出並更正下列電子郵件中標點符號的錯誤。

Dear Customer Service Manager;

I am writing to let you know that your sales specialist [Maggie] has been unable to process my order for one week, I talked to her twice on the phone and sent her several e-mails!!! Each time she said I will try my best- but she didn't do anything!!

"This is not good service". Is there anything you can do to expedite my order.

I look forward to your quick reply.

Sincerely:
James

---

2. 用 ¶ 符號標示出段落應該從哪裡開始，並用□符號指出哪裡應該加空行。

Hi Bob,
Did you receive my e-mail regarding moving the production line to Shanghai? I sent it several days ago but didn't receive a reply. Perhaps the e-mail was lost, so I will retype the general contents below.
We would like you to move the production line from Hsinchu to Shanghai for the following reasons.
1. We can save a lot of labor cost. 2. We already have a branch office near the Shanghai Industrial Zone, so we can more easily meet with your pro-duction engineers and monitor the production process. 3. We will save

---

money on shipping costs, since most of our customers are in China.
My vice president would like to know your initial assessment. Is it possible
to move the production to Shanghai?
Thanks for considering our request
Yours,
Lavonne

＊解答請見 361 頁

第 **8** 章

E-mail 寫作技巧與慣用語

Common Business Usage

本章要談的是，電子郵件要怎麼寫，看起來才專業。誠如前一章所述，寫電子郵件最重要的一點就是要一目了然。你不必費心試圖在電子郵件中填滿特殊的商務行話。你要做的就是學會使用一些關鍵的商用片語，來幫助你以商務人士熟悉的方式陳述特定重點。你的溝通必須兼顧效率和效果。我蒐集了一些和商業用法有關的秘訣，以及一些各位必須徹底了解的關鍵片語，這些都是專業電子郵件寫作的核心。

This chapter presents how to word your e-mails so that they sound professional. As shown in the previous chapter, the most important thing about writing e-mail, by far, is being clear. You needn't worry about trying to fill your e-mails with special business jargon. All you need to do is learn to use a few key business phrases that can help you address specific points in ways that businesspeople are used to. You need to communicate efficiently and effectively. I have assembled a handful of tips related to business-usage and some key phrases that you need to know inside and out — they lie at the core of writing professional e-mails.

1 簡短扼要 Be Brief

　　要寫好商業電子郵件最重要的一點，就是要讓訊息簡短扼要。關鍵就在於：只寫重點，並盡量保持簡短。你無須費心把電子郵件寫成既特殊又講究的「商業文體」，只要簡明扼要傳達出訊息即可。

　　這麼做有兩個理由：
1. 在這個網際網路的年代，我們都已感受到資訊超載。研究顯示，現代人並不是「閱讀」電子郵件，而是「瀏覽」電子郵件。其原因在於，處理電子郵件可能浪費大量的時間。我們都接收了太多無用、冗長或是包含不重要資訊的訊息。你不應該把自己的時間——也不應該把別人的時間——浪費在寫得不好的電子郵件上。
2. 電子郵件不是很正式的溝通媒介。商務人士每天必須寫很多電子郵件，而且他們必須寫得很快。他們沒有足夠的時間像古時候在寫信一樣字斟句酌。因此，電子郵件的寫法很像是人在面對面地說話。把句子寫得像面對面溝通能節省時間，而且只要稍加練習即可上手。

　　這並不是說，書寫英文沒有特殊的形式或特定的商業修辭。當然有！本章稍後會提到。我要各位了解的重點是：應盡量以簡短明白為重點。你不必大費周章地嘗試以某種特別正式或潤飾的商業文體來寫作。

　　在現今 E 化的世界裡，能把電子郵件寫得既簡短又清楚，也就同時能展現專業、思考周密與成熟的一面。廢話太多、過度冗長的電子郵件等於是告訴讀者，作者缺乏判斷力、無法專注在重要的訊息上，而且不尊重其他人的時間。這樣說聽來可能很嚴苛，但這就是在商業世界溝通的殘酷現實。未來對於簡短電子郵件的渴望只會變得更強烈！

✗ 錯誤範例

Hi Malcolm,

How are you today? Last night there was a big party hosted by one of our clients. We sang and danced and drank a lot of wine. But I am pretty tired now because I went to bed late.

Anyway, I want to ask you some questions about the payment methods for our order. I hope you are not too busy today. Well, if you are, it is okay. You can answer the questions later if you like. Maybe you had a party last night, too, and feel tired now! Ha ha!

Question one: Are you sure that you require a letter of credit for new customers? It might be more convenient to just <u>wire</u> the money to you. I <u>encountered</u> the same situation once, and we were able to use wire transfer instead of letter of credit.

Question two: In the future, can we <u>combine</u> some of the payments so that we don't need to go to the bank so often? The bank we use is a little far away, and it takes too much time if we have to go there a lot. You should see the traffic here. It is unbelievably crowded!

Okay, those are my two questions. I hope they make sense. If they don't make sense, please ask me to clarify. I would be glad to do so.

Thanks <u>in advance</u> for your reply. Talk to you soon. Have a nice day!

Ian

□ 翻譯

嗨，莫康姆：

今天好嗎？昨天晚上我們有位客戶辦了一場盛大的派對，我們又是唱歌又是跳舞的，並且喝了很多酒。不過我現在很累，因為我很晚才睡。

不管怎樣，我想要問你一些和我們訂單的付款方式有關的問題。我希望你今天不

Word List

wire [waɪr] v. 電匯；用電報發送
encounter [ɪn`kaʊntɚ] v. 碰上；遇見

combine [kəm`baɪn] v. 使……合併；結合
in advance 預先

會太忙，假如你忙的話，那也沒關係。如果你願意的話，可以晚點再回答我的問題。搞不好你昨天晚上也有個派對，而且現在覺得很累，哈哈！

問題一：你確定你們的新客戶需要使用信用狀嗎？直接把錢匯給你們可能會比較方便。我遇過一次同樣的狀況，我們那一次就可以用轉帳來代替信用狀。

問題二：將來我們可不可以把一些款項合併起來，這樣我們就不用那麼常跑銀行？我們往來的銀行有點遠，假如我們必須常跑，就會花很多時間。你應該瞧瞧這裡的交通，簡直是塞到令人不敢相信的地步！

好，這就是我的兩個問題，希望還清楚。假如不清楚，就麻煩要求我釐清，我會很樂意的。

先謝謝你的回覆，希望能盡快與你談話。祝你今天順心！

伊恩

☑ 正確範例

Hi Malcolm,

How are you today?

I have two questions about the payment methods for our order.

1. Are you sure that you require a letter of credit for new customers? It might be more convenient to just wire the money to you.

2. In the future, can we combine some of the payments so that we don't need to go to the bank so often?

Thanks in advance for your reply.

Ian

☐ 翻譯

嗨，莫康姆：

今天好嗎？

我有兩個和我們訂單的付款方式有關的問題：

1. 您確定你們的新客戶需要使用信用狀嗎？直接把錢匯給你們可能會比較方便。

2. 將來我們可不可以把一些款項合併起來，這樣我們就不用那麼常跑銀行？

先謝謝你的回覆。

伊恩

✏ **Memo**

---

2 說明目的 Stating the Purpose

2.1 主旨列 Subject Line

　　主旨列很重要，可是會認真看待它的人少之又少。由於資訊的超載，所以商務人士會很仔細地把值得花時間閱讀的 E-mail 篩選出來。大家會「快速瀏覽」電子郵件信箱，以找出哪些電子郵件要刪、哪些要立刻看、哪些要晚點看。除了看電子郵件是誰寄來的之外，如果要知道電子郵件在講什麼以及它的重要性如何，唯一的線索就是主旨列了。因此，寫出好的主旨列就成了你必須精通的重要任務。

　　對於寫出好的主旨列，我個人的原則（規則）如下：
　　1. 清楚易懂，且確實是與電子郵件內容相符的主題。
　　2. 盡量使用最切題的措詞，即使用帶有足夠資訊的字。
　　3. 用英文標題的方式呈現，把該大寫的字大寫。
　　4. 盡可能保持簡短。
　　5. 假如可能的話，就用主旨列當做電子郵件。

✗ something useful for you
對你有幫助的東西
✊ 違反規則 1、2、3。
✓ New Engineering Software
新工程軟體

✗ Do you have time?
你有時間嗎？
✊ 違反規則 1、2、3。

✗ I Would Like to Invite You for Dinner
我想請你吃晚餐
✊ 違反規則 4。
✓ Dinner Invitation
晚餐邀約

Note

電子郵件「主旨」的意思是，「這封電子郵件有關……」。所以不應該把「about」當成主旨列的第一個字。

✗ About Your Product Order

有關您的產品訂單

💬 此主旨列的意思是：「這封郵件是有關有關您的產品訂單。」

✓ Your Product Order

您的產品訂單

💬 此主旨列的意思是：「這封郵件是關於您的產品訂單。」

✗ sickness

生病

💬 違反規則 1、2、3。再者，收件人必須開啟郵件才能了解它的重要性。

✓ Irene Sick Today. Will Return Tomorrow.

艾琳今天生病，明天會來。

💬 這個主旨列一針見血，足以當成一封電子郵件。它符合規則 5，所以收件人不需要開啟訊息。這樣既省時間，又能增進效率。

2.2 引言 Introduction

在電子郵件中應該盡快說明目的。目的可以視情況在第一或第二段說明。在下列的情況中，你可以在第二段說明目的：

- 你想先說一些寒暄的話。
- 你必須先向收件人介紹自己。

在其他所有的情況下，電子郵件的目的都應該在第一段說明。假如可能的話，你甚至可以在主旨列中說明。

BIZ 必通句型

I AM WRITING TO ....

我寫這封郵件是要⋯⋯。

例 I am writing to inform you that we have a new business manager.

我寫這封郵件是要通知您，我們有了一位新的業務經理。

I AM E-MAILING YOU BECAUSE ....

我寄這封電子郵件給您是因為⋯⋯。

例 I am e-mailing you because your payment is <u>overdue</u>.

我寄這封電子郵件給您是因為您的付款過期了。

I AM E-MAILING TO LET YOU KNOW ....

我寄這封電子郵件是要讓您知道⋯⋯。

例 I am e-mailing to let you know that your report has been forwarded to the manager.

我寄這封電子郵件是要讓您知道，您的報告已經轉呈給經理。

I AM WRITING TO TELL YOU ....

我寫這封郵件是要跟你說⋯⋯。

例 I am writing to tell you some good news.

我寫這封郵件是要跟你說一些好消息。

I AM WRITING ABOUT ....

我寫這封郵件是要談⋯⋯。

例 I am writing about the fax you sent this morning.

我寫這封郵件是要談你今天早上傳過來的傳真。

　　有時候電子郵件的訊息和它的目的相同。在這種情況下，電子郵件只會有一段，甚至就只有一句。例如：

Word List

overdue [ˌovəˈdju] *adj.* 過期的；逾期未付的

Hi Felix,

I just want to acknowledge receipt of your shipment. Thanks.

Ramona

□ 翻譯

嗨，菲力克斯：

我只是想要告訴你，我收到你的貨了，謝謝。

雷夢娜

電子郵件的目的經常不必說明。假如你要回覆電子郵件，電子郵件系統會自動在主旨列加上「RE:」。如此一來，電子郵件的主旨就很清楚，所以你不必寫新的主旨列，或是在引言中說明目的。例如：

原始郵件主旨： Packing Invoices Needed
　　　　　　　　需要包裝的發票
回覆郵件主旨： RE: Packing Invoices Needed
　　　　　　　　RE: 需要包裝的發票

🖉 Note

每當有人回覆主旨列中有「RE:」的電子郵件時，電子郵件系統可能就會在主旨列的開頭加上另一個「RE:」。假如發生這種狀況，就刪掉主旨列中不必要的「RE:」。這在現在的專業電子郵件系統中不成問題，但在舊系統中卻很常見。

✗ RE: RE: RE: RE: Part Number 5432 Is Broken
　 RE: RE: RE: RE: 零件 5432 號壞了
✓ RE: Part Number 5432 Is Broken
　 RE: 零件 5432 號壞了

3 開場 Opening

3.1 稱呼語 <u>Salutation</u>

　　稱呼語列在電子郵件中並不是很重要。電子郵件在本質上就不算正式，而且是快速寫下的。當你要寫電子郵件給熟識或者經常通信的人時，下列的稱呼語都是可以接受的。

Hi Fred:	Hi Fred,
嗨，弗列得：	嗨，弗列得，
Hello Fred:	Hello Fred,
哈囉，弗列得：	哈囉，弗列得，
Fred:	Fred,
弗列得：	弗列得，

> 🖉 **Note**
>
> 　　使用冒號或逗號並沒有真正的差別。此外，等你和對方熟了以後，比方已經有過十次左右的郵件往來，你就可以把稱呼語完全刪除。

　　當你第一次寫電子郵件給某人時，或是寫重要且正式的電子郵件給認識的人時，你可以用比較正式的稱呼語：

Dear Fred:	Dear Fred,
親愛的弗列得：	親愛的弗列得，
Dear Mr. Jones:	Dear Mr. Jones,
敬愛的瓊斯先生：	敬愛的瓊斯先生，

Word **List**

salutation [ˌsæljəˋteʃən] *n.* （信函開頭的）稱呼語

Note

當你寫標準的電子郵件給某個你很熟或經常通信的人時，使用正式的稱呼語「Dear …」（親／敬愛的……）通常是個錯誤。大部分的人都會有這樣的想法：「你幹嘛這麼正式？不認識我嗎？我們都已經互相通信兩年了！」

假如你不知道寫信對象的姓名，可以用下列正式稱呼語的其中一個：

Dear Sir:	Dear Sir,
敬愛的先生：	敬愛的先生，
Dear Sirs:	Dear Sirs,
各位敬愛的先生：	各位敬愛的先生，
Dear Madam:	Dear Madam,
敬愛的女士：	敬愛的女士，
Dear Sir/Madam:	Dear Sir/Madam,
敬愛的先生／女士：	敬愛的先生／女士，
Gentlemen:	Gentlemen,
各位先生：	各位先生，
Ladies and Gentlemen:	Ladies and Gentlemen,
各位先生、女士：	各位先生、女士，

3.2 溫馨的開場用語 Warm Opening Words

根據不同的情況或你和收信人的關係，你可能會想以一些溫馨的字詞為你的電子郵件開場。

BIZ 必通句型

HOW ARE YOU?
你好嗎？

HOW IS EVERYTHING?
一切都好嗎？

HOW HAVE YOU BEEN?
你近來如何？

I HOPE YOU ARE WELL.
希望你很好。

GREETINGS FROM (PLACE/COMPANY).
來自（地點／公司）的問候。
例 Greetings from Taiwan.
　來自台灣的問候。
例 Greetings from Giant Fruit Company.
　來自碩果公司的問候。

4 結語 Closing

4.1 禮貌的結束用語 Polite Closing Words

就很短的電子郵件而言，結束用語通常不是很必要。但假如你想用的話，還是可寫下一句加入電子郵件。對長篇的電子郵件來說，結束用語則很有幫助，因為加入一些令人覺得溫馨或有人情味的結語，可以凸顯雙方的商業關係並不僅止於討論電子郵件中的公事而已。

BIZ 必通句型

● 提及未來的溝通 References to Future Communication

I LOOK FORWARD TO YOUR REPLY.
期盼您的回覆。

I LOOK FORWARD TO HEARING FROM YOU.
期盼收到您的消息。

I HOPE TO HEAR FROM YOU SOON.
希望很快收到您的消息。

STAY IN TOUCH.
保持聯絡。

● 祝福用語 Pleasant Words

TAKE CARE.
保重。

BEST WISHES.
衷心祝福。

說謝謝 Saying Thanks

THANKS.
謝謝。

THANKS FOR ....
謝謝……。
例 Thanks for helping with the problem.
謝謝您幫忙處理這個問題。

THANKS IN ADVANCE.
先謝謝了。

4.2 署名列 Signature Line

　　跟稱呼語一樣，結尾辭在電子郵件中也不是很重要。在寫標準式的電子郵件給熟識或經常通信的人時，以下是可以接受的結尾辭：

Regards,　　　　　　Yours,　　　　　　Daniel (your name only)
上　　　　　　　　　草　　　　　　　　丹尼爾（只寫你的名字）

　　當你要寫比較正式的電子郵件，比如寫電子郵件給不認識的人，或是寫議題敏感的電子郵件給認識的人時，你可以用正式的結尾辭：

Sincerely (yours),　　　　Respectfully (yours),
謹上　　　　　　　　　　敬上

Cordially (yours),　　　　Yours (truly),
謹啓　　　　　　　　　　敬啓

Sincere Regards,　　　　Best Regards,
謹啓　　　　　　　　　　敬上

Note

不要使用固定的署名列！假如你有個非正式的固定署名列，它並不適合用在正式的電子郵件中。相反地，假如你有正式的固定署名列，它也不適合用在非正式的電子郵件中。凡是有固定署名列的人，他們的正式署名列跟他們所寫的絕大部分電子郵件幾乎都互相衝突，因為絕大部分的電子郵件都不正式。這條規則只有一個例外：假如你在電子郵件的結尾只寫你的名字，你當然可以使用只包含名字的固定署名列。無論如何，在寄出下一封電子郵件之前，你都要視狀況來設定電子郵件格式和相關用語！

Memo

5 正確的開場與結束範例 Examples of Correct Openings & Closings

5.1 非正式電子郵件 Informal E-mail

☑ 正確範例 1

Hi Barney,

How have you been recently?

I just want to ask if you can send me a list of your suppliers.

Regards,
Jill

☐ 翻譯

嗨，巴尼：

最近好嗎？

我只是想問問，你可不可以把你們的供應商名單寄給我？

吉兒
上

☑ 正確範例 2

Barney:

How are you these days?

I just want to ask if you can send me a list of your suppliers.

Thanks in advance.

Jill

☐ 翻譯

巴尼：

最近好嗎？

我只是想問問，你可不可以把你們的供應商名單寄給我？

先謝謝了。

吉兒

5.2 正式電子郵件 Formal E-mail

☑ 正確範例 1

Dear Mr. Roberts,

Greetings. I am Ramona, a salesperson at Rainbow Candy Company.

I am writing to tell you that we would like to discuss using your company as our exclusive sugar supplier. Can you tell me a day and time that is convenient to have a meeting to discuss this?

I look forward to hearing from you.

Sincerely yours,
Ramona Lambert

☐ 翻譯

> 敬愛的羅伯特先生：
>
> 您好，我是彩虹糖果公司的業務員雷夢娜。
>
> 我寫這封信是要告訴您，我們想討論請貴公司擔任我們獨家糖品供應商的事。您可以告訴我方便開會討論此事的日期和時間嗎？
>
> 期盼收到您的消息。
>
> 雷夢娜‧藍伯特
> 謹上

☑ 正確範例 2

> Dear Kieran:
>
> Greetings. I am Ramona, a salesperson at Rainbow Candy Company.
>
> I am writing to tell you that we would like to discuss using your company as our exclusive sugar supplier. Can you tell me a day and time that is convenient to have a meeting to discuss this?
>
> I look forward to your reply.
>
> Cordially yours,
> Ramona

☐ 翻譯

> 親愛的奇亞倫：
>
> 你好，我是彩虹糖果公司的業務員雷夢娜。

我寫這封信是要告訴你，我們想討論請貴公司擔任我們獨家糖品供應商的事。你可不可以告訴我方便開會討論此事的日期和時間？

期盼您的回覆。

雷夢娜
謹啓

 Note

　　署名列的結尾辭和姓名之間並不空行，這兩行合起來算一個部分。

Memo

6 ： 常用商業片語 Common Business Phrases

6.1 提及先前的溝通（電子郵件、電話、傳真等）
Referring to Prior Communication (E-mail, Phone, Fax, etc.)

BIZ 必通句型

... PER ....

……依照……。

例 I have sent the brochure to you per your request.

我已經依照你的要求把簡介寄給你了。

AS FOR ..., ...

至於…… , ……。

例 As for your suggestion, can you provide me more details?

至於你的建議，可不可以告訴我更多細節？

REGARDING ..., ...

關於…… , ……。

例 Regarding your idea, I think we can go for it.

關於你的想法，我認為我們可以試試看。

IN/WITH REGARD TO ..., ...

關於…… , ……。

例 In regard to the complaint, I am still checking the details.

關於那項抱怨，我還在查看詳細內容。

例 With regard to your question, I will get back with you soon.

關於您的問題，我會很快回覆您。

Word List

go for sth. 嘗試獲得某物；嘗試達成某事

IN REFERENCE TO ..., ...

關於……，……。

例 In reference to your problem, I think I can help you.

關於你的問題，我想我可以幫你。

ACCORDING TO ..., ...

根據……，……。

例 According to your first e-mail, the policy <u>prohibits</u> us from doing anything.

根據你的第一封電子郵件，政策禁止我們做任何事。

IN RESPONSE TO ..., ...

回應……，……。

例 In response to your last message, the rework is almost finished.

回應你最後的訊息，重做的工作幾乎已經完成。

PLEASE REFER TO ....

請參考……。

例 Please refer to the meeting notes I sent you two days ago.

請參考我兩天前寄給你的會議記錄。

6.2 提及電子郵件裡的訊息 Referring to Information Inside an E-mail

BIZ 必通句型

○ 上述訊息 Information Above

AS YOU CAN SEE ABOVE, ...

您在上面可以看到，……。

例 As you can see above, all the questions have been answered.

您在上面可以看到，所有的問題都已經回答。

Word List

prohibit [prə`hɪbɪt] v.（根據法令、規定等）禁止；阻止

327

PER THE ABOVE, ...

依照上述內容，……。

例 Per the above, your company has two months to <u>submit</u> a request.

依照上述內容，貴公司有兩個月時間可以提出要求。

• 下列訊息 Information Below

AS YOU CAN SEE BELOW, ...

您可以在下面看到，……。

例 As you can see below, some numbers have been <u>transposed</u>.

您可以在下面看到，一些號碼已經被調換了。

... AS FOLLOWS ....

……如下。

例 My <u>recommendations</u> for the case are as follows.

我對這案子的建議如下。

... PER THE FOLLOWING ....

……依照下列……。

例 Please set up the test procedures per the following information.

請依照下列訊息設定測試程序。

THE FOLLOWING IS/ARE ....

以下是……。

例 The following is my supervisor's reply to your question.

以下是我們主管針對你的問題所給予的回覆。

例 The following are the figures you requested.

以下是你要的數據。

Word List

submit [səb`mɪt] v.（向……）提出

transpose [træns`poz] v. 把（位置、順序等）調換

recommendation [ˌrɛkəmɛn`deʃən] n. 建議；勸告

6.3 表示了解 Stating Understanding

BIZ 必通句型

I UNDERSTAND (THAT) ....

我明白……。

例 I understand the issue is important for you.

我明白那個問題對你而言很重要。

例 I understand that your budget is limited, but our price is still <u>competitive</u>.

我明白您的預算有限,但我們的價格還是很便宜。

I AM AWARE THAT ....

我知道……。

例 I am aware that the project should be finished soon.

我知道這案子應該要盡快完成。

6.4 確認 Confirmation

BIZ 必通句型

I WANT TO CONFIRM ....

我想要確認……。

例 I want to confirm that we will finalize the changes by this weekend.

我想要確認,我們會在這星期前將變更定案。

THIS IS TO CONFIRM ....

這封郵件的目的是要確認……。

例 This is to confirm that your order has been processed.

這封郵件的目的是要確認您的訂單已經在處理了。

Word List

competitive [kəmˋpɛtətɪv] *adj.* (價格、產品等)具有競爭力的

6.5 通知收到 Acknowledging Receipt

BIZ 必通句型

I RECEIVED ....

我收到了……。

例 I received your e-mail.

我收到了你的電子郵件。

I ACKNOWLEDGE RECEIPT OF ....

我要通知你我已經收到……。

例 I acknowledge receipt of your claim.

我要通知你我已經收到你的要求了。

... WAS RECEIVED.

……收到了。

例 Your letter was received.

你的信收到了。

6.6 建議 Making Suggestions

BIZ 必通句型

I WOULD LIKE TO SUGGEST ....

我想要建議……。

例 I would like to suggest that you check everything again.

我想要建議你再把每樣東西都檢查一遍。

Word List

acknowledge [ək`nɑlɪdʒ] v. 通知收到（函件、信件等）；函謝

IT MIGHT BE A GOOD IDEA TO ....

……可能是個好主意。

例 It might be a good idea to call the warehouse.

打電話給倉庫可能是個好主意。

MIGHT I SUGGEST ...?

我可不可以建議……？

例 Might I suggest that you ask the Quality Control Department for assistance?

我可不可以建議你請品管部門幫忙？

6.7 引起注意 Drawing Attention

BIZ 必通句型

PLEASE NOTE ....

請注意……。

例 Please note the expiration date.

請注意終止日期。

PLEASE TAKE NOTE THAT ....

請注意……。

例 Please take note that a return form must accompany all returns.

請注意，所有的退貨都必須附上退貨單。

PLEASE NOTICE THAT ....

請注意……。

例 Please notice that the contract requires your signature.

請注意，合約需要你的簽名。

PLEASE BE AWARE THAT ....

請了解……。

例 Please be aware that we are not responsible for any misuse of the product.

請了解我們對於任何產品的不當使用概不負責。

PLEASE UNDERSTAND THAT ....

請了解……。

例 Please understand that our offices will be closed for two days because of the holiday.

請了解因為放假的關係，我們的辦公室將關閉兩天。

6.8 請求 Making Requests

BIZ 必通句型

DO YOU MIND IF ...?

您是否介意……？

例 Do you mind if I send you a customer survey?

您是否介意我寄一份顧客調查給您？

IS IT ALRIGHT IF ...?

……可以嗎？

例 Is it alright if we bring some friends with us?

我們帶一些朋友一起來可以嗎？

COULD YOU ALLOW ME TO ...?

您可不可以讓我……？

例 Could you allow me to record the meeting tomorrow?

您可不可以讓我把明天的會議錄下來？

COULD YOU POSSIBLY ...?

您是不是能夠……？

例 Could you possibly send the attachment again?

您是不是能夠再寄一次附件？

WOULD IT BE POSSIBLE TO ...?

有沒有可能可以……？

例 Would it be possible to start the conference call a little late?

有沒有可能可以晚一點再開電話會議？

6.9 強調 Emphasizing

BIZ 必通句型

I WOULD LIKE TO EMPHASIZE ....

我想要強調……。

例 I would like to emphasize that you can <u>stipulate</u> the vendor we will use.

我想要強調，你們可以明定我們要選擇哪一家廠商。

I SHOULD EMPHASIZE ....

我必須強調……。

例 I should emphasize that my colleague is working on this problem now.

我必須強調，我的同事現在正在想辦法解決這個問題。

Word **List**

stipulate [ˈstɪpjəˌlet] v. 規定；講明（條件等）

6.10 道謝 Saying Thanks

BIZ 必通句型

I APPRECIATE ....

我很感謝……。

例 I appreciate your continued <u>expertise</u> in this matter.

我很感謝您在這件事上持續提供專業見解。

THANK YOU FOR ....

謝謝您……。

例 Thank you for your <u>constructive</u> comments.

謝謝您建設性的意見。

MANY THANKS FOR ....

非常謝謝……。

例 Many thanks for <u>going the extra mile</u> for us.

非常謝謝您為我們額外地付出。

THANK YOU IN ADVANCE FOR ....

先謝謝您……。

例 Thank you in advance for verifying the product code.

先謝謝您核對產品代碼。

I AM GRATEFUL FOR ....

我很感激……

例 I am grateful for the information you provided.

我很感激您所提供的資訊。

Word List

expertise [ˌɛkspɚˋtiz] *n.* 專業知識；專門技術
constructive [kənˋstrʌktɪv] *adj.* 建設性的；積極的
go the extra mile 額外地努力、付出

.... THANKS IN ADVANCE.

…。先謝謝了。

例 Can you mail me a hard copy of the memo? Thanks in advance.

你可不可以寄一份備忘錄的列印本給我？先謝謝了。

6.11 表示愉快 Expressing Happiness

BIZ 必通句型

I AM GLAD/HAPPY/PLEASED THAT ....

我很高興……。

例 I am pleased that you received such good news.

我很高興你收到這麼好的消息。

I AM GLAD/HAPPY/PLEASED TO HEAR ....

我很高興聽到……。

例 I am glad to hear that you found the answer.

我很高興聽到你找到了答案。

6.12 給予保證 Giving Assurance

BIZ 必通句型

I ASSURE YOU THAT ....

我向你保證……。

例 I assure you that the task will be completed on time.

我向你保證，任務一定會準時完成。

YOU CAN BE ASSURED THAT ....

您可以放心……。

例 You can be assured that we will take care of all your needs.

　　您可以放心，我們會處理好您所有的需求。

REST ASSURED THAT ....

放心……。

例 Rest assured that we can fulfill any request.

　　放心，我們能滿足任何要求。

6.13 要求迅速回覆 Asking for a Quick Reply

BIZ 必通句型

YOUR PROMPT REPLY IS APPRECIATED.

請立即回覆，感謝您。

I LOOK FORWARD TO YOUR QUICK REPLY.

期盼您盡快回覆。

6.14 提及附件 Noting Attachments

BIZ 必通句型

PLEASE SEE ....

……請見……。

例 Please see the attached file for more information.

　　更多的資訊請見附檔。

THE ... IS ATTACHED.

附上……。

例 The PowerPoint file is attached.

附上 PowerPoint 檔案。

THE ATTACHED ....

附加的……。

例 The attached document should be reviewed carefully.

附加的文件應該要仔細查閱。

ATTACHED IS/ARE ....

附檔是……。

例 Attached is the financial statistics I promised.

附檔是我答應給你的財務統計資料。

ATTACHED PLEASE FIND ....

……請見附檔。

例 Attached please find the photos that you asked for.

你要的照片請見附檔。

ATTACHED YOU WILL FIND ....

你在附件中可以看到……。

例 Attached you will find the schematics for the new handheld GPS system.

你在附檔中可以看到新款手持 GPS 系統的草圖。

🖉 **Note**

不可以用「enclosed」來指附件。「Enclosed」專門指與信一起裝在信封裡的資料。

Word List

schematic [ski`mætɪk] *n.* 草圖

handheld [`hænd,hɛld] *adj.* 手持式的

6.15 告知突發訊息 Informing of Sudden Information

BIZ 必通句型

I JUST FOUND OUT ....

我剛剛才發現……。

例 I just found out that the package was already sent.

我剛剛才發現包裹已經寄出去了。

I JUST REALIZED THAT ....

我剛剛才了解……。

例 I just realized that the prices are <u>outdated</u>.

我剛剛才了解價格原來是舊的。

IT HAS JUST COME TO MY ATTENTION THAT ....

我剛剛才注意到……。

例 It has just come to my attention that the item is out of stock.

我剛剛才注意到那一項東西缺貨。

6.16 要求訊息 Asking for Information

BIZ 必通句型

PLEASE LET ME KNOW ....

請告訴我……。

例 Please let me know how you want to handle the problem.

請告訴我，你想要怎麼處理這個問題。

Word List

outdated [ˌaʊtˋdetɪd] *adj.* 過時的；不再使用的

PLEASE INFORM ME OF ....

請告知我……。

例 Please inform me of your shipping requirements.

請告知我你們的運送要求。

PLEASE ADVISE ....

請通知……。

例 Please advise me who will make the decision.

請通知我誰會作決定。

WOULD YOU PLEASE ADVISE ...?

可否請您建議……？

例 Would you please advise how fax orders should be handled?

可否請您建議傳真訂單該怎麼處理？

PLEASE ADVISE.

請提供建議。

例 We are still confused about the cause of the glitch. Please advise.

我們還是搞不清楚故障的原因。請提供建議。

✐ **Memo**

7 實戰演練 Practice

找出並刪除這封電子郵件中不必要的部分，然後重新改寫。

Subject: Maybe you would be so kind to fill out the attached survey

Dear Customers,

First, thank you for years of letting us serve you. We really cherish our business relationship. It seems things are going well, and we expect many more years of doing business together.

Every year, we like to conduct a survey of our customers. This survey helps us learn about the quality of our services. We want to improve our service every year. If we improve every year, that is good for all of us.

I hope you don't mind filling out a survey for us. The survey is attached to this e-mail. You can send the completed survey back to us by e-mail or fax. Either way is okay. We will just be glad to receive the survey back. Thanks for your time to fill out the survey!

Finally, we wish you great success in the upcoming quarter, the last of this year. We look forward to being your partner next year.

Sincerely yours,
Betsy Moss

＊解答請見 364 頁

第 9 章

語氣

Tone

說英文時要讓語氣正確已經夠難了，更別提要在寫英文時掌握它。以電子郵件來說，由於文化上的差異，語氣可能會是個棘手的問題。因為只從一段文字很容易就誤解對方的態度和情緒，所以我主張電子郵件的寫作要跟口語一樣清楚（請見第七章）。只要專注在寫出能清楚表達客觀事實和訊息的郵件上，你就不用太擔心語氣的問題。不過，還是必須注意幾件事，以免在電子郵件中不經意地表現出錯誤的語氣，而這也是本章所要探討的內容。

Getting your tone right while speaking English is difficult enough, let alone nailing it while writing English. In e-mail, owing to cultural differences, tone can be a prickly problem. Because it is very easy to misinterpret attitudes and emotions in a piece of writing, I advocate clarity in e-mail writing as well as in speech (see Chapter 7). By focusing on writing clear e-mails that are objective and information-based, you need not worry so much about the issue of tone. There are, however, some things you need to know in order to avoid accidentally conveying the wrong tone with your e-mail, and that is what this chapter is all about.

1 ┃ 否定語氣 Negative Tone

1.1 避免以高姿態說話 Avoid Talking Down

在寫商務電子郵件時，應該避免讓人覺得你是老闆而收件者是部屬，或者你是父母而讀者是孩子。語氣應該傳達出寄件者和收件者身分地位相當。不要賣弄文筆或以恩人自居！你要做的是分享想法、給予建議，並提供有幫助的忠告或訊息。不要試圖告訴別人他們應該做什麼或相信什麼，至少不要讓人感覺是那個樣子，文句要保持簡單明瞭。

✘ Intelligent people will choose our new product instead of our competitor's product.
聰明人會選擇我們的新產品，而不是我們競爭對手的產品。

✔ We think that our product is superior to our competitor's product, and we hope you will take a look at it.
我們認為我們的產品比競爭對手的產品要好，希望您能看一下。

. . . .

✘ Send your order to us right away so we can ship the items to you quickly.
立刻把你們的訂單寄給我們，這樣我們才能快點把貨品運送給您。

✔ 1. The faster you send us your order, the faster we can ship it.
您越快把訂單寄給我們，我們就能越快把貨送去給您。

2. If you want the items quickly, we suggest that you send your order right away.
如果您想快點拿到貨品，我們建議您立刻把訂單寄給我們。

. . . .

✘ Please tell me exactly how you want me to solve the problem. And please send me a file with the specifications you are referring to.
請告訴我您到底希望我怎麼解決問題，並請把您提到的規格檔案寄給我。

✔ Could you give me exact details about how you want me to solve the problem? If you can send me a file with the specifications you are referring to, it will be easier for me to help you.
您可不可以把希望我如何解決問題的確切細節告訴我？如果您可以把您提到的規格的檔案寄給我，我就更容易幫您。

342

Note

我見過的一種典型錯誤是，為了緩和語氣而在命令句中勉強加上「please」（請）這個字。命令句以動詞開頭，例如「Finish your work.」（完成你的工作。）。命令是採取由上而下的邏輯。如果你在命令的開頭加上「Please」，那還是個命令！「Please do it now.」（請現在做。）和「Do it now.」（現在做。）基本上是同樣的命令，兩者都是以高姿態對讀者說話。為了表示客氣，這類句子最好以「Could you」（你可以）或「We should」（我們應該）等用語開頭，例如：「Could you do it now, please?」（可以麻煩你現在做嗎？）或「We should finish our work.」（我們應該完成我們的工作）。

1.2 避免顯得虛偽 Avoid Appearing Fake

1.1a 不真誠 Insincerity

避免在寫作中使用大量的甜言蜜語。生意就是生意，商場人士不需要花俏的語言。他們做生意是為了賺錢，而不是為了當你最好的朋友。如果你用了很多推心置腹的言詞，讀者反而可能會覺得你很虛假。就我所知，中國文化很強調使用聽起來令人愉悅的字眼。也許這正是為什麼有這麼多學生喜歡在英文電子郵件中使用這類措詞，而犯下令人覺得不真誠的錯誤。語言就是文化，所以在用英語寫作時，一定要記得下列重點，並注意簡潔的重要性。

✗ Thank you so much for your reply. I am so happy to receive it. You are really a kind customer.
非常感謝您回覆。能收到您的信我非常高興。您真是一位親切的顧客。

✓ Thanks for your reply.
感謝您的回覆。

✗ I really appreciate your kindness when I was in Canada for my business trip. The places you showed me were the most wonderful places in the world. I can't imagine a better way to spend my time than to chat with you while drinking coffee. Your kind assistance will stay in my heart forever.
非常感激您在我到加拿大出差時親切的接待。您帶我去的地方是世界上最棒的地方。我無法想像有什麼會比和您邊喝咖啡邊聊天更好的消磨時間方式。您貼心的協助將永遠銘

記在我心中。

✓ I appreciate your kindness. While I was in Canada on my business trip, you showed me some nice places and helped me a lot. Thank you.

感激您親切的接待。在我到加拿大出差時,您帶我去了一些很不錯地方,而且幫了我很多忙。謝謝您。

1.2b 誇大 Exaggeration

　　盡量使用客觀性的言語。把焦點擺在事實上,並提供精確的訊息。如果你用很多主觀性的言語,而沒有把焦點擺在提供精確的細節上,收件人很可能會懷疑你所寫的內容。務實為上!

✗ Our new product is so <u>fabulous</u> that you won't believe your eyes.　When you just look at it, you will feel like you are a king holding a valuable jewel.

我們的新產品棒極了,你絕不會相信自己的眼睛。只要看它一眼,你就會覺得自己像是個拿著奇珍異寶的國王。

✓ Our new product is quite unique on the market. When you see it, you will be impressed by the bright yellow color and shiny surface.

我們的新產品在市場上非常獨特。你看到它的時候,你會對它鮮明的黃色和閃亮的外表留下深刻的印象。

1.2c 不斷道歉 <u>Profuse</u> Apologizing

　　如果你用了太多字表示歉意,它們就會失去意義。這可能會讓讀者覺得你的言詞不真誠,甚至會覺得你其實並「不覺得」抱歉。道歉過多的另一個問題是,讀者可能會覺得你能力不夠,而且不是可以依賴的人。正確的做法是,說一次抱歉,然後轉入正題,說明補救方案。

✗ I am really sorry for the error. I don't know what happened. It is a really stupid mistake. Please forgive me.

我對那個錯誤感到非常抱歉。我不知道發生了什麼事。那是個很愚蠢的錯誤,請原諒我。

Ｗord List

exaggeration [ˌɪgzædʒəˈreʃən] *n.* 誇張;誇大　　　　profuse [prəˈfjus] *adj.* 極其豐富的;過多的

fabulous [ˈfæbjələs] *adj.* 【口】極好的

✓ I am sorry for the error. I don't know what happened, but I will take a careful look and fix it immediately.
我對那個錯誤感到抱歉。我不知道發生了什麼事，但我會仔細檢查並立刻補救。

📎 **Note**

太常用「Sorry」（抱歉）是很常見的錯誤。只要一有問題，不管問題的本質是什麼或是誰的錯，很多人都會以「Sorry」當作句子的開頭。其實應盡量簡潔。如果你真的需要道歉（如：抱歉，我寄錯了附檔），或是要麻煩某人（如：抱歉打擾您，但我需要戴納的電話號碼），才用「Sorry」，否則就不要用。

✗ Sorry, the information you sent us is incorrect. Can you send us the correct information?
抱歉，你寄給我們的訊息不正確。你可不可以寄正確的訊息給我們？

✓ The information you sent us is incorrect. Can you send us the correct information?
你寄給我們的訊息不正確。你可不可以寄正確的訊息給我們？

1.2d 推諉塞責 Passing the Blame

當你犯錯時，應該要主動為錯誤負責。不過，假如是你公司的其他人犯了錯，通常最好不要提。假如你推諉責任（請見下例），儘管有些事的確不是你的錯，但讀者可能會覺得你不老實。你可以做的一件事是，用「我們」代替「我」。這是一種策略，既然你是公司的一份子，個人的錯誤就可以視為整個公司的錯。

✗ The shipping mistake was not my fault. It was my colleague's fault. She gave me the wrong information. Sorry about that.
運送錯誤不是我的錯，是我同事的錯。她給了我錯誤的訊息，很抱歉。

✓ Sorry for the shipping error. I made a note and am sure it will not happen again.
抱歉運送出了錯。我已經記下來了，保證不會再發生。

✓ I apologize for the shipping error. We won't make that error again.
我要為運送的錯誤道歉。我們不會再犯那種錯了。

當錯誤發生時，沒有理由要把焦點擺在犯錯的人身上。你可以用被動的動詞結構來把焦點從人轉移到錯誤上。這在商業寫作中很常見。

✗ Sorry, the Quality Control section didn't analyze the <u>raw</u> material yet.
抱歉，品管部門沒有分析原料。

✓ Sorry, the raw material hasn't been analyzed yet.
抱歉，原料還沒有分析。

✗ I apologize that my boss didn't follow your guidelines.
我為我們老闆沒有遵照你們的指導方針道歉。

✓ I am sorry that your guidelines were not followed.
我很抱歉沒有遵照你們的指導方針。

1.3 避免讓人覺得失禮 Avoid Seeming Disrespectful

1.3a 暗示懷疑 Implying Doubt

你不應該暗示你懷疑或不相信客戶說的事，即使你真的懷疑或不信任客戶。要把焦點擺在訊息及事實上，把問題個人化只會讓解決之道變得更複雜。仔細研究下列範例。

✗ Did you really send me the updated schedule? I didn't receive it.
你真的有把更新的時程表寄給我嗎？我並沒有收到。

✓ I didn't receive the updated schedule. Can you send me the schedule again?
我沒有收到更新的時程表。你可不可以把時程表再寄一次給我？

✗ It seems you didn't test the machine thoroughly as you said. It needs to be tested according to the guidelines I sent you. Please do the tests correctly and send me the data.
你似乎並未如你所說的徹底測試了機器。它必須根據我寄給你的指導方針來測試。請正確地測試並把資料寄給我。

✓ Did you remember to follow all the guidelines when testing the machine? There are many guidelines, so it is easy to <u>overlook</u> some of them.
你測試機器時是否記得要遵照所有的指導方針？方針很多，所以很容易忽略掉其中的一些。

Word List

raw [rɔ] *adj.* 仍為原料的；未加工的   overlook [ˌovəˈlʊk] *v.* 忽略；漏看

1.3b 缺乏人情味的用語 Avoid Impersonal Language

你寫電子郵件，一定是寫給特定對象的。因此，用字應該表現出你認為這個人是獨立的個體，而不只是一般顧客。

✗ We always do our best for all our customers. If there are any questions, a customer can contact us at any time.

我們一向會為所有的顧客盡我們最大的努力。假如有任何問題，顧客隨時都可以和我們聯絡。

✓ We will always do our best to help you. If you have any question, you can contact me at any time.

我們永遠會盡我們最大的努力幫助你。假如你有任何問題，隨時都可以跟我聯絡。

Memo

2 正面語氣 Positive Tone

2.1 著重事實 Focus on Facts

表達正面語氣最重要的是要忘掉個人，記住你是為公司做事，你是在做生意。廠商不會故意犯錯來傷害你個人；一切都是為了生意。假如顧客有所抱怨，他們抱怨的對象並不是你，而是你所服務的公司。你是公司的代表，不要把事情個人化。

2.1a 感覺不重要 Feeling Is Not Important

我的學生經常認為「正面」的意思是「很快樂的感覺」，這其實是大錯特錯。當你在寫任何一種電子郵件時，盡量寫重要且相關的事實，而不要管感覺，包括快樂的感覺在內。不用特別表達情緒，除非電子郵件的目的明確要求這樣做，比方說表達「感謝」的電子郵件。只要提出讀者需要的訊息，他們就會對你的郵件感到滿意。記住，這是商業電子郵件，不是給心上人的郵件。

✗ I am happy to send the information to you. Thanks a lot for asking me. If you have any questions, I will be so glad to answer you!
我很高興寄這些資料給你。非常謝謝你問我。假如有任何問題，我會十分樂意回答你！

✓ I am happy to send the information to you. If you have any questions, just let me know.
我很高興寄這些資料給你。假如有任何問題，請通知我一聲。

2.1b 避免生氣 Avoid Anger

假如你太過自我中心，你就會對在電子郵件上所看到的內容產生情緒化的反應。不過，假如你視自己為公司的員工，你就會客觀地思考。客觀思考是指把焦點放在事實上。假如你收到一封負面或粗魯的電子郵件，應該忽略當中令人不悅的詞語，並從電子郵件中找出事實。要回應事實，而不是回應令人不快的詞語。千萬不要寄出氣憤的電子郵件！它會回過頭來困擾你。

顧客來信：

> I was not satisfied with your response at all. Where is your sincerity? Can't you finish any job on time? I have been waiting for your Excel file for two days. How much longer do I have to wait?

☐ 翻譯

> 我對你的回應一點都不滿意。你的誠意在哪裡？你什麼事都無法準時完成嗎？我等你的 Excel 檔等了兩天了。我還得再等多久？

☒ 錯誤回應：

> I always try to do the best I can. It is not fair to say such mean words to me. I am working on the Excel file and will send it when I am finished.

☐ 翻譯

> 我一直試著盡最大的努力。對我說這麼惡毒的話不公平。我正在做 Excel 檔，一完成就會寄給你。

　　上述的回應只會使已經不悅的收信人更不開心。寫電子郵件的人很自我，郵件中也沒有提供有用的訊息。看起來他／她只想爭辯。

☑ 正確回應：

> The file is much longer than I expected. I am working on it now and will send it to you by tomorrow.

☐ 翻譯

> 這個檔案比我預期的大多了。我現在正在努力，明天以前會寄給你。

2.2 以正面思考取代負面思考
Replace Negative Ideas with Positive Ideas

　　盡可能把焦點放在正面的思考上。即使是必須包含像是抱怨或壞消息等負面元素的電子郵件，也要盡量強調事情的積極面。

✗ I'm afraid we cannot accept such a long delay. That will <u>set back</u> our operations and cost a lot of money.
我們恐怕不能接受這麼久的延期。那樣會延宕我們的營運，並耗費很多金錢。

✓ I'm afraid we cannot accept such a long delay. Can you suggest a shorter delay that will still satisfy your needs?
我們恐怕不能接受這麼久的延期。你可不可以提出較短但還是能滿足你們需求的延期？

✓ I'm afraid we cannot accept such a long delay. How about postponing for one week instead of two weeks?
恐怕我們不能接受這麼久的延期。把延後兩星期改成一星期怎麼樣？

- -

✗ The sample you sent is not good enough. The LCD <u>panel</u> is much too small. How can anyone see the picture?
你寄來的樣品不夠好。液晶面板小太多了。誰看得清楚畫面？

✓ Can you send us a different sample? One with a larger LCD panel would be easier to use.
你可以寄別的樣品給我們嗎？液晶面板比較大的樣品會比較好用。

2.3 強調你能為讀者做什麼 Emphasize What You Can Do for the Reader

　　事情都有一體兩面。在商場上，甲與乙從事交易的原因是，雙方都能從中獲利。你能提供給別人的東西愈有吸引力，他們給你的回報也就會愈具有吸引力。因此，要強調你能提供什麼，如此才能得到你想得到的東西。

Word List

set back 使（進度）落後、延後
panel [ˋpænl] *n.*【機】控制版；儀表版

✗ If you want to receive the payment on time, you had better send the parts according to schedule.
假如你想準時收到付款，最好照時程表把零件送來。

✓ We will pay you promptly when we receive the parts.
我們一收到零件就會立刻付款給你。

✗ You sent us the wrong information, so of course the customization looks bad. If you want the customization to be done again, you have to send the correct information.
你寄給我們的資料有誤，所以訂製的東西看起來當然不好。假如你想重新訂製，必須把正確的資料寄給我們。

✓ We customized the layout according to your information. If you can send us the new information, we will customize the order accordingly.
我們是根據您的資料來訂製設計圖的。假如您能夠把新的資料寄給我們，我們就會據以訂製您訂的貨。

Memo

3 處理壞消息 Dealing With Bad News

　　商場就像人生，常常有很多壞消息要處理，有時是小錯誤，有時是大錯誤，甚至是全盤皆錯。因此，處理壞消息也是電子郵件很重要的部分。我整理出向他人傳達壞消息的三大準則：

1. 要直接
2. 要準確
3. 強調你的解決辦法

3.1 要直接 Be Direct

　　電子郵件的第一段決定了整封電子郵件的調性。假如電子郵件是以開心的語氣開頭，讀者就會覺得這是一封開心的電子郵件。假如讀者接著在第二或第三段突然看到壞消息，後果就會像撞上了山腰。假如有壞消息，不要拐彎抹角，直接說！

☒ 錯誤範例：

Hi Willy,

Greetings from Taiwan! I hope everything is going well in Australia. Maybe I will see you next week at the trade show in Tokyo.

Today I was going over my records to make sure they are up to date. Then, I noticed something. The order I shipped to you yesterday contained the wrong items. Sorry about that. I will send the right items to you today.

Heather

☐ 翻譯

嗨，威利：

我在台灣向你問好！希望你在澳洲一切順利。也許我會在下星期的東京貿易展上見到你。

我今天查看了我的記錄，想確定內容都是最新的。我發現一件事。我昨天寄給你的訂貨裡有幾項弄錯了，很抱歉。今天我會把正確的貨品寄給你。

海瑟

☑ 正確範例：

Hi Willy,

Greetings.

Today I noticed that the order I shipped to you yesterday contained the wrong items. Sorry about that. I will send the right items to you today.

Heather

☐ 翻譯

嗨，威利：

你好。

我今天發現昨天寄給你的訂貨裡有幾項弄錯了，很抱歉。今天我會把正確的貨品寄給你。

海瑟

BIZ 必通句型

I REGRET TO INFORM YOU THAT ....

我很遺憾地通知你……。

例 I regret to inform you that we cannot accept your order at this time.

我很遺憾地通知你，我們這個時候無法接受你們的訂單。

I REGRET TO SAY THAT ....

我很遺憾地說……。

例 I regret to say that we lost the receipt.

我很遺憾地說，我們把收據弄丟了。

I NEED TO LET YOU KNOW THAT ....

我必須讓你知道……。

例 I need to let you know that Bill cannot attend the meeting.

我必須讓你知道，比爾不能參加會議。

I NEED TO TELL YOU THAT ....

我必須告訴你……。

例 I need to tell you that our main vendor closed its business.

我必須告訴你，我們的主要廠商結束營業了。

I AM AFRAID THAT ....

恐怕……。

例 I am afraid that the <u>mainframe</u> was <u>down</u> for two days.

主機恐怕已經當機兩天了。

Word List

mainframe [ˈmenˌfrem] *n.* 【電腦】主機；中央處理機

down [daʊn] *adj.* 【電腦】不再工作；當機

3.2 要精確 Be <u>Accurate</u>

在告訴別人壞消息時，我們常會很想以模糊的用語把消息輕描淡寫地帶過。然而，在傳達任何訊息時精確性都很重要。假如你不精確地說明訊息，往後它只會造成更多的麻煩。事實上，假如你試圖輕描淡寫帶過一些壞消息，一旦客戶了解壞消息實際的嚴重性，他／她反而可能會認為你是個騙子。所以勇敢說出讀者需要的一切訊息，讓他們充分了解你所要傳達的壞消息有多嚴重。

✗ I am afraid that there is a small delay with your order.
您的訂貨恐怕會稍微延期。

✓ I am afraid that your order will be two weeks late.
您的訂貨恐怕會延後兩個星期。

. . . .

✗ I need to tell you there might be a slight malfunction in the battery-powered toy.
我必須告訴你，以電池驅動的玩具可能有點小故障。

✓ I need to tell you that the battery-powered toy is defective. The control chip doesn't work. We need to replace all of them.
我必須告訴你，以電池驅動的玩具有瑕疵。控制晶片不靈光，我們得全部更換。

3.3 強調你的解決辦法 Emphasize Your Solution

每個人不時都會碰到問題。假如問題有解決之道，那它就不是問題了。真正的問題是那些沒有人願意解決或是沒有人能有效解決的問題。所以，每當你把問題告訴別人時，一定也要說清楚你會如何解決這個問題。你必須展現出會善盡本分的熱忱。研究顯示，顧客並不怎麼在意問題，他們在意的是解決之道。如果顧客的問題能有效且完全被解決，他／她就會是「最忠實的顧客」。

Word List

accurate [ˈækjərɪt] *adj.* 精確的；準確的

☒ 錯誤範例：

Hi Mr. Taylor,

I regret to say that the approaching typhoon has <u>grounded</u> all flights, so our <u>courier</u> cannot deliver the prototype to you tomorrow. Please accept our apologies.

Nancy

☐ 翻譯

嗨，泰勒先生：

我很遺憾地說，由於颱風即將來襲所有的班機全部停飛，因此我們的快遞明天無法把原型送交給您。請接受我們的道歉。

南西

☑ 正確範例：

Hi Mr. Taylor,

I regret to say that the approaching typhoon has grounded all flights, so our courier cannot deliver the prototype to you tomorrow. We expect flights to <u>resume</u> tomorrow night, so we will send the courier on the first available flight. He will probably arrive the day after tomorrow. I will confirm this as soon as we know the flight schedule.

Meanwhile, we have taken some <u>digital</u> photos of the prototype for you to

Word List

ground [graʊnd] v. 使停飛

courier [ˋkʊrɪɚ] n. 快遞人員

resume [rɪˋzum] v. 重新開始；再繼續

digital [ˋdɪdʒɪtl] adj. 數位的

check. They are attached to this e-mail. If there is anything else I can do for you, please let me know.

Nancy

□ 翻譯

嗨，泰勒先生：

我很遺憾地說，由於颱風即將來襲所有的班機全部停飛，因此我們的快遞明天無法把原型送交給您。我們預計班機會在明天晚上恢復起飛，所以我們會派我們的快遞搭第一班班機。他大概會在後天到達。我們一得知飛機班次，就會立刻確認這點。

在此同時，我們拍了一些原型的數位照片供您檢視。它們就附在這封電子郵件裡。假如還有什麼我能為您效勞的事，請通知我一聲。

南西

Memo

4 敏感用語 Sensitive Language

4.1 特定性別用語 Gender-specific Language

　　長久以來，英文有個普遍的慣例，那就是要避免使用暗示性別的字詞。這一點要注意，因為如果你使用了特定性別的字語可能會困擾，甚至冒犯某些人，尤其是西方女性。由於很多人對性別用語非常敏感，所以請仔細閱讀本單元的範例，以了解你要在什麼時候和什麼地方使用「salesman」及「saleswoman」之類的字眼。

4.1a 特定性別字彙 Gender-specific Words

Gender-specific 特定性別	Neutral 中性
businessman 商場人士	businessperson 商場人士
chairman 主席	chairperson, chair 主席
fireman 消防隊員	firefighter 消防隊員
housewife 家庭主婦	homemaker 持家者
insurance man 保險員	insurance agent 保險經紀人
mailman 郵差	mail carrier 郵差
policeman 警察	police officer 警員
salesman 銷售人員	salesperson 銷售人員
spokesman 發言人	spokesperson 發言人
stewardess 空中小姐	flight attendant 空服員
weatherman 氣象預報員	weather reporter 氣象播報員
actress 女演員	actor 演員

4.1b 「他」與「他的」He vs. Him

　　避免使用「he」及「him」有三個方法：
1. 使用複數而不用單數。
2. 採用不同的字。
3. 使用「he/she」或「him/her」。

Word List

gender [ˋdʒɛdə] *n.*【口語】性別
stewardess [ˋstjuwədɪs] *n.* （客機、輪船）女服務員

特定性別用法：

If you ever have a **customer** complaint about a product that we manufactured, you can tell **him** to contact us directly.

假如你有任何一位顧客抱怨我們所製造的產品，你可以請他直接跟我們聯絡。

中性用法 1 ：

If **customers** ever complain about a product that we manufactured, you can tell **them** to contact us directly.

假如有顧客抱怨我們所製造的產品，你可以請他們直接跟我們聯絡。

中性用法 2 ：

If you ever have a **customer** complaint about a product that we manufactured, you can tell the **customer** to contact us directly.

假如你有任何一位顧客抱怨我們所製造的產品，你可以請那位顧客直接跟我們聯絡。

中性用法 3 ：

If you ever have a **customer** complaint about a product that we manufactured, you can tell **him/her** to contact us directly.

假如你有任何一位顧客抱怨我們所製造的產品，你可以請他／她直接跟我們聯絡。

4.2 小姐、女士和夫人的用法 Miss, Ms., and Mrs.

有些女性對女性稱呼的用法很敏感。以下是正確的用法。

- **Miss** [mɪs] 小姐（年輕女性）
- **Ms.** [mɪz] 女士（不清楚這位女性是已婚還是單身）
- **Mrs.** [ˋmɪsɪz] 夫人（已婚女性）

要小心這些稱呼的發音，尤其是「Ms.」。大多數的人都會把它唸錯。

不幸的是，使用「Miss」或「Ms.」的時機很難掌握。有些年輕的女性偏好「Miss」，但有些年輕女性則認為「Miss」聽起來不專業，所以她們希望被稱為「Ms.」。假如你不確定要怎麼稱呼某位女性，可以直接問她：

Shall I call you Miss or Ms.?

我該稱呼你小姐還是女士？

5 實戰演練 Practice

找出並重寫你認爲這封電子郵件中語氣可能不對的部分。

Dear Denny,

Thanks for being such a great customer! I have enjoyed communicating with you for several years. You always reply to my mails so fast, and that helps me a lot.

By the way, can you do me a favor? I need to reschedule our conference call. There is a huge problem with one of our vendors, and it is taking all of my time. You can't believe how difficult it is to deal with this vendor. It is really terrible!

Anyway, I know you understand. But please accept my apology. I am really so sorry! If you can forgive me this time, I will be so grateful.

＊解答請見 365 頁

實戰演練解答 Answer Keys

Chapter 7

1. 圈出並更正下列電子郵件中標點符號的錯誤。

解答：

> Dear Customer Service Manager,
>
> I am writing to let you know that your sales specialist, Maggie, has been unable to process my order for one week. I talked to her twice on the phone and sent her several e-mails. Each time she said "I will try my best," but she didn't do anything.
>
> *This is not good service.* Is there anything you can do to expedite my order?
>
> I look forward to your quick reply.
>
> Sincerely,
> James

翻譯：

> 敬愛的客服經理：
>
> 我寫這封信是要讓您知道，貴公司的業務專員瑪姬已經有一個星期沒處理好我的訂單了。我和她在電話上說過兩次並寄了好幾封電子郵件給她，她每次都說「我會盡最大的努力」，但她什麼都沒做。
>
> * 這不是好的服務。 * 您可以做些什麼來加快我的訂單嗎？

期盼您盡快回覆。

詹姆斯
謹上

錯誤分析：

1. 稱呼語：在稱呼語中習慣用逗號或冒號，而非分號。
2. 第一段：第一行中的方括弧用得不恰當，名字應該要用逗號隔開。第二行中的逗號不能用來連接句子，應該用句號來表示前後兩句是分開的。不要像第三行那樣使用驚嘆號（尤其是連用三個），而要用句號。在第四行中，要用引號來指出直接引述，並把驚嘆號改成句號。
3. 第二段：由於這不是直接引述，所以不要用引號。在這種情況下，如果要強調的話，就用一對星號或粗體字。此外，由於第二句子是個問句，所以要以問號來結尾。
4. 結尾辭：像「Sincerely」（誠摯的）這種字後面要加逗號，而不是冒號。

2. 用 ¶ 符號標示出段落應該從哪裡開始，並用□符號指出哪裡應該加空行。

解答：

Hi Bob,
□
¶Did you receive my e-mail regarding moving the production line to Shanghai? I sent it several days ago but didn't receive a reply. Perhaps the e-mail was lost, so I will retype the general contents below.
□
¶We would like you to move the production line from Hsinchu to Shanghai for the following reasons.
□
¶1. We can save a lot of labor cost.
□
¶2. We already have a branch office near the Shanghai Industrial Zone, so

we can more easily meet with your production engineers and monitor the production process.

☐

¶3. We will save money on shipping costs, since most of our customers are in China.

☐

¶My vice president would like to know your initial assessment. Is it possible to move the production to Shanghai?

☐

¶Thanks for considering our request.

☐

Yours,
Lavonne

翻譯：

嗨，巴伯：

你有沒有收到我那封關於將生產線移到上海的電子郵件？我在幾天前就寄了，可是沒有收到回覆。也許郵件寄丟了，所以我在下面把大致的內容再寫一遍。

我們希望你們把生產線從新竹移到上海的理由如下：

1. 我們可以省下很多勞動成本。

2. 我們在上海工業區附近已經有一家分公司，所以我們在跟你們的產品工程師見面以及監控生產流程時會更容易。

3. 我們可以省下運送費用，因為我們大部分的顧客都在中國。

我們副總經理想要知道你的初步評估。有沒有可能把生產移到上海？

謝謝你考慮我們的請求。

蕾馮
上

錯誤分析：

　　主要的問題在版面安排。記得要在段落間加空行。假如你想要像這則訊息中的三個原因一樣把事情編號，那所有的號碼都要置於左邊界。

Chapter 8

1. 圈出並刪除這封電子郵件中不必要的部分，然後重寫。

解答：

Subject: Please Complete the Survey

Dear Customers,

Would you be so kind to fill out the attached survey for us? The survey will help us improve our performance so that we can serve you even better in the coming year.

You can send the survey back by e-mail or fax. Thanks for your time to fill out the survey!

Sincerely yours,
Betsy Moss

翻譯：

主旨：填寫問卷

親愛的顧客：

您願不願意費心幫我們填寫附件中的問卷調查？這份調查將有助於我們改善我們的作業，好讓我們在來年可以為您提供更好的服務。

您可以電子郵件或傳真寄回問卷，感謝您撥空填寫！

貝西·摩絲
謹上

錯誤分析：

記得要立刻切入重點！讀者想知道你為什麼寄這封電子郵件。假如讀者必須要等到信的結尾才知道目的，他／她會感到不悅。以簡潔的主旨列起頭。原郵件頭兩段的客套話並不會讓讀者感到開心，它們聽起來就像是浪費讀者寶貴時間的典型行銷用語。只要鎖定和主要議題相關的事實就好。

Chapter 9

1. 找出並重寫你覺得這封電子郵件中語氣可能不對的部分。

解答：

Dear Denny,

Can you do me a favor? I need to reschedule our conference call because of a problem with one of our vendors. Could we delay the call for two days? Instead of tomorrow evening, I can talk with you Friday evening at the same time.

I am sorry to ask for this postponement. This kind of postponement rarely happens, fortunately.

Judy

翻譯：

> 敬愛的丹尼：
>
> 你能幫我個忙嗎？我必須重新排訂我們的電話會議，因為我們的一家廠商出個了問題。我們可以把通話延後兩天嗎？從明天晚上改成星期五晚上的同一個時間，我再跟你談。
>
> 很抱歉要求這樣的延期，幸好這種延期很少發生。
>
> 茱蒂

錯誤分析：

1. 第一段所採用的語氣不對。這段的語氣是開心的，但電子郵件裡卻是壞消息。
2. 電子郵件聽起來很虛假。(1) 第一段說了一大堆好話，但郵件的目的卻是要請人幫忙。(2) 廠商的問題被情緒用語嚴重誇大。(3) 道歉太多次，反而給人不可靠的感覺。
3. 「我知道你會了解」是負面的句子。記得不要以高姿態對讀者說話。
4. 這封電子郵件並沒有針對電話會議延期的問題提出積極的解決之道，讀者不知道會延期多久。對方必須浪費時間寫另一封電子郵件來問電話會議要重訂在什麼時間。要主動提出解決之道。

Memo

國家圖書館出版品預行編目資料

搞定進階商務口說＝Advanced business
communication / Dana Forsythe著；戴至中譯.
－－初版. －－臺北市；貝塔，2006〔民95〕
　　面；　　公分
　　ISBN 978-957-729-605-4（平裝）
　　1. 商業英語－會話　2. 商業書信
805.188　　　　　　　　　　　　95014904

搞定進階商務口說
Advanced Business Communication

作　　者／Dana Forsythe
總 編 審／王復國
譯　　者／戴至中
執行編輯／莊碧娟

出　　版／貝塔出版有限公司
地　　址／台北市 100 館前路 12 號 11 樓
電　　話／(02) 2314-2525
傳　　真／(02) 2312-3535
客服專線／(02) 2314-3535
客服信箱／btservice@betamedia.com.tw
郵撥帳號／19493777
帳戶名稱／貝塔出版有限公司

總 經 銷／時報文化出版企業股份有限公司
地　　址／桃園縣龜山鄉萬壽路二段 351 號
電　　話／(02) 2306-6842

出版日期／2011年2月初版二刷
定　　價／380元
ISBN-13：978-957-729-605-4
ISBN-10：957-729-605-X

Advanced Business Communication
Copyright © 2006 by Dana Forsythe
Published by Beta Multimedia Publishing
All Rights Reserved.

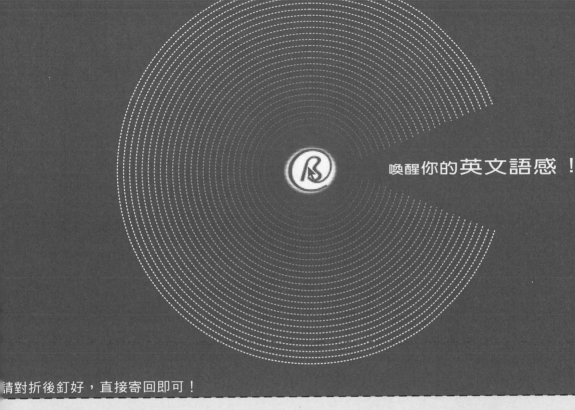

喚醒你的英文語感！

請對折後釘好，直接寄回即可！

100 台北市中正區館前路12號11樓

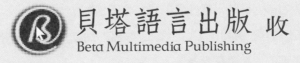

貝塔語言出版 收
Beta Multimedia Publishing

寄件者住址 ☐ ☐ ☐

貝塔語言出版
Beta Multimedia Publishing

讀者服務專線（02）2314-3535　　讀者服務傳真（02）2312-3535
客戶服務信箱　btservice@betamedia.com.tw
www.betamedia.com.tw

謝謝您購買本書！！

貝塔語言擁有最優良之英文學習書籍，為提供您最佳的英語學習資訊，您可填妥此表後寄回（免貼郵票）將可不定期收到本公司最新發行書訊及活動訊息！

姓名：＿＿＿＿＿＿＿＿＿＿＿＿　性別：□男 □女　生日：＿＿＿年＿＿＿月＿＿＿日

電話：(公)＿＿＿＿＿＿＿＿＿(宅)＿＿＿＿＿＿＿＿＿(手機)＿＿＿＿＿＿＿＿＿

電子信箱：＿＿＿＿＿＿＿＿＿＿＿＿＿＿＿＿＿＿＿＿＿＿＿＿

學歷：□高中職含以下 □專科 □大學 □研究所含以上

職業：□金融 □服務 □傳播 □製造 □資訊 □軍公教 □出版

　　　□自由 □教育 □學生 □其他

職級：□企業負責人 □高階主管 □中階主管 □職員 □專業人士

1. 您購買的書籍是？＿＿＿＿＿＿＿＿＿＿＿＿＿＿＿＿

2. 您從何處得知本產品？(可複選)

　　　□書店 □網路 □書展 □校園活動 □廣告信函 □他人推薦 □新聞報導 □其他

3. 您覺得本產品價格：

　　　□偏高 □合理 □偏低

4. 請問目前您每週花了多少時間學英語？

　　　□ 不到十分鐘 □ 十分鐘以上，但不到半小時 □ 半小時以上，但不到一小時

　　　□ 一小時以上，但不到兩小時 □ 兩個小時以上 □ 不一定

5. 通常在選擇語言學習書時，哪些因素是您會考慮的？

　　　□ 封面 □ 內容、實用性 □ 品牌 □ 媒體、朋友推薦 □ 價格□ 其他＿＿＿＿＿

6. 市面上您最需要的語言書種類為？

　　　□ 聽力 □ 閱讀 □ 文法 □ 口說 □ 寫作 □ 其他＿＿＿＿＿＿

7. 通常您會透過何種方式選購語言學習書籍？

　　　□ 書店門市 □ 網路書店 □ 郵購 □ 直接找出版社 □ 學校或公司團購

　　　□ 其他＿＿＿＿＿＿

8. 給我們的建議：＿＿＿＿＿＿＿＿＿＿＿＿＿＿＿＿＿＿＿＿＿＿＿＿

＿＿＿＿＿＿＿＿＿＿＿＿＿＿＿＿＿＿＿＿＿＿＿＿＿＿＿＿＿＿＿

喚醒你的英文語感！

Get a Feel for English !

喚醒你的英文語感！

Get a Feel for English !